A RING IN TIME

Linda Sawley

Linda Sawley

LINRIC PUBLISHING
ENGLAND

Published in 2002 by LinRic publishing
18 Victoria Lodge
Read, Lancs
BB12 7SZ

British Cataloguing in publication data
Sawley, Linda
TITLE
A Ring in Time
I. Title
Classification: Historical Romantic Fiction
ISBN   0-9534329-1-2

Cover design by David Eaves

Digitally Printed by Beacon – DM
Unit 2, Valley Road Business Park
Gas Works Road
Keighley, BD21 4LY

For Judith Habiak,
my encourager.

Chapter 1

Sarah pressed her face against the bus window. Peering out into the dark, she looked at the Christmas lights coming into view as the bus entered Whalley, the small Lancashire town, whose ancient abbey nestled on the banks of the River Calder. It was the night that the Christmas lights would be turned on and all the shops were staying open. Excitement rising, Sarah jumped up and hurried to the stairs at the front of the bus, so that she could get off the bus quickly. She caught a reflection of herself in the mirror on the stairs. A small slim figure, well wrapped up against the cold peered back at her, her bob-cap covering her long auburn hair. The dark polo neck jumper that she was wearing seemed to accentuate the paleness of her face. As the bus slowed, Sarah jumped off the bus and hurried towards the centre of the town.

'I'm glad I decided to leave the car at home tonight', she mused, 'It seems more fitting to come by bus. Besides, the parking would have been horrendous. If only Darren could have come tonight'. Her pretty face clouded over as she thought about her boyfriend. Well, hardly a boyfriend as he was 33, but man friend didn't seem to have the same ring to it. Their deepening relationship was exciting, but he was so busy with his business and he had to work away from home a great deal. They only managed to see each other about twice a week and full weekends together were rare. Always the business had to come first and Sarah pondered that this could be a problem between them in the future. But he always insisted that the business was young and he had to work hard to establish it.

Her steps slowed as she reached the shops, gazing in childlike wonder as she looked at the trimmings and bright lights everywhere. The Christmas theme was Pickwick from Dickens, and all the shopkeepers were hoping to win the prize for best shop display. Many of them had dressed up in keeping with the theme. The first shop that she saw was the funeral director. Sarah laughed to herself. She couldn't believe that the funeral director's shop was open on a night like this. But there seemed to be plenty of people going in. Perhaps they are going to book a discount funeral, or 'pay now - die later' sort of arrangement. Whatever it was, it seemed a bizarre kind of shop to be open tonight. Just wait until she told Darren tomorrow. He wouldn't believe it.

As Sarah passed the ironmongers, she stopped to look at a stall that was selling home-made fudge. She stood looking at the stall, savouring the lovely smells drifting up from the fudge, unable to decide which flavour to try. After much deliberation, she bought the Christmas Pudding flavour in keeping with the time of year. The next stall had white chocolate teddy bears and, on an impulse, she bought Darren one. She would give it to him tomorrow night. Walking through the town, she was amazed at how many stalls there were. She bought raffle tickets and a few last Christmas gifts for the girls at the library where she worked. Further down the road, Sarah waved at the staff at the hairdressers and one of the owners, Mel, shouted 'Come and join us for a drink afterwards.'

'I will, don't worry, you know I always like a free drink,' replied Sarah laughing. With having travelled on the bus, she could risk taking a drink tonight. A brass band was playing carols in the square. 'All it needs now is some snow', thought Sarah, but the sky was clear, with the stars shining bright. Sarah wondered about how she would spend Christmas this year. In the past few years since her parents had died in the car crash, she had been invited to different friends' houses each year. This year, she had been suitably vague about her arrangements to her friends. Darren had told her that he always spent Christmas with his mother, who was a frail elderly widow and lived in Suffolk. Sarah had waited for an invitation to join them but up to now, it had not been forthcoming and there were only three weeks left to go. Sarah sighed as she thought about Christmas, but then laughed at herself and decided to enjoy herself tonight, with or without Darren.

Her only brother, James, had emigrated to America straight after getting his degree. He had eventually married an

American girl but, for many years, had stayed single whilst he built his computer business up. Because of this, she could understand Darren's total commitment to his business but, even so, it was hard to live with when in the first throes of love. James and his wife, Donna, had twin sons who would be one year old on Boxing Day. James was seven years older than Sarah. He had been born on the day when President Kennedy had been assassinated in 1963. Their mother always used to laugh when people asked, 'What were you doing when President Kennedy died?' She could never forget that date, as she was having a long and hard labour with her firstborn child. But, as with all new mothers, as soon as she held the miraculous baby in her arms the pain was forgotten, as she searched the tiny face for family characteristics.

Because of the age gap, James and Sarah had not been particularly close. They kept in touch fairly infrequently by e-mail, as they both had such busy lives. Photos had been sent through the e-mail, but it was not the same as seeing the twins in real life. James had urged her to go and visit this Christmas, but she had been reluctant to go, not only because of Darren, but also because of the money. There always seemed to be something else to do with her money. She had bought a little modern mews-type house in the next village so that she was handy for her work as a librarian in the small town where the lights were being turned on. Clients from the library stopped to say hello to Sarah whilst she was walking through town. She waved at a group of small children who were regular visitors to her after-school reading sessions. It felt good to belong to a small community like this, even though she didn't live in the town. She would have liked to buy a house in the town, but the house prices were exorbitant, so she settled for a house in the next village, which was called Read.

The opening ceremony was due to start shortly and Sarah edged to the front of the crowd. She started looking round at the jostling crowds. Her favourite hobby was people watching. A small family of three children, all under seven years of age, jumped about impatiently on the pavement next to her. Excited cries erupted as the children shrieked to each other. An elderly gentleman was standing across the road, nearly as excited as the small children. The whole atmosphere was vibrant and exciting.

Looking to the side of her, Sarah saw a tall blond woman, a toddler hanging on each hand. The woman was searching the crowds expectantly, framed against the bright lights of the window. She looked worried and Sarah felt sorry for her, as her worried expression marred her beautiful features. A noise from the far side of the square distracted Sarah, and she strained forward to see if it was Father Christmas and his sleigh coming, as the children were suggesting. But it was a false alarm. A crowd of youths started to sing, 'Why are we waiting?' and the little boy next to her started to cry because his sister had trodden on his foot. Sarah watched the interaction between the mother and her children, as she sorted the dispute out, lovingly yet firmly. Sarah wondered when she would ever have children, and longed for that day. She turned away from the family and looked back to the light window where the anxious woman had been. She was still there.

Sarah turned round, wondering when the festivities were going to start. As she looked across the square, she suddenly froze to the spot. There, hurrying across the street was Darren. Her heart surged with joy as she waved and shouted to attract his attention, but he didn't hear or see her. He hurried across the road to a spot further away from Sarah. Sarah watched his progress as he wove his way through the crowds. As she turned, she noticed that the tall blonde woman was now smiling and laughing. Suddenly, the blonde woman was enveloped in a big hug, as a man swirled her round in his arms. As they turned towards Sarah, she saw the man's face. It was Darren. He was hugging the blond woman and the two toddlers were clutching at his coat shouting 'daddy, daddy'. At that moment, Darren saw Sarah, froze, then turned away, guiding his wife and children quickly away from Sarah.

Sarah couldn't move. She felt as if her feet had turned to lead, and yet her heart was pounding. The little girl next to her screamed at her, 'Look, look, Father Christmas is here'. Her excited cries made Sarah try and smile but she couldn't feel anything at present. She pushed her way through the crowds and back towards the bus shelter. She had to get home before she broke down altogether. How stupid she had been. Married. Why had she never suspected it before? She must be really gullible. All those stories about not being able to see her because he was building his business up, or away on business. And all the time, he was not only married but had two small children. She would never have gone out with him if she had known. But how was she to know? Men of his age didn't go round with 'married' tattooed on their forehead, worse luck. 'It would make my life a lot easier', mused Sarah despondently.

Sarah got back to the bus stop. The bus driver jumped as she got to the mini-bus, disturbed from his forty winks.

'Going home already, love?' he asked, 'Why the fun has only just started'.

'I'm not feeling too well' replied Sarah, 'Is there any chance that you could take me home to Read?

'You do look a little bit peaky. Go on then, I'll take you home, there'll be nothing else to do for the next hour or two'. Sarah got on the mini-bus, smiling her grateful thanks.

'Probably women's troubles,' mused the bus driver to himself. Having a wife and four teenage daughters made him somewhat of an expert in these matters. Not that he ever professed to understand women.

Sarah sat slumped in her seat, avoiding looking at the bus driver, so that she wouldn't feel obliged to talk to him. It was so unlike her, normally she would talk to anyone and everyone. You had to be able to converse easily with all kinds of people when you worked in a library. As the bus approached her house, she walked to the front, trying to smile at the bus driver as he made small talk about the weather. She paid the fare and hopped off the bus, walking quickly along the street to her house.

Unlocking the front door, Sarah ran upstairs and threw herself on the bed, still fully dressed. She sobbed and sobbed for a long time, until she had a terrible headache. Sarah slowly got off the bed and went into the bathroom. She looked in the mirror and saw a reddened, blotchy face staring back at her. All traces of the pretty woman of three hours ago had gone. Just looking at her reflection set the tears off again. Looking away from the mirror, Sarah went downstairs and made for the kitchen. She automatically turned the kettle on and got a teabag out of the jar. The clock on the oven said that it was half past nine. Sarah had to make a decision quickly. The thought of going into work tomorrow morning was unbearable. She needed some time to pull herself together before she could face anyone. Sarah picked the phone up and dialled the number of her friend Jackie who worked part-time in the tiny library in Read. The ringing tones sounded shrill in her ear. Her whole body ached, especially her head. Jackie's husband answered the phone, and she quickly asked for Jackie without saying who it was.

'Hi Jackie' Sarah said, trying to keep her voice light, 'Can you do me a massive favour? Could you cover for me at Whalley tomorrow? I know it's short notice, but I've got a terrible migraine and I know that I won't be able to work tomorrow. If I stay in bed all day tomorrow, I'll be OK for Saturday. Can you help, please?'

Jackie paused for a second before answering. 'A migraine, you say. Yes, yes, of course I can work for you. As you know, my mother-in law is here for the week, so I'll just check that she will look after the children for me.' Jackie put the phone down and Sarah could hear her talking in the background. Very quickly she came back to the phone. 'Yes, that's fine Sarah. Do you want me all day?'

'Yes please', replied Sarah. 'Margaret is on from 9 until 1pm, but you'll be on your own in the afternoon. Jenny doesn't work Fridays. Will you be OK?

'I'll be fine', reassured Jackie, 'Just you get yourself better. I'll call round in the evening to see how you are'.

'Thanks Jackie, you're a real star. I owe you one for this.'

'Just you wait 'til I need a babysitter, I'll be round at your house to claim the favour back.'

'That's fine; you know I'll have the children anytime I can. They're such brilliant children', said Sarah.

'Huh, you wouldn't say that if you had them all the time. They can be really naughty at times. But I know, they're always good for you. They daren't be anything else. They'd be frightened you wouldn't take them out again. D'y'know, you'd make a lovely mother. It's about time you had your own children, never mind looking after mine.'

Sarah tried to stifle a sob and quickly finish the conversation. 'I'll have to go, Jackie, My head's really pounding now. Thanks a lot. Margaret has the keys and will let you in. Can you tell her what's happened? I really need to get to bed now. Bye'

Sarah put the phone down quickly, and started making sure that all the doors were locked; the central heating was turned down, her actions automatic. Blow the empty milk bottle, she thought savagely, it will have to wait until tomorrow. I'm sure Mr Pickering the milkman won't mind for once. She noticed that the ansaphone was flashing, but ignored it. She couldn't face talking to anyone else tonight. Sarah walked wearily upstairs, still on automatic pilot. She went to the loo, cleaned her teeth, and dumped her dirty clothes on the bathroom floor, so unlike her meticulous self. Dragging her nightie over her head, she walked into the bedroom. As she closed the curtains and turned towards the bed, she suddenly remembered the last time Darren had been here. They had only recently become lovers. He had teased her, as it was her first time ever, and Darren couldn't believe that she was still a virgin at the ripe old age of 29. She had defended herself by saying that she had been saving herself for the right man. Whilst her friends at University had had multiple partners, she had never met anyone that she had wanted to make love to until now. Until Darren. The tears returned with a vengeance.

'How could I be so stupid?' Sarah wailed to herself. 'Why could I not see what was before my very eyes? Why did I believe everything he told me?' Sarah started reliving all the times that she had spent with Darren, making herself more and more miserable as the evening wore on. 'Because I wanted to believe him,' she answered herself. No wonder they say that all who love are blind. The more she recalled their conversations, the more she realised what a fool she had been. Sarah tossed and turned in her bed, pummelling the pillow, and trying to get comfortable. She looked at the clock. It was well after midnight. Sarah tried to think about nice things in her life. Her job, her friends, her brother and his family, but they only served to make her feel lonelier. This Millennium year had been very special for her up to now, but so quickly it was all in ruins. Her eyes throbbing and her head pounding, eventually sleep overtook Sarah and she slept fitfully until dawn.

Chapter 2

The phone ringing woke Sarah next morning. She slowly turned to look at the bedside clock, her head throbbing and her eyes smarting. It was 8 o'clock. For a split second, she wondered why she felt so terrible and then she remembered. The pain and anguish came flooding back. She listened as the ansaphone kicked in with the recorded message. 'Well, who ever it was,' thought Sarah, 'I'm not getting up to speak to them,' and tried to drift back to sleep.

But sleep would not come to help her forget Darren's betrayal. 'How could he?' she cried to her bedroom ceiling. Eventually she got up and went downstairs to make herself a cup of tea. 'Cup of tea,' she mused, 'the panacea for all ills. If only it would cure all,' she muttered to herself miserably. Going into the lounge, she noticed the ansaphone flashing. There were three messages. Sitting in the chair, she settled down to listen to the messages. The first one was from Tracey, her friend from University, ringing up for a girly chat. The bleep of the phone denoted the end of the first message and then Darren's voice flooded into the room.

'Sarah, sorry about tonight, I've been meaning to tell you. I'm so sorry that you found out that way. Don't ring me tonight, I'll be with my wife. I'll ring you tomorrow. Bye for now, and sorry.' Wife. The word cut into Sarah's heart as if a real knife had been plunged there. Fumbling in her dressing gown pocket for her hanky to stem the flow of tears, Sarah was surprised when Darren's voice burst into her room again.

'Hi, it's Darren. We need to talk. Please ring me on the office number or my mobile. It doesn't need to be the end. We can work something out. Please, Sarah, I love you. Please ring me.'

'Love me? Love me?' screeched Sarah at the ansaphone, 'You lying, cheating, scheming, no good, evil, married bastard'. She stopped dead in her flow, horrified at the words that had just come out of her mouth. She never used words like that normally. What was she turning into, all because of that man? 'Well, no man will treat me like that ever again,' she determined. 'I'm off men for a very long time now.'

As she started to calm down, and started sipping her tea, the phone rang again. She waited until the message finished and listened to the caller. It was Darren. She couldn't believe it. She dashed across the room, viciously grabbed the receiver and screamed a string of abuse down the phone at him, telling him to get back to his wife and stay away from her. 'And don't ever, ever, ring me again' she finished with before slamming the phone down. Shaking visibly, she picked up the cup off the floor, from where it had gone flying when she had jumped up to answer the phone.

Crying uncontrollably and shaking with rage by now, Sarah crawled back upstairs to her bed, but not before unplugging the phone. She sobbed and sobbed and made herself far worse than she had been when she woke up. Her hatred of Darren and her rage against him were frightening. Only yesterday she had been deeply in love with him, so how could all these feelings of hatred be here today? 'Quite easily,' she mused, 'after what he's done to me.' She dozed fitfully until lunchtime and then decided to get up. After making another cup of tea, Sarah filled the bath with lovely hot water and poured in her new expensive bubble bath that she had treated herself to last week. She caught a glimpse of her hair in the bathroom mirror. It looked like she had been through a hedge backwards. Sarah groaned at the state of her hair, which was usually her pride and joy.

'Well, it will just have to stay like that today,' she said to the glum face in the mirror. 'I can't be bothered with that today.' Sarah sank into the bath and let the bubbles swish round her, healing her aching body and making her more relaxed. She filled up the bath with hot water again, each time it started to cool. Once her skin started wrinkling, Sarah decided that it was time to get out and get dry. She rubbed herself vigorously with the thick bath towel and slipped on her jeans and sweatshirt over her underwear. She ran the brush through her hair without even looking at the mirror, fastened her hair back with a band, and then went back downstairs. She looked behind the front door to see if there was any mail. There were three Christmas cards. 'Perhaps that is something I could do today. Write my Christmas cards. Keep my mind active and away from him.' As she thought of Darren again, the tears welled up in her eyes, but the anger wasn't there this time. Just an awful feeling of loss. 'How am I going to get through Christmas without him?' she asked herself. 'Just the same as you did last Christmas, she answered herself. You hadn't even met him then.'

'Christmas,' thought Sarah, 'what on earth am I going to do this year? I can't face the thought of being on my own. Well, I won't worry about that at the moment. I've a lot more to sort out before Christmas comes. Like my life,' she mused miserably to herself.

'Think positive, girl, think positive and count your blessings. That's what your granny always used to say and there was a lot of sense in it. Remember Granny and get those Christmas cards out.' Sarah went upstairs to the spare bedroom. It was set up as a study rather than a bedroom and she also had a chest of deep drawers where she kept presents and cards. She got the Christmas card list and the boxes of cards out of the drawer and went back downstairs, putting the cards on the dining table. Sarah realised that her tummy was rumbling, but didn't really feel like eating. She went into the kitchen and made a cup of soup and a coffee, and went back into the lounge. She picked the cards out of the boxes and spread them out on the table in front of herself, looking at them whilst she drank her soup. She tried to match cards to the people that she was sending them to. Sarah had bought the cards from Save the Children, Cancer Research and the Royal National Lifeboat Institute this year. She always liked to choose them from the Christmas card charity catalogues and chose different charities each year.

'Why am I so late in sending out my cards this year? I've usually got them out by the 1st December,' Sarah asked herself. She was one of those irritating people who send them out really early and make people feel guilty because they haven't even thought about theirs. Sarah then realised that she had been waiting for an invite to Darren's mothers for Christmas, so that she could tell people about Darren at the same time. Tears threatened to spill down her cheeks again, so Sarah jumped up and went upstairs to the spare bedroom to get a small gift that she had bought for Louise, a friend she had met at University. She concentrated on wrapping the parcel up and brought it back downstairs. 'Now,' said Sarah to herself sternly, 'No more tears, he's not worth it.' She got a padded bag out of the bureau drawer and packaged the gift and card up together. Sarah made a determined effort and wrote the rest of her Christmas cards, but didn't send the chatty letters that she usually included in some of her cards. It was dark outside by the time she had finished the cards, and Sarah stretched her back, uncomfortable from all the writing that she had been doing. It was too late now to go to the post office to get the special Christmas stamps, so she would have to do that tomorrow.

Sarah went to put the kettle on and whilst waiting for it to boil, noticed that the phone was still unplugged. She walked across to plug it in and dialled 1471 to see if anyone had rung. It was Darren's mobile number at 2.05 pm. Not again. She couldn't believe the arrogance of him, to keep trying to get in touch with her. Well, she certainly wasn't going to return that call. Sarah sat down with her drink and turned the TV on to catch the news. She had missed most of it, but caught the tail end, and then the local news programme. A lot of the stories were about

Christmas and it only made Sarah feel even lonelier. She must have dozed off because she was suddenly woken by the doorbell ringing. Sarah jumped up to answer it, then stopped in her tracks. What if it was Darren? What would she say? She tried to peep through the kitchen window, but couldn't see who was there. Sarah went into the porch and shouted, 'Who's there?' through the door.

'Hi Sarah, it's only me' shouted a female voice. Relief flooded through Sarah as she opened her door to Mrs Foote, her next door neighbour.

'Noticed that you weren't at work, lovey, and wondered if you were all right. You look a bit peaky', said Mrs Foote. 'Is there anything that I can do to help?'

'No thanks, Mrs Foote, I'm fine. Just had a migraine that's all. I'm much better now', smiled Sarah. Mrs Foote was a dear, but she did tend to want to put the world to rights and enjoyed knowing everyone's business in the village. 'Mind you,' thought Sarah, 'she's never malicious. Such a heart of gold and really caring. She'd do anything for anyone and loved to help everyone. It seemed to keep her going. She'd been like that since her husband had died and she'd moved to the smaller house.

'Well, you don't look it to me', said Mrs Foote, 'Downright peaky, I'd say. Is Darren coming tonight? That'll put the shine back in your eyes.'

Sarah stared at Mrs Foote, then burst into tears.

'Why, what ever is to do, lovey? Here let me come and have a better look at you.' Mrs Foote put her arm round Sarah and sat her down on the settee. 'Now you tell me all about it. What's made you so unhappy?'

Sarah told Mrs Foote about Darren in between gulping sobs. 'Why, I'd never have believed it of him, he was such a nice young man. Oh, the cruel thing, and just at Christmas, too.' Sarah went and got a long piece of kitchen roll to mop up her tears and eventually calmed down.

'Shall I make you a cup of tea, lovey?' asked Mrs Foote.

'No thanks', replied Sarah, 'I think I'll drown if I have any more drinks. I just feel so stupid and gullible'.

'Well, never you mind, lovey. There's plenty more fish in the sea, as they say. You're a bonny lass and you'll soon find someone else. At least you've found out before it got any more serious'. Sarah laughed in spite of herself. 'I thought it was serious', she said. 'Ah well, we all know what thought did'.

'Are you going to be alright, tonight? I can't stay any longer as I'm going out. Shall I pop round when I get home?'

'No thanks, Mrs Foote, I'm going to get an early night. I'm working in the morning. But thanks all the same. It's really good of you.'

'Well, I'll have to be going now. Just you take care of yourself. And let me know if there is anything you want me to do for you.'

'Thanks, I will,' replied Sarah and walked Mrs Foote to the door. As she opened the door, Jackie was just about to knock. Mrs Foote and Jackie greeted each other and Sarah invited Jackie in as Mrs Foote left.

'Okay, Sarah, what's all this about a migraine? Margaret and I were saying that we've never known you have one before. Besides, you sounded like you were upset last night. So, come on, what's the matter?'

Sarah wasn't sure that she could tell the story again so soon, but knew she had to. She owed that to Jackie.

'You're right, Jackie, you know me so well. I did have a headache, that was no lie. But there was a real cause for my headache.' Sarah started to tell her about Darren and Jackie's face became more and more shocked.

'Oh, how could he do this to you? He seemed such a nice bloke.'

'Well, he wasn't' snapped Sarah, and then immediately felt remorse. 'Oh I'm sorry Jackie, I shouldn't take it out on you. It's not your fault.'

'That's okay' replied Jackie, 'you can shout at me all you want. Are you sure that you can work tomorrow?'

'I'll be fine,' replied Sarah. 'I've got to get back to work as soon as I can. Besides, it will keep my mind off things. Thanks for covering for today'.

'Will you be all right? I have to get home now. I've visitors coming tomorrow, my brother and his wife and four children. It will be like a mad house.'

'Yes, you go, and thanks for everything. Bye'.

Sarah came back into the house and sank into the settee. She felt drained and curiously empty. She went over the two conversations that she had had with Mrs Foote and Jackie. At least she had told two people now, but would it get any easier? She certainly hoped so. She couldn't afford to keep breaking down every time somebody mentioned Darren. Deciding that she would have an early night, Sarah made her way slowly upstairs and fell asleep as soon as her head hit the pillow.

Next morning Sarah got to work early, determined to make up for being off sick the day before. As soon as she got in the library, she got the kettle on and started making herself and Jenny a drink. Saturday mornings were always busy and they often didn't get a chance for a drink all morning. Jenny came hurtling through the door as usual. She was always in a rush and would have already done several errands before coming to work. 'Hi Sarah, better today? You still look peaky,' asked Jenny in staccato fashion.

'Jenny,' said Sarah quietly. Jenny stopped rushing round and turned to look at Sarah. 'I need to tell you what has happened. I've found out Darren is married. It's all over. I'm just beginning to be able to talk about it without crying, but I'm still very fragile, so could we leave it for now?' Jenny stood frozen to the spot, a look of horror on her face.

'Sarah, I'm so sorry, I thought . . .'

'I know Jenny,' Sarah interrupted. 'Please leave it for now. Oh look, here are Mr and Mrs Ormerod. Good morning to you, bright and early as usual.' Sarah forced a smile for her clients. They came in early every Saturday morning. 'How's the family tree going?'

'Good morning, Sarah. We had a successful day on the internet yesterday and got on to the IGI register that the Mormon church have. I'm dreading the phone bill, but it was fascinating.'

'He's not kidding', said Mrs Ormerod. 'He was like a child with a new toy yesterday, but at least I got a bit of peace to catch up with my jobs'.

'We've got back to 1749 now, but one person is proving very hard to find' continued Mr Ormerod. 'We've got his marriage and death, but not his birth. I'm beginning to think that he came from Mars.'

'Knowing your family, that wouldn't surprise me,' quipped Mrs Ormerod.

'Now, now,' laughed Sarah, 'no falling out. The library is supposed to be a peaceful place. Besides, I've just got a new book in about being a family tree detective and I haven't put it on the shelf yet. Would you like to look at it?'

'Would I? Where is it?' asked Mr Ormerod, with a glint in his eye. Mr and Mrs Ormerod ran the local family history society in the village. It was another thing that Sarah intended to join one day, when she had time. She'd always enjoyed history at school and had kept up the interest since and had done her dissertation on a historical theme at University. As Mr and Mrs Ormerod wandered off down the library, Sarah thought that perhaps that was one thing she could do now. She felt sad as she remembered Darren and her new need to find hobbies to occupy herself.

'Are you OK, Sarah?' asked Jenny. 'You've gone all thoughtful again.'

'I'm fine, Jenny, thanks. I'll be all right, honestly'.

The day passed quickly after that, leaving Sarah little time to dwell on her own problems. After work, she went to Zigzags hairdressers in the village, where she had a regular appointment on a Saturday afternoon. Sarah loved having her hair done and it was her one little luxury that she went to the hairdressers every week, knowing that work was finished until Monday. From the minute she walked in, she felt at ease. It was a lovely feeling of being pampered. As soon as she arrived the apprentice, Caroline, guided her to the sink to wash her hair. Sarah loved the feel of the gentle massage as her hair was washed, and it always made her feel relaxed. After that she was guided to a chair, and a cup of coffee was placed on the table by young Ellie, the Saturday girl. Ellie didn't need to ask if she wanted one, Sarah always said 'yes, please'.

'Give me a new image, Mel' Sarah asked.

Mel always loved a gossip with her clients. In fact, with coming regularly, it was a little like a soap opera as Sarah got caught up in other people's lives. Mel loved to tease the people she worked with, too. It was Ellie's turn to be teased this week, as Caroline had seen her out with a boy in town. A blushing Ellie was keeping quiet.

'Right,' said Mel turning back to Sarah. 'A new image? Is there something exciting in your life that I don't know about?'

'No, nothing new. I just need something to cheer me up.'

'Where did you get to last Thursday at the Christmas opening?' asked Mel. 'I saw you early in the evening but then didn't see you again. You said that you were going to call in for a glass of wine and a mince pie. You don't usually refuse a glass of wine.'

'Oh, er, well, er, oh I might as well tell you.' She told Mel about Darren and received commiserations from all the staff.

'I'm so sorry,' said Mel. 'Me going on about something new in your life. I feel awful now. Never mind, we'll sort your hair out and then you'll feel better if nothing else. Now how do you want it?'

Sarah looked in the mirror and said, 'I don't want to lose much of the length, but could you trim some off the bottom and make a better shape round my face, more of a bob I think, what do you think?'

Mel said she thought that sounded fine and started to cut her hair.

'When you come in next week, I won't be here. I'm taking Luke to Lapland. But Jenny will look after you.'

'Yes, that will be fine, book me in with Jenny. I bet Luke is excited about Lapland.'

'Well not really,' said Mel laughing. 'I think I'm more excited than he is.' Mel soon finished Sarah's hair.

'Yes, that's better,' Sarah said. 'Thanks Mel, I do feel better, I always do when my hair looks good.'

'I've never seen you with your hair not looking good,' replied Mel. 'It's so thick and such a lovely colour.'

'You wouldn't think so if it was yours, I've always wanted blonde hair like yours.'

'I don't think anybody is ever satisfied about their hair', replied Mel. 'If it's curly they want it straightened, if it's straight they want it permed. Mind you, I'm not complaining, it keeps me in business.'

'Well, I'd best be off, Tesco calls. Have a lovely time in Lapland. See the rest of you next week. Bye.'

'Bye,' they all chorused back.

Sarah drove to Clitheroe to Tescos and did the shopping that she usually did on Thursday evenings. 'Just think,' mused Sarah, 'if I'd gone to Tesco's as usual on Thursday instead of the Christmas opening, I might never have known about Darren's wife and children. At least I know now, even though I'm miserable.' The longer the relationship had gone on, the worse it would have been for her. But she couldn't imagine it being any worse than it was now. Tears started to fill her eyes, so she got her hanky out and started to blow her nose furiously to try and make it look like she was full of cold. Children from a local school were singing carols outside the store and Sarah stayed to listen to them. She loved Christmas and all that went with it. Sarah decided there and then that she would go to church this Christmas, if not before.

She'd been promising to go to the Parish church in the village ever since she moved in, so perhaps the time was now ripe. For the Millennium, the church was producing a Rock Nativity that week, and it would be a gentle introduction to the church. She went to the Rock Nativity that night and felt lulled by the age old story of Christ's nativity. The girl playing Mary was as gentle and caring as the man playing Herod was nasty. Sarah was able to laugh at the antics of the people playing the sheep which brought a laugh to many of the congregation. Sarah decided that the church seemed friendly and decided to attend the family service next morning. Hearing the distantly familiar words, Sarah felt a measure of comfort in the service, which brought back memories of her childhood. A baptism took place during the service and it reminded her again about her new nephews. 'I will go and visit them soon,' she promised herself. But it also brought a sadness to her, as she saw the look of love pass between the new parents and their child, and it reminded her again of the keenness of her loss. Sarah thought again about her longing for marriage and her own child, but decided that she must enjoy the good life that she had, and be thankful for it. As she left the church, many of the people came to talk to her and welcome her to the church. One of the ladies recognised her from the previous night and asked her if she had enjoyed the Rock Nativity.

'It was marvellous,' answered Sarah, 'I really enjoyed it.' As she was leaving, the lady asked Sarah's name. The lady laughed. 'Well at least I won't forget your name, as it is my name too although I'm usually called Sally. I'm the churchwarden here, so do contact me anytime you want to and we look forward to seeing you again.'

'Thanks' said Sarah, 'I must go now,' and hurried down the drive, anxious not to have to make any commitment to anything at this stage. But walking back down the hill through the village, Sarah felt strangely warmed by the welcome that the other Sarah had given her.

Chapter 3

Sarah soon got back into the busy life that she had. As the days went by, it got easier and she thought about Darren less frequently, but there were still times when the sadness overwhelmed her, often at unexpected times. She immersed herself in her work and went to aerobics classes in the village, feeling fitter than she had done in a long time. Slowly and surely she rebuilt her life. She had a lot to look forward to. When she e-mailed James about Darren, he had sent her a promise of an airline ticket for her next Christmas present. He had said laughingly that that was the only way he could guarantee that his sons saw their only aunty. She had been thrilled to receive it and decided that she wouldn't have a major holiday this year, but would save up so that she could have plenty of spending money when she went to Garland in Texas, where James lived. Sarah had found a leaflet from the National Trust in her annual membership pack that advertised holidays. One of them was for a week's holiday spent visiting a selection of stately homes around the country.

Sarah had sent for more details. It was the sort of holiday that you could go on alone and make friends there. It was an awful realisation that, this year, she would have no one to go on holiday with. Her two closest friends were otherwise engaged this year. She had usually gone abroad with Louise and Tracey, but Tracey was getting married later in the year and Louise was expecting her first baby. That was another thing to look forward to, reflected Sarah. She was to be a bridesmaid for Tracey in August. Who knows, she might meet someone at the wedding who was single. 'Some hopes,' she reflected grimly.

The next day at work, Sarah slipped out to the shops during her lunch break. She got bread and cooked meat from the Spar shop to save going after work, then picked up the Clitheroe Advertiser from the paper shop. Still having a few minutes to spare, she went into the sweet shop. Sarah always liked calling in the sweet shop. She and the girls liked to keep a supply of mints under the shelf in the library. But Sarah also liked to see the owner, Joyce. She was a local councillor and started telling Sarah about the rows that were going on about the lack of parking in Whalley.

'I've never known anything like this, in all my years as a councillor,' she moaned. 'The council meetings have been terrible. Nobody can agree on anything. I don't know where it is all going to end.' Sarah commiserated with her then, picking up the selection of mints, walked back to work. When she got back, it was Margaret's turn to go for a break.

'Could I borrow your Clitheroe Advertiser whilst I'm on my break?' asked Margaret.

Sarah handed it over, and Margaret left the library. During a lull in the afternoon, Margaret started telling Sarah about an article that she had been reading in the paper.

'It's about a young boy called Philip who lives in Clitheroe. He's got cerebral palsy and has been on one of those courses where they learn to do intensive exercises to make them better. His mum is now appealing for people to help her with the exercises, to give her a break.'

'Poor woman,' replied Sarah, but the conversation got no further, as a group of schoolchildren arrived for the weekly story telling session. Sarah forgot all about the article until late that evening, when she was curled up on the settee reading the paper. Her heart went out to the young woman who was a single parent. Philip's father had walked out on them when he found out that Philip had cerebral palsy. She was determined to do her best by her son, but was finding it hard to keep up with the round the clock exercises. As Sarah looked at the picture of Philip and his mum, she felt a tremendous sympathy for them. But it went further than that. She felt that she wanted to help them. She noticed a phone number at the end of the article and slowly walked over to the phone and dialled the number. After a few rings, a lady answered.

'Hello, Victoria here'.

'Er, hello, er, I'm Sarah Evans, and I've seen the article about you in the Clitheroe Advertiser. I don't know if I could help you, I haven't any medical background'.

'Hi Sarah, you don't need any medical background, just a lot of patience, a sense of humour and plenty of enthusiasm. I'd teach you all you needed to know. Would you like to come and meet us? We could talk about it, and you could watch me do the exercises and see if you think that you could help. There's no commitment if you find it harder than you thought.'

'Yes, I'd love to come round, when's convenient?

'Do you work, Sarah?'

'Yes, full time, but I'm free most evenings. And I have Tuesdays and Sundays off.'

'Why not come round tomorrow night then? About six? Then you can see me do the exercises.'

'Six would be fine', said Sarah. 'Now, where do you live?'

Victoria described how to get to the house and then Sarah rang off. She settled back on to the settee and felt strangely calm. Although she was worried about the exercises, she felt that this could be something that would keep her occupied and find a new focus to her life, as well as helping young Philip and his mum.

Next evening, Sarah parked outside Victoria's house and hesitantly knocked on the door. The door was soon opened by a tiny woman in her early thirties with black curly hair falling all over her shoulders and forehead. She greeted Sarah with a big grin.

'Hi, you must be Sarah. Come in.' She led the way through the hall into the lounge.

'Would you like a coffee whilst we chat, Sarah?'

'That would be lovely. No sugar and plenty of milk, please.'

'You sit down on the settee whilst I make it. I won't be long.'

Sarah looked round the room whilst she was waiting. It was decorated in bright bold colours that Sarah wouldn't have thought would go well together. Bright reds, yellows and oranges were everywhere, with a stunning effect. 'I wouldn't have dared use these colours together in my lounge, but it works' thought Sarah, but then her lounge was much smaller than this. Hearing Victoria talking, Sarah turned towards the kitchen door, then realised that Victoria wasn't talking to her. She was wheeling a chair through the doorway, which contained a small boy.

'Now, Philip, say hello to Sarah. She's come to watch us do our exercises.'

Philip grinned at Sarah and said 'hello', and a few more words but it was very difficult to make out what he was saying, so Sarah just smiled back.

'He's saying thank you for coming, red haired lady,' laughed Victoria. 'He has a fascination for redheads, I don't know why.'

At that point, Philip reached out and tried to touch Sarah's hair but his movements were jerky and uncoordinated and he couldn't reach. Sarah leaned her head forward so that Philip could reach, and he jerkily stroked her hair.

'It's lovely hair, mummy,' said Philip to his mum, who then translated it for Sarah's benefit.

'That's Philip's main problem. He's bright and intelligent, but his body won't do what his brain tells him to do. He gets so frustrated, especially when people don't understand what he is saying. Or treat him like he is simple.' Sarah felt guilty and a little worried. Would she ever be able to understand him and how could she possibly be of any use to Philip? As if she had read her mind, Victoria started reassuring Sarah.

'It's surprising how quickly you'll get use to understanding him. Everybody panics at first. Come on, I'll start showing you the exercises. We call them patterns.'

Victoria lifted Philip out of his chair and laid him on his back, on a mat on the floor. She started to move Philip's legs up and down, then bent and stretched them at the knee. The manoeuvres were quite simple and followed a pattern, eventually working the muscles all over his body.

'What do you think so far?' asked Victoria. 'Do you think that you could do it?'

'Well, I'm not sure. I'd have to have a go first.'

'Feel free,' said Victoria, and moved over on the mat. Sarah crouched down on the mat and picked up Philip's leg and tried to copy the movement that Victoria had done.

'How do I know whether I'm hurting him or not?' asked Sarah, tremulously.

'He'll let you know if you are, won't you Philip?'

Philip grinned and nodded his head. 'How am I doing then?' asked Sarah.

'Doing OK' said Philip jerkily.

'Oh,' gasped Sarah, 'thank you, I understood you then.'

'There, you two are getting on famously already,' smiled Victoria.

Sarah kept up the exercises for twenty minutes and then Victoria took over. Sarah felt exhausted. She hadn't realised how tense she had been whilst going thorough the patterns.

'How do you keep this up every day?' asked Sarah. 'I'm exhausted after a few minutes.'

'That's why I've appealed for help,' replied Victoria. 'It does get easier. At first, you are very tense because it is all new. But later you will relax into the exercises and find that they are quite relaxing. Of course, it's easy for me; I learnt to do them very gradually. You seem to have picked them up very quickly though, and I know that Philip likes you, as he soon lets you know if he doesn't! How do you feel about coming to help?'

'Well, if you think I'll be any good, I'd love to come and help.'

'Brilliant. I know that we are all going to get on well together. How much can you offer a week? You said that you were free on Tuesdays. Is there any chance that you could come and help on Tuesdays? That would be great. It's the one day when I can't get any help.'

'Yes, I could come every Tuesday. What time does the school bus come for him?'

'About half past nine, and then he's back at half past three. But he finishes for the Easter holidays this week.'

'Well, shall I come next Tuesday morning about ten o'clock? And then you could have a break, if we're OK together.'

'That would be great. I love to have a quick visit to the market if I can. I love Clitheroe market. If you are sure that you don't mind.'

'No, that will be fine. I'd better come again before Tuesday then Philip can get to know me better, and I can do more of the exercises. What about Saturday night?'

Victoria stared at Sarah and then said, 'Saturday night? Are you sure? Nobody comes on a Saturday night.'

Sarah laughed, 'Well I'll come.'

Victoria decided that it was Philip's bedtime and started to take him up to bed.

'I think I'll get going, then,' said Sarah, 'I'll see you Saturday. I'll see myself out.'

'Thanks Sarah, I know we're going to get on great, the three of us. I know about people straight away. I always have done. See you Saturday, then, if you don't mind.'

'Bye Victoria, bye Philip,' said Sarah as she left the house, hearing their farewells as she closed the door. Sarah got in her car and sat for a while before starting the engine up. She felt very humble and realised that life had treated her very kindly up to now. She had been feeling very miserable about Darren, but what was that to the lifetime of commitment that Victoria was giving to Philip. And with never a grumble about her lot, or any sign of resentment. Sarah decided there and then that she would do all in her power to make Philip's life more comfortable, but also to help this brave woman and try and give her some of her life back. As she arrived home and got ready for bed, Sarah started to realise that her life would be better when she was focusing on someone else instead of herself. As she turned the light out, Sarah felt strangely calm for the first time in many months, and fell asleep as soon as her head touched the pillow.

Tuesday dawned all too early. After a lie in, Sarah got up and showered. She put on her jeans and a t-shirt, with a sweatshirt on top. She suspected that working with Philip on his patterns could be hot work. She arrived exactly on time and Victoria opened the door.

'Hi Sarah, you haven't changed your mind after Saturday night, then? Come in. Do you want a coffee before you start?'

'No, off you go,' said Sarah. 'Enjoy the break while you can.'

'I won't argue, I'll be off up town before you can say Jack Robinson,' laughed Victoria. 'Now you're sure you'll be OK with Philip?'

'Get off with you, before I change my mind. Philip and I will be fine.'

'Do you want anything bringing back from town?' asked Victoria.

'No, I'll go up to the market afterwards myself. Bye Victoria.'

'OK, OK, I'm going.'

Sarah turned and laughed with Philip. 'Isn't your mum hard work?' and Philip laughed. They started work on the patterns and Sarah was amazed how quickly the time had flown. She was surprised when Victoria opened the door and realised how late it was. 'Is it that time already?' she asked, looking at the clock. Victoria went straight to the kettle and made Sarah a drink.

'You'll need this now,' she laughed.

Sarah thanked her for the drink and sat companionably with Victoria. They had talked for a long time on Saturday night, after Philip had gone to bed. She eventually told Victoria about Darren, but although Victoria sympathised with her, she told Sarah not to let it ruin her life. That was the mistake that she had made, advised Victoria. Sarah had thought long and hard after their chat and felt much stronger and determined to get on with her own life. After the coffee, Sarah got ready to leave.

'I'll be on my way, thanks for the snack you left us. We both enjoyed it. I'll see you on Sunday.'

'Bye,' said Philip and Victoria in unison as she closed the door. Sarah walked up the hill into town and mooched round the market, buying several items. She decided to go for a coffee and something to eat before going home, so that would save time later and save her cooking. She went to Halfpenny's café. The first time that she had been there, she thought that it was a strange choice of name for a café, until she found out that it was the proprietor's name. Another strange feature was that it was a café and needlework shop, and it was also the old toll house for Clitheroe. After a toasted sandwich and a cappuccino, Sarah went in to talk to Tessa Halfpenny who ran the needlework part of the business. Tessa smiled her beaming smile.

'Erm, do you have, er, sort of, very easy to do needlework? I haven't a clue really. I've never done it before. Could you help me?' Sarah stumbled. Tessa smiled.

'I'll gladly help you. What would you like to start with?'

'I haven't a clue, you tell me. I asked a lady in the village to do a sampler for my twin nephews when they were born and ever since I've been meaning to get started.'

'Well, I don't think you're ready for a sampler yet, but why not try an initial, perhaps yours, or a special person?'

'My initial will be fine,' Sarah replied rather quickly. Sarah and Tessa chatted about the stitches and colours and eventually she was ready to start on her own. Sarah thanked Tessa and made her way to the door. Tessa's husband opened the door for Sarah and as she thanked him, he quipped, 'Always ready to help someone who spends money here.' Sarah laughed; he was quite a tease at times.

When she got home, she decided to start the needlework straight away and was quite proud of her achievement by the end of the night although she had had to pull a few stitches out again. Tessa had told her to call back in next time she was in town if she required any more help. 'She'll be sick of me before I've finished,' thought Sarah. As she went to bed, she mused over the new skills that she was learning lately, both with Philip and now the needlework with Tessa. As her head hit the pillow, Sarah realised that she felt happier than she had for a long time, and she sighed pleasurably as she drifted into sleep.

The weeks and months passed by and, before she knew it, it was time to go on her holiday. The girls at the library were worried about her going on holiday on her own, but Sarah said that, when she had rung up about it, the lady had said that many single people came on the holidays, and she should not worry. She told the girls that if she was bored by the holiday, she would know not to go again, but going to several stately homes in a week would be sheer bliss, as she always felt uncomfortable going to them on her own. And anyway, it was better than staying at home alone for her holidays.

Sarah finished work on the Thursday so that she had plenty of time to get ready for the holiday. She chose the clothes that she was taking and at the last minute put an iron in the case, just in case there wasn't one at the different hotels they were staying at.

The coach was picking her up from Blackburn and so she left her car at home and got a taxi.

Chapter 4

Sarah sat on the coach that was to take her down to meet the other holidaymakers who were going on the National Trust holiday. It seemed a long journey on this hot sticky day, but the holiday was starting near London. It would end up in Yorkshire, ironically, so she had negotiated with the organisers that she wouldn't return with the others but would drop off in Yorkshire and get a bus back home. It would be strange not seeing Philip and Victoria for a week, but it had turned out incredibly well as Philip was going on a holiday for disabled children and Victoria was going to visit a cousin in Huddersfield. The coach pulled into a bus station. They had arrived at the destination with an hour to spare, so there was time for a snack and a freshen up before they got on another coach. Sarah went to wait by stand 18 on the bus station, which was where the trip was going from. The coach was already waiting so Sarah got on, showing the driver where her luggage was. He told her that she was the first to arrive, so they wouldn't be setting off just yet, but at least she could have her pick of the seats. She smiled in return and thanking him, she climbed up and sat on the first seat across from the driver.

'I like to see where I'm going,' she quipped. The coach slowly filled up and within 15 minutes they were ready to set off. Sarah watched her fellow passengers as they got on the coach. There were a lot of couples, but a few people on their own, too. They were all at least twenty years older than her. 'No danger of romance here,' she mused. She felt like she was on a Saga holiday for the over 50's. But that was the trouble when you were getting older and were still unmarried. One by one, your friends dropped off as they married, or even worse, had babies, and then it seemed that you had nothing in common anymore.

'Gosh Sarah,' she said to herself, 'pull yourself together. You're beginning to sound maudlin. You've a lot going for you, girl, so remember Granny and think positive.' Sarah started reflecting on her life. It wasn't all that bad, considering. She had her house and no money worries like a lot of her married friends, as her mortgage was very small. Mind you, if her parents hadn't been killed in the car crash six years ago, she would probably still have been living at home. Sarah relaxed back and closed her eyes. She must have dozed because suddenly she was woken by an elderly lady's voice asking if the seat was taken.

'Pardon?' said Sarah, a little embarrassed.

'Is this seat taken?' replied the lady much louder, as if Sarah was deaf.

'No', stammered Sarah, by now feeling rather foolish. The lady swung her shopping bag onto the rack and sat down heavily.

'Carter, Evelyn Carter, Miss, retired headmistress, spinster but not of this parish,' said the lady in loud, jerky tones. Sarah stared at her. 'Well, what about you, then?' Evelyn asked, beaming.

'Er, Sarah Evans, librarian, not married,' she replied.

'Good, we've got the introductions out of the way. On this trip on your own, then?'

'Er, yes,' replied Sarah, a little awestruck.

'And what parish do you live in then?'

'I live in a little village called Read,' replied Sarah regaining her wits. 'It's in the Ribble Valley in Lancashire, near Whalley or Clitheroe, if you've heard of them.'

'Read, um, now, let me think. Yes that's right, Read Hall was mentioned in the book 'Mist Over Pendle.' Is Read Hall near you?'

'Yes, it is. I sometimes walk through the grounds. It's beautiful,' said Sarah.

'Been to Whalley too,' boomed Evelyn. 'Went to the Whalley Abbey Conference Centre to a retreat. Marvellous place. Very atmospheric. You almost expect the mediaeval monks to come round the corner. You can really enjoy the silence there.'
Sarah tried to smother a smile, imagining Evelyn being totally silent.

'And the food,' she boomed again. 'Wonderful. In fact all of the staff are a delight. But the vicar of the place is a hoot. Good man, him, good man.'

'Yes, I know Whalley very well, I work there,' said Sarah quickly whilst she could get a word in edgeways. 'I often go to the coffee shop in the Abbey grounds for my lunch. I know what you mean about the vicar. He's recently broken the world record for preaching the longest sermon. He's hoping to go in the Guinness book of records. I went to listen to him one day. He was amazing. And all without the use of notes.'

'Ha' boomed Evelyn, 'just the sort of thing I'd expect from him. Tell him well done from me, next time you see him. I'm sure he'll remember me.'

'I'm sure he could never forget you,' mumbled Sarah.

'What was that, my dear? I'm a little deaf.'

'Er, nothing much, I was just saying that the vicar would probably remember you. He's got a very good memory.'
'Phew,' thought Sarah to herself, 'that was close.'
The coach rumbled on and Evelyn seemed to have temporarily dried up, for which Sarah was very grateful. She closed her eyes and relaxed, hoping that Evelyn would take the hint.

Sarah woke with a jolt. The coach had stopped outside a hotel.

'This is our first port of call, ladies and gentlemen', said the driver. 'We'll be staying here tonight and will visit the first stately home tomorrow. Your courier will join you here.' As if on cue, a middle-aged lady jumped on the bus. She was tall and solid, with a large face and square figure. Her tweed suit was rather masculine and severe. She bounded around the bus saying 'hello' to everyone.

'Definitely a jolly hockey sticks sort,' mused Sarah. She could just imagine her on the hockey field, or chief scorer at netball. She eventually got to Evelyn and Sarah.

'Last, but by no means least, you two, welcome to the tour. I'm Margaret Spencer. I hope you'll have a very happy time on our tour. Have you had a good journey so far? I do hope so; it's terrible to have an uncomfortable journey at the beginning of the holiday, isn't it? Well, must stop chatting and then we can all get on with the holiday.' With that, Miss Spencer hurried off the bus shouting, 'follow me'. Sarah and Evelyn let out a sigh of relief. Evelyn was the first to recover.

'My, she can talk,' said Evelyn. Sarah nodded in agreement, secretly admiring anyone who could out-talk Evelyn. Perhaps Evelyn had met her match!

The bus slowly emptied as all the passengers got off, leaving Evelyn and Sarah to the last. As they got into the foyer of the hotel, Miss Davenport was directing the group towards a notice-board. On the board was a list of all the room numbers. Sarah fervently hoped that she was not sharing with Evelyn. As she scanned the lists, her heart sank as she saw her name linked with Evelyn's.

'Oh goody,' boomed Evelyn, 'we're sharing. I'm glad we sat together, we've had such a lovely chat already.' Sarah smiled, thinking that it had been more of a monologue than a chat. She followed the porter up the stairs to the twin bedroom. Evelyn got in first and dumped her bag quickly onto the bed next to the window, which overlooked the gardens.

'Next time,' Sarah promised herself, 'however much the single supplement is, I'll go for it. Just my luck.'

'I'm going to have a little nap before supper,' said Evelyn. 'Will you shout me in an hour, please?'

'Of course,' said Sarah, relieved at the prospect of silence. After putting her things away, Sarah decided to go for a walk. Sitting still in a coach all day was pretty uncomfortable, even though the coach itself was very well-sprung and luxurious. She walked outside and headed towards a little rose garden that was at the side of the hotel. Such formal gardens were quickly going out of fashion now. She remembered her grandfather's formal garden, with carefully cut out borders, all with roses in the beds. The only relief from the roses were clumps of pinks, and Sarah could almost smell the sweet scent in her imagination as she thought of her childhood. Nowadays, people wanted instant, low maintenance gardens, which had been popularised by Alan Titchmarsh and Charlie Dimmock on TV. And not to forget the water features. The name Charlie Dimmock had become synonymous with water features. Actually, the young couple next door had got a water feature in their garden and Sarah loved to hear the water trickling. But then the young man next door was a landscape gardener, so she expected great things from him. One day, she would ask him to sort her garden out, but that was a long way in the future. The most important thing to budget for, after this holiday, was her holiday to see her nephews.

Sarah wandered back into the hotel and went to the bar to order herself a drink. Some of the party were coming downstairs ready for evening dinner. Sarah was relieved to see that they had not changed for dinner, so she nipped into the cloakroom and freshened up for the meal, collecting her drink on the way out. She wandered in to the residents' lounge and walked towards the large bay window, that had stained glass at the top of each panel, giving them almost a saintly look. She sat down in the large leather armchair and placed her drink onto the mat. As a lady came in, she looked up. Sarah recognised her as one of her own party. The lady appeared very nervous and approached Sarah, asking very quietly if the seat was free. Sarah looked round at the two large settees and three chairs, and wondered if she was joking. Seeing her looking so nervous, Sarah said, 'No, of course not, do sit down.' The lady smiled and quickly sat in the nearest chair, frowning into her cup of coffee. 'Are you on your own, on this holiday? I am,' asked Sarah.

'Yes, I am. I've never been on holiday on my own before. Have you?'

'No,' replied Sarah. 'It's my first time, too. It's quite nerve wracking, isn't it? Wondering whom you will meet. I'm Sarah by the way.'

The lady smiled and looked a little more relaxed and smiled at Sarah.

'My name's Irene. Irene Scanlon. I, er, I'm a widow. I've never been on holiday without my husband before. It feels really strange. The children were very good; they took me away for Christmas and New Year last year, y'know, for the Millennium. That was really good of them. I was dreading my first Christmas on my own'.

'I'm so sorry,' said Sarah, 'when did you lose your husband?'

'A year ago tomorrow. That's why I came on this trip. To take my mind off things. Mind you, I'd never have come on a holiday like this when my husband was alive, he couldn't stand stately homes. Used to go on about the poor workers who had to skivvy for the Lords and Ladies who thought themselves better than we were. Bit of a revolutionist was my Jack. Mind you, he never did anything, more an armchair revolutionist than a real one.' Irene started to laugh to herself, and Sarah watched as Irene's face suffused with pleasure, as she recalled her husband's foibles with love. When she lifted her face, Sarah could see tears forming on her eyelids. Desperate to change the subject, Sarah asked which stately home she was looking forward to most. Irene replied, 'All of them, I'll be in my element. Just to be able to crawl round them at my own speed, rather than hurrying up because Jack was bored with looking at the house and wanted to get to the gardens. Oh, look, they're calling us into dinner. Can I sit with you?' asked Irene.

'With pleasure,' replied Sarah, and they walked to a small table at the side of the dining room. This is better than sitting with Evelyn, thought Sarah, and then was cross at herself for being so catty. As if to punish her for her thoughts, Evelyn appeared and made a beeline for Sarah and Irene's table. Sarah guiltily remembered that she had promised to wake Evelyn up for dinner.

'I was just going to come up and check that you were awake,' said Sarah lamely, hoping that Evelyn couldn't tell that she was lying.

'No problem,' boomed Evelyn, 'now who's your friend?'

'This is Irene Scanlon. Irene, this is Evelyn Carter. The two ladies replied that they were pleased to meet each other. 'Oh dear,' thought Sarah to herself, 'she'll eat Irene alive.' Sarah watched as Evelyn started her direct tactics to get to know Irene. Feeling embarrassed for Irene, Sarah looked away and pretended to study the wine list, but ready to pounce in and rescue Irene her if necessary. Sarah was worrying unnecessarily. Irene seemed to be blossoming under Evelyn's questioning techniques. It was almost as if Sarah had broken the ice with Irene, and now she was slowly coming back to life again. Sarah hoped that this tentative friendship would work out. Perhaps Evelyn was just what Irene needed.

The waiters arrived with the food and, for a while, the ladies ate in companionable silence. At the end of the meal, the guests were asked to go into the lounge, where a representative from the costumiers would be waiting for them. The lounge had taken on the look of a ladies' boudoir, with dresses, suits, wigs and accessories covering all the tables and many of the chairs. When they had booked the holiday, they had been required to fill in quite a lot of personal details such as age, height, weight, sex, colouring. Sarah had laughed when they asked these questions, but was assured that they were simply to match people up with the characters that would have lived in the house during a particular era. A lot of hilarity ensued during the evening, as people tried on the outfits that the costumiers had selected for them. They then had the unenviable task of altering them to fit the people who would be wearing them on Friday night. No mean feat for one lady and her assistant. But she assured the guests that she had never been beaten yet. Evelyn had been chosen to play the part of Lady Grace, the dowager mother of the Lord of the Manor, and she looked very regal in her flowing robes.

After the impromptu fashion show, Irene said goodnight to both Sarah and Evelyn and thanked them for a lovely evening. Sarah was pleased at that. She had been worried that Irene might have been overawed by Evelyn, but the opposite was the fact. As Sarah walked upstairs behind Evelyn, she felt a little guilty that she had been critical of her new found friend, and decided to be more tolerant for the rest of the holiday. 'Well, tomorrow at least, she wasn't sure she could keep it up for the whole holiday,' she chuckled to herself as she went upstairs.

The first stately home that they visited was Hughenden Manor. This had been the home of Benjamin Disraeli, where he used to like to escape from the pressures of his working life. Sarah spent much of the day with Evelyn, and they were pleased to see that many of the books, pictures and furniture were still the original ones. The gardens had been designed by his wife, Mary, and the woodland walks were beautiful.

The following day they visited Blickling Hall in Norfolk. Here, Sarah was fascinated by the mellow brick Jacobean building and especially by the ornate ceilings. There seemed to be several stately homes in this area, and Sarah decided that she would like to visit this area again, as Felbrigg Hall also looked interesting.

Tuesday found them in Grantham, visiting Belton House. This house had also been built in the seventeenth century and was from around the same era as Blickling Hall. The gardens contained some exciting adventure playgrounds, set apart for different ages, and Sarah could envisage that this would be popular with families with children, who may get bored looking at yet another old house. Mr and Mrs Wallbank decided that they would bring their grandchildren here some day. Sarah was awash with history by Tuesday night, but enjoyed reading the booklets in detail, that she had bought from each house. The hotels that they stayed at each night were all very different, but they were all of a very high standard.

Derbyshire was their next port of call, and Sarah was thrilled that they were visiting Sudbury Hall. She knew that there was an exciting museum of childhood here, as one of her friends from

University had lived near the Hall and had worked in the tearooms whilst she was at Sixth Form College. Sarah was not disappointed. She spent most of the time in the museum on her own, and had only a short time to explore the rest of the house, before they set off to their hotel. Her most vivid memories were of the great staircase at Sudbury Hall, and she knew that she would remember this place for a long time to come.

From Derbyshire, they came to Dunham Massey in Greater Manchester. For Sarah, they were getting nearer home. As well as enjoying the beautiful house, Sarah found the gardens to be lovely, too. She and Irene bought an ice cream and sat in the gardens watching the deer roam through the grounds. Later they spent time walking round the lakes and ponds. Some local young boys were fishing in one of the ponds, and seemed to be having a great time. All too soon, they were travelling to their last overnight accommodation before the ball. Sarah was tired, but exhilarated by all that she had seen during the week, and such contrasts of styles that the tour had included. She would remember them for a long time.

Chapter 5

Sarah leaned back into her seat, as the coach sped along the motorway. She looked at her watch, trying to work out how long it would be before the next stop. Sarah smiled as she looked at her watch, remembering that Darren had bought it for her, and the romantic way he had given it to her. He had taken her to the Moorcock Inn near Waddington. It had been their first weekend away together. The hotel was halfway up Waddington Moor and had a stunning view over Clitheroe and the surrounding areas. As there hadn't been a wedding booked for that weekend the proprietors, Susan and Peter, gave them the bridal suite. Darren had put the watch on the tea tray the next morning. Sarah's eyes started to fill with tears.

'Now just stop all that,' she said to herself, 'look where it got you. Nowhere, with a lot of heartache to boot.' 'Well,' she answered herself, 'I didn't know he was married. He didn't look or act married, he never let anything slip that might have alerted me. How was I to know? If I hadn't seen him and his wife in Whalley, I would still have been seeing him. And those children, so innocent, so trusting, looking up at their father with those big brown eyes. How I hate brown eyes, especially big ones. Oh, I'm so naïve. I'll never trust another man again.' She stretched a little in the seat, and then laughed to herself. 'Well, not until the next time anyway!' The loudspeaker above her head crackled into life and woke her from her reverie.

'We'll be arriving at the hotel in ten minutes,' said the driver, 'just in time for afternoon tea.' Sarah sat up and put her book away in the large handbag she carried everywhere with her on holiday. The coach pulled into the driveway of a large red brick building that had been a private house previously. Margaret Spencer leaped off the coach to welcome everyone.

'Welcome to the Mayflower. We'll be staying here for two nights, so that you can recover from the ball tonight. We've to be ready to set off for the ball at 6 pm so there will only be a snack provided at about 4 pm to put you on. Can't have you all too full to eat tonight, can we?' she grinned to everyone.

Sarah was looking forward to the ball. It was the highlight of the whole holiday. Tonight, they were going to another stately home that was on the outskirts of a city in Yorkshire. She was almost home, being back up in the north of England. It had been arranged that her suitcases would be taken to an hotel near the stately home, so that she could stay the night and return to Lancashire the next day, rather than travel back down country to the Mayflower. Sarah was relieved that she wouldn't have to make the journey back down to London by coach, as it had seemed to take forever.

They were to dress in authentic period costumes and eat food that would have been served many years ago. In the cool clean bedroom, Sarah started to get ready for the ball, with some trepidation. Apparently her dress was the replica of a dress that was on a picture in the stately home where they were going. It was in rich dark green velvet, which complemented the colour of her eyes. The dress was gathered under the bust, then fell in gentle folds down to the floor. Sarah walked carefully round the room. The pale green satin slippers were a little tight, but at least the dress was comfy.

'It could have been worse,' she thought, 'it could have been the crinoline era when they all had tiny waists. I wouldn't have been able to eat much with a nipped in waist,' she mused to herself. She wasn't allowed to wear her watch, though, because it didn't fit in with the era. 'Perhaps as well,' she thought, 'it will stop me thinking about him. I'll even have to leave the mobile at home, which will make me feel even more vulnerable. Mind you I don't suppose I need it tonight, as we will be accompanied at all times.' Remembering how reluctant she had been to buy a mobile phone, she laughed at herself, not believing that she could feel vulnerable without it. 'I suppose it's like a comfort blanket,' she mused.

Fastening the black velvet choker round her neck, Sarah looked in the ornate mirror and wondered at the size of the enormous emerald that was fastened to the choker. 'I hope this is just imitation, otherwise I'd be frightened of losing it,' she thought. She turned her attention to her hair. A picture was on the dressing table beside her. The costumiers had ordered her a wig for the evening but, when they saw her hair, they had suggested that she didn't need it.

'It would be an insult to give you a wig, my dear, your hair is just too perfect', oozed the woman. As she took the tiny heated rollers out of her thick, shiny auburn hair, Sarah shook her head and then brushed her hair into a sort of loose ponytail. The little curls bobbed and bounced around the nape of her neck and she pulled some ringlets free to frame her face, fastening the pink flowers into her hair behind each ear, copying the style of the picture on her dressing table.

Sarah looked again at herself in the mirror. The new hairstyle framed her elfin face and the dress made her seem taller and thinner than she was. 'I think I should have been born in this era, I don't look too bad,' she laughed to herself. Buoyed up with confidence, Sarah swept down the stairs to where the rest of the guests were waiting for the coach. As they were about to set off, Sarah noticed that Evelyn was not amongst the guests.

'Where's Evelyn?' she shouted to nobody in particular.

'Oh, she's got a tummy upset,' replied Irene. 'I'm sorry Sarah, I was supposed to be letting you know. She went to the local doctor and he advised her to miss out on the evening. She's gone into town to the chemist.'

'Oh, poor Evelyn, she'll be really sorry to miss tonight's entertainment. She was really looking forward to being Lady Grace; she definitely looked the part. I wondered where she had got to when I was getting ready.' At that point the driver shouted that he was setting off, so Sarah had to sit down quickly and fasten her seatbelt.

They drove for about an hour through countryside and then took the ring road round the outskirts of the city. They had just driven through a built up area when the driver shouted 'Here we are'. At first, Sarah thought that it was a joke. They were still in the middle of the built up area. The driver swung the coach into a small gateway that looked to be in the middle of a housing estate.

As they entered the drive, it was as if they had entered another age. A long curving drive curled round to the front of an eighteenth century house. Lights were shining from all the windows and the sounds of a string quartet could be heard. The guests were greeted by a man in his thirties, dressed in a period outfit from many years ago.

'Welcome to Roding Hall. I hope you will enjoy your stay here. I'm the curator of the hall, and your host for this evening. I am dressed as, and taking the part of, Lord Josiah Grace for tonight. We will start by having a tour of the hall and I will tell you a little of its history. Then we'll dine, followed by the ball. Let's start by going up these fine carved stairs. The house was built in 1775 for the younger son of Lord Grace on the occasion of his marriage. It then passed to his eldest son, Josiah, who remained unmarried and died without issue, as they say in the history books.' The man appeared very knowledgeable about the house as he showed them round the ground floor.

They started to ascend the wide staircase. The top of the stairs led into a gallery that had many paintings lining the walls. One of the men in the party was very interested in all the portraits and asked the curator who they were. Sarah lost interest; art wasn't a favourite subject of hers. She wandered over to the other side of the gallery and looked out of the window. It was getting dusk, so there was little to see. Sarah noticed that there was another wing built onto the back of the house. It spoilt the look of it really. It would never have passed the planning committee in the Ribble Valley, she reflected to herself. It made the house look quite odd. The back of the house looked like a T shape from the window. A bit different from all the E shaped houses that had been so common in Elizabethan days. She turned round and leaned against the wall, weighing up the curator, Joe.

'Pleasant enough chap,' she thought, 'nice beard, lovely dark brown hair cut in a neat style, tall and slim. Mmm, very nice,' thought Sarah, 'and he certainly knows his stuff about this hall.' Still, I suppose they have to do their homework. Haven't been out with a Joe before.' She pulled herself up sharp. 'That's enough, my girl, he's probably married with six kids.' As she thought this, her eyes surreptitiously moved to his ring finger. 'No wedding ring,' she thought, 'but then, many men didn't wear them nowadays. Darren certainly didn't. Stop it,' she reprimanded herself, 'no thoughts of him today, or any other day for that matter. He's history.'

A maid came up to Joe and said that the dinner was ready to be served. As she turned to walk back down the stairs, she gasped as she passed Sarah.

'What's the matter?' said Sarah, a little concerned.

'Nothing Miss, you just gave me a turn. You look so like her.' The maid pointed to the picture behind Sarah and, as she turned to look, Sarah too gasped.

'That must be the picture that my outfit is modelled on,' she said. 'I can see what you mean, I do have a look of her.' Sarah carefully examined the painting and noticed the large choker similar to her own but also an enormous emerald ring on the lady's ring finger. Sarah wondered why the costumiers had missed the ring out of her outfit if they were trying to be so accurate, but then realised that it would be too difficult to gauge ring sizes, unlike a choker that could be adjusted to fit. One or two other guests started commenting on the likeness, but by then Joe was halfway down the stairs at the far side of the gallery, telling more of the history as they passed through. Sarah hurried after everyone else.

'This isn't the original dining room. That was at the far side of the house, miles away from the kitchens. It must have driven the maids mad in those days. They had to run along an underground passage and up two flights of stairs up to the old dining room with all the dishes. The wife of the sixth Lord Grace had it all changed, but I'm afraid that we couldn't change it back just for tonight,' he laughed. He led the way into the sumptuous dining room, ablaze with candles everywhere. No electric lights allowed tonight!

Most of the guests had walked into the room in couples so Sarah hung back whilst everyone sat down. Joe sat at the head of the table, looking very much like the Lord of the Manor.

'Well miss, looks like you'll have to do the honours and sit in Lady Grace's own chair, opposite me at the other end of the table, although you are not dressed as her. It was a shame that the other lady could not come tonight'. It was difficult to see his expression because of the candlelight, so Sarah simply thanked him and sat down. As soon as she was seated, the servants swept into the room with the food. Sarah looked at the phenomenal array of cutlery and glasses, and hoped that she didn't use the wrong implements.

The first course was Summer Pease Soup. This appeared to be a combination of cucumber, mint, lettuce, peas, peppers and onion. It tasted refreshingly different from the tinned soup that Sarah was used to. Joe explained that, in 1825, there would then have been a separate fish dish prior to the meat dish but, in order to cater for vegetarians, both courses would be served at the same time. But everybody was welcome to try both dishes if desired. The fish course was sole with mushroom and wine sauce, and the meat dish was Pheasant a la Braise. There was an amazing variety of vegetables and potatoes to meet all needs and tastes. Sarah was feeling quite full by this time, and grateful for the loose flowing garment that she had on, with no waist restrictions. The sweet course soon arrived and Sarah was about to refuse, but the tempting smell of the fresh fruit that made up the syllabub soon changed her mind. Also Joe was explaining that the recipe, or receipt as they used to be called, was an original one. It had been created by a cook who lived in the house in 1825.

It was delicious and very light, the tangy taste of apricots and nectarines very refreshing. Sarah groaned as small dishes of sweets were brought into the room, and large displays of fresh fruit were also put on the table. Tea and coffee were also served. This wasn't how it would have happened in 1825, Joe explained. The ladies would have taken their tea in another room, whilst the gentlemen would have retired to drink porter or brandy and smoke their cigars in the billiards room. But as there was to be a ball, Joe had changed the plans for tonight. After the sumptuous meal had finished, Sarah felt like she could have had a snooze, but there was no chance of that. Joe jumped up and shouted to all the guests.

'Now follow me into the ballroom, the string quartet are just tuning their instruments. Come, Lady Grace,' he laughed at Sarah, 'let's lead the way.' Joe leaned over to Sarah and said, 'I hope you don't mind, I love to play the part at these dinners.'
'Not at all,' stammered Sarah thinking that she could be doing a lot worse than being with this man. He really was very attractive, she thought to herself. He must be at least six foot tall, and his beard was so luxuriant and full, his dark hair shiny and neatly groomed, and he had blue eyes, a great improvement on brown ones, she decided. She was so busy weighing him up that she suddenly realised that he had asked her a question and was waiting for an answer.

'I'm so sorry,' she stammered, feeling a blush colour her cheeks, 'I was miles away then. What did you say?'

'I'm sorry if I'm boring you,' said Joe.

'Not a bit,' replied Sarah hurriedly, 'I was just thinking, er, er, how careful you have been to keep all the detail to how things were done in the nineteenth century. In fact, it's just the opposite, I'm fascinated by this house.'

'Yes,' said Joe, 'it is rather special to me.' By now they had arrived at the ballroom on the next floor. Joe was still holding her hand, even though there was no need to anymore. 'Will you have the first dance with me, Sarah? It is the tradition at Roding Hall balls. Mind you, I'd have wanted the first dance with you whether or not.' By now, Sarah was recovering a little and teased him back.

'Yes, I bet you made that up just so that you could dance with me.'

'No,' said Joe protesting, 'it really is a tradition. But you're right. I would have made it up just to dance with you. But I must warn you that I can't have all the dances with you, as another tradition was that the current Lord had to dance with all the ladies. It would have been good fun as a young man, I expect, but not so good when the Lord was an old man. Mind you, I don't think any of the Lord Graces lived to be old men.'

Joe led Sarah on to the dance floor and a dancing master, who had been hired for the night, explained how the dances would have been. They were very elegant and slow, and Sarah was glad that the age of the polka wasn't fashionable. As she whirled round the floor in Joe's arms, she had a wonderful feeling of safety and well-being. She relaxed in his arms as they twisted and turned through the dances. Feeling that Joe was looking down at her, Sarah tried to start up a conversation, to hide her embarrassment. Or was it just pleasure at being looked at so tenderly by a man?

'This beats going down the disco,' she said with a lightness that she didn't feel, 'dancing was so much more elegant in those days.'

'You can say that again, but my disco dancing days are over. Can't stand the smoke and noise nowadays. Must be a sign that I'm getting older. I can't stand the way you have to keep a finger over your bottle of beer all evening, to make sure somebody doesn't spike your drink. Too many idiots about nowadays for my liking.'

'I couldn't agree more,' replied Sarah. 'My friends think I'm an old fuddy duddy 'cos I don't like going clubbing. I'm glad to meet someone else who feels the same way.'

As the dance came to a close, Joe led Sarah back to a chair and helped her to sit down. 'I'll be back later for you,' he promised, giving her hand a little squeeze as he let go.

'Shouldn't you be marking my card, or something, or is that another era?' said Sarah with a flirtatious grin.

'You're probably right, but there aren't enough of us to bother about that. Well here goes, wish me luck. I'll go and dance with the oldest looking lady in the room now, and then work my way round them all. See you later.'

Sarah watched as he walked away. He was smiling at everyone in the room and seemed to cheer up everyone that he came into contact with. He really was a lovely, lovely man. Sarah sighed. 'Here I go again,' she thought, 'going down a slippery slope of romance.' She laughed at herself, remembering that she had only met him two hours ago. But as he danced with all the other ladies, she kept watching him, and often caught his eye, as he seemed to be watching her as well.

'May I have the honour of this dance, ma'am?' asked an elderly gentleman, making Sarah jump.

'Oh, thank you, of course you may,' replied Sarah as she jumped to her feet. The gentleman led her slowly onto the floor and they joined the dance. She remembered that it was Mr Wallbank. He and his wife had come on this holiday as the first one after retiring. They had had a shoe shop that had been in the family for years, but their sons did not want to carry on in the business and were both making their own different careers.

'Are you enjoying yourself, Sarah?' asked the gentleman, 'you seemed to be smiling to yourself when I approached you.'

'Oh, I'm having a lovely time,' she smiled, 'it's all so authentic, they must have had to do a lot of planning to make it so perfect.'

'Yes, even to your shoes, Sarah. They are a replica of the shoes that young ladies would have been wearing to go dancing in the nineteenth century. We had quite a few books on the history of shoes, some that were passed down through the generations. We also had some of the shoe lasts that belonged to the richer and affluent people in the town where we lived. They were kept at the shoe shop, for their shoes to be handmade. It's a dying art nowadays, though. Very few people can afford to have shoes made for them.'

'I don't think that these were made for me,' said Sarah, 'I keep sliding on the floor in them. I just hope that I don't go flying.' Mr Wallbank chuckled as the music came to an end, and he took her back to her seat. Sarah sat and watched the dances, occasionally having a dance with the other guests, but always, her eyes seeking Joe wherever he was dancing. Eventually, Joe came over to her and took her hand in his, drawing her to her feet. They seemed to mould into each other when they danced, and Sarah felt that her heart was pounding, far more than the exertion of the dance warranted. After two more dances, the music stopped and the string quartet left the little stage and went off to get some refreshments.

'Come with me,' said Joe, 'I want to show you something.' And he gently pulled her away from the ballroom and towards the stairs. 'Don't worry, I'm not going to seduce you' laughed Joe. 'Pity,' thought Sarah to herself, and then was shocked at her own thoughts. How could she feel like that so quickly after meeting a person? Joe led her to the end of the corridor and through a door. They were standing in a minstrels' gallery that overlooked the ballroom, but was positioned so that the people in the ballroom couldn't see them. Joe led Sarah to the side of the thick damask curtains that were at the end of the minstrels' gallery, and showed her the detail of the ornate sculptured roof. He stood closely behind her, and she could feel his breath on her neck.

As he pointed out a detail on the chandelier, he leaned closer to her, and she sank back against his body. Her heart was pounding as he carefully touched her hair, and then gently kissed the side of her neck, like a butterfly. Sarah started trembling and turned round to face Joe. As she did, he gently kissed her on her lips, drawing her closer to him. They drew apart and stared at each other for what felt like a long time, but was probably only seconds.

'I've been wanting to do that all night, Sarah, ever since I met you. It's quite incredible, I've never felt like this before with anyone.'

'Neither have I,' croaked Sarah, barely able to speak. Joe bent down and kissed her again, with more strength and passion this time. Sarah felt like she was drowning, or sinking, or something. She wasn't quite sure what. But she held on to him tightly, just in case she did fall. Her heart was pounding so much she thought that it was going to burst, and she could feel through his shirt, that his heart was pounding in the same way. They drew away at the end of the kiss and gazed into each other's eyes. His blue eyes were the colour of pale sapphires and, as he looked at her, they seemed to deepen in colour.

Sarah couldn't believe her feelings. She was totally and fully in love with this man. She felt that she knew all about him, even though they had just met. And she knew that she wanted to go on being with him for a long time, the rest of her life even. How could she feel like this so suddenly? Sarah realised that the feelings that she had had for Darren had been nothing compared with this, and yet she thought that she had been in love with him then. The thought of Darren brought her suddenly back to her senses. She couldn't go through all that again.

'What will your wife think about all this?' Sarah asked, in a very cool voice.

'Wife? I have no wife,' said Joe with a look of bewilderment at the icy tones of her voice. Sarah persisted.

'Yes, that's what they all say.'

'Sarah, I have no wife, I assure you. Got near once and got engaged, but never went through with it, there was just something missing, I didn't know what. I just knew that she wasn't right for me. Why did you say it so forcefully? What's happened?'

Sarah leaned against him, her head hidden in his shoulder.

'I'm sorry, I have been hurt before. I feel so vulnerable. I'm frightened of my feelings.'

'Why, what are your feelings right now, Sarah? Tell me.'

'I, I, er, I can't,' stammered Sarah, keeping her head firmly against his shoulder. Joe lifted her head up by her chin and looked deeply into her eyes.

'Okay, I'll tell you how I feel, Sarah. You'll probably think I'm mad, but I've fallen in love with you. I can't explain it, and I don't believe in love at first sight. I've even scoffed at others before. But I've never, ever felt like this before'. Sarah stared into Joe's eyes, unable to believe what she was hearing.

'Me too,' she whispered, without taking her eyes away from his.

'What,' said Joe, 'what did you say?'

'Me too,' she whispered only slightly louder.

'Can't tell what you're saying, say it properly.'

'I love you too, Joe, and I don't understand it either.' Joe let out a sigh of relief. 'Oh Sarah, I thought that it was just me, or I was going mad or something. I had to make you say it. I had to be sure about you.' They looked at each other with new eyes as they tenderly took in all the features that were new to each other, as if they were going to fade away if they stopped looking. Suddenly they were disturbed by the sound of the string quartet tuning up again.

'Come on you temptress, you're making me neglect my duties. We've got the rest of our lives to catch up.' They started walking back down the stairs to the ballroom and, after a tiny hand squeeze, separated, promising to exchange addresses before they went home tonight.

Sarah sat down alone, near to the string quartet. She needed time to think. Everything had gone far too fast. She watched Joe dancing, but the feelings were still there. She knew without a shadow of a doubt that this was the man that she wanted to spend the rest of her life with. And yet she didn't really know anything about him apart from the fact that he was a curator at this house. She was shattered by the strength of her feeling, and looked forward to long talks with Joe after the holiday was over. She had so much to find out about him, and he about her. After a couple more dances with the other guests, Sarah felt desperately thirsty. She looked round the ballroom, but all the drinks had been cleared away, ready for the supper that was due in half an hour's time. Sarah didn't feel that she could wait that long, so she decided to go and find the kitchen and get herself a drink. She went down the two flights of stairs, to the lower regions of the house. She knew vaguely where the kitchens were, and eventually found where the entrance was. A narrow, twisty flight of steps led down into the kitchen and, as she hurried down the stairs, she slipped in her satin slippers and fell down the last few stairs, hitting her head on the stone flagged floor. An excruciating pain shot through her head, and then blackness closed in, and she knew no more.

Chapter 6

Sarah vaguely became aware of voices before she was fully back to her senses. It was an older lady and a young girl talking to each other about Sarah.

'Peggy, go and get t' mistress, I think she's comin' round, go on be quick, don't thee stand gawping, girl'. Young Peggy suddenly rushed off up the stairs, as if the Devil was after her. The older lady knelt beside Sarah wafting a teacloth in her hands, near to Sarah's face.

'There, miss, don't move, young Peggy 'as gone to get 'elp',' the older woman soothed in a broad Yorkshire accent. Sarah, feeling vaguely bemused about what was happening, marvelled at the lengths that the firm had gone to, to make this evening authentic. Even to hiring actresses to work in the kitchen who could mimic the local accent of years gone by.   She tried to sit up.

'Nay, lass, tha' musn't. Mistress'll kill us if you cum ter any harm.   She'll go mad that yer slipped on mi steps. She's allus saying I polish stuff too much, but I can't 'elp it. It's the way I am.   Ooh, look, t' mistress is cumin' now.' A tall regal lady wearing a black high necked satin dress appeared in the kitchen, followed shortly by Peggy, who slunk away to the fireside, as if in awe of this great personage.

'Now what's happening here, Martha, Peggy is all of a stir. What's been going on?'

'Well, yer Ladyship, I was just washin' up after th' meal, and this 'ere young lady fell inter me kitchen. I aint sin her before, and I dunno 'ow she got 'ere,' stammered Martha, curtsying to the lady.

'Never mind that now, let's look at the young lady's injuries. Peggy, get me some hot water and a clean cloth, quickly.' Peggy suddenly galvanised herself into action and ran around the kitchen, collecting the requested things.

'Ere yer are, mum,' muttered Peggy, passing them to the lady.

''Ow many times do I have ter tell thi that its yer ladyship, not mum, girl. I am sorry, Lady Grace, I 'ave told 'er.'

'Oh stop that Martha, Peggy will soon learn the ropes. If you keep shouting at her she'll spill this water, and make the situation far worse. Now let's clean up this cut on her head, and see how much damage has been done,' reprimanded Lady Grace sharply. Sarah weakly listened to all this and wondered if she should tell them that they didn't need to keep up the charade for her. They could just act normally now, but the severe headache made her lie passively against the cushion that Martha had put under her head. Besides, she must have had a worse head injury than she thought, because she didn't remember seeing this lady at the dinner.

'Did she lose consciousness Martha?' asked Lady Grace

'Er, yes, yer Ladyship, fer abaht five minutes I think. Well, it might not 'ave bin that long, like, but it felt a long time.'

'Well, we'd better get the doctor anyway to check her over. Where's Williams?'

'Mr William's is in the long gallery, supervising the maids setting up the supper for the dancers,' answered Martha.

'Good, well get him to come down here now. Peggy, go up to the Long Gallery and find Mr Williams.'

Peggy started to speak, but Martha gave her such a look, that she scuttled off up the stairs to find the butler.

'Now, young lady, what is your name?'

'Er, Sarah,' she replied, 'Sarah Evans.'

'Well Sarah, I'm not sure who you are, or who you came with, but we won't worry about that at the moment. Are you able to sit up?' Sarah nodded but, as she moved to sit up, she instantly felt woozy and sank back against Lady Grace.

'Oh, I'm so sorry,' stammered Sarah, 'I feel dreadful.'

'Well, just lie there until we get help. Peggy, go and find Mrs Hardcastle, Myrtle and Agnes and tell them to come here.' This time Peggy needed no second telling. Another step was heard on the stairs, and an elegantly dressed man about her own age came into the kitchen, closely followed by two young girls dressed as maids, and an elderly man dressed as a butler.

'Mama, what is going on? Williams seems all of a dither, these two were scurrying across the landing, and Peggy looked like death when I caught her on the stairs just now. Has she been accused of running off with the family silver or something?'

'Oh Josiah, thank goodness you're here. Williams, send young Johnny to get Doctor Griffiths.' Williams, looking slightly disconcerted at being described as 'all of a dither', bowed to Lady Grace and went out of the kitchen again.

'Josiah, I can't seem to get any sense out of these servants. This young lady has fallen and knocked herself unconscious, and needs seeing to.'

The elegant young man stared at Sarah and asked where she had come from.

'Why is everybody asking that question? Never mind that now,' said his mother, 'we can find that out later. Do you think that it would be safe to move her before Doctor Griffiths gets here? I'm sure that she must be very uncomfortable down here.' Josiah knelt down and asked Sarah if she thought that she had broken anything.

'I don't think so,' replied Sarah, 'but I do feel woozy.'

'Woozy, what ever do you mean?' he asked laughing.

'Er, light headed, faint.'

'Well,' he drawled, 'that is a new word. I quite like it. Well, Miss Woozy, perhaps you would allow me to carry you up to your bedroom. Which one is it, Mama?' Lady Grace looked at the oldest of the two maids and asked which room.

'I'm not sure, yer Ladyship, I've not sin 'er before,' said Myrtle. 'Mrs Hardcastle said ter get the Blue room ready. I could get a warming pan there right away.'

'Good idea, Myrtle, we'll put her in there and sort it out later. You and Agnes go and sort the bedroom out. Martha, get Sarah a drink of hot sweet tea. Peggy, get a bowl of water in the drawing room for the doctor. Josiah, take her into the drawing room. Doctor Griffiths will examine her there.' The whole room suddenly turned into action, as if she was an army colonel commanding her troops. Mrs Hardcastle told Agnes to fill the warming pan with coals and for her and Myrtle to follow her upstairs as soon as possible. Martha rushed to the enormous kettle to make a cup of tea, almost falling over Peggy as she did so.

Josiah leant over and picked Sarah up in strong arms, as if she was a child and carried her up the fateful steps where she had fallen earlier. Sarah was very confused. It was as if she had landed in the middle of a play, and all the players knew their parts, but she didn't understand either the play or her part. It was all very strange. Surely one of these actors would forget and slip into modern English, but they had certainly been well schooled for their parts. Remembering the earlier scene in the Minstrels' Gallery, Sarah suddenly asked the question, 'Where's Joe?'

'Joe? Joe who? There's nobody staying here by that Christian name,' replied Josiah. Sarah tried to work out what this could mean. Where was Joe? Was all this just a charade that was being played for her benefit? Would Joe turn up dressed as the doctor? She hoped so because she was beginning to get a little frightened by the events that had overtaken her. Josiah laid her very carefully on the couch, fussing around her, and placing a blanket very tenderly on her. His mother came in and shooed him away.

'Josiah, leave her alone, you're like a mother hen fussing like that.'

A loud knocking on the front door cut short any further conversation. 'That'll be Griffiths,' said Josiah, 'about time too.'

A gentle rap on the drawing room door was followed by Williams opening it. Sarah turned to look at who was coming in, in a vain hope that it might be Joe. Williams escorted a small rounded figure into the room, who appeared to be puffing and panting.

'I came as soon as I could, Lord Grace, but I was out at the time. Lady Morrison is near her time and I had gone to check on her. Now what seems to have been happening?' Whilst Lord Grace explained the situation to the doctor, Sarah stared at him. Lord Grace. Now something was really wrong. Joe had been playing the part of Lord Grace, and this man was certainly not Joe. A feeling of unease crept over Sarah and she began to feel frightened. Why was everybody acting like this? If only she could ask them what was going on. She watched as Dr Griffiths opened his old leather bag, and marvelled at the antiquity of his instruments. The stethoscope looked like something out of a museum, and didn't have the usual ear pieces. The doctor seemed to be making a great fuss of feeling her head and looking into her eyes, and checking her pulse, but he didn't measure her blood pressure or test her reflexes, like they had when she had knocked herself unconscious as a child. 'Perhaps he would just refer her to the local hospital and take some X-rays,' mused Sarah to herself. After a lot of humming and hah-ing, the doctor prescribed his treatment.

'You should keep her lying down for at least one week, and give her only thin soup at first. If that stays down, she can have some light food, but nothing fatty or heavy. I'll leave the food side of things to your excellent cook. I know from past experience that she can rise to any occasion. And keep a fire in her bedroom, and don't let her get in any draughts. A chill on her head could be very serious at this stage. And put some oil of lavender on her pillow, that will aid the concussion, or a little oil of rosemary. Now, my dear,' he leaned over to Sarah, speaking slowly as if to a child, 'you just lie there and do as you are told. Do you understand? I'll come and see you each day.' Sarah nodded, too frightened to answer. That's probably why he spoke to me like a child, thought Sarah, I haven't said a sensible thing since he came.

As Sarah looked at Dr Griffiths, she noticed that his jacket was not too clean. If she didn't know any better, she would have said that he had blood on his jacket. A terrible thought came back to Sarah. He had just come from visiting a lady in labour. Surely it wasn't blood. Not with all the scrubbing of hands that went on nowadays. Dr Griffiths was giving last minute instructions to Lady Grace and was walking towards the door. Lord Grace came into the room just as Dr Griffiths was leaving.

'Send your man round with your bill, Griffiths, and we'll attend to it right away.'

'Not much point, Lord Grace, as I've told your mother, I'll have to attend for a few days to make sure that the lady doesn't get a fever or chill, or any complications from this fall. It's all too easy to get an inflammation of the brain after a fall like this. She'll need careful nursing. Shall I arrange for a nurse to be in attendance?'

'No, that won't be necessary. Mama prides herself on the standard of care that she and her staff give to anyone who is a little under par. I'm sure she would feel slighted if I suggested it.'

'What's that, Josiah? Who will feel slighted?' asked Lady Grace.

'Nothing Mama. I was just telling Griffiths what excellent care the young lady will get here, and there is no need for a nurse.'

'Oh, thank you my dear, that's kind of you to say so. I suppose you remember all those times when you were ill as a child and we stayed up for hours on end with you. He gave us some scary moments didn't he, Griffiths? The worst was the diphtheria, I really thought that I was going to lose him that time. It was only your administrations that saved his life. I can never thank you enough. And it was so soon after losing our two little girls, Miriam and Louise, with the measles. I couldn't have borne the loss of another child so soon after them. I thought my heart would break.' The tears started to flow.

'Mama, don't upset yourself. You've still got seven of us left. And some lovely grandchildren. It is good that you have managed to raise so many children to adult life. Now let's be sorting this young lady out.'

Sarah lay quietly during this conversation, feeling more and more worried and confused by what she was hearing. Paying a doctors bill? Inflammation of the brain? Children dying of measles and getting diphtheria? Only seven children surviving? Dear God, she really had landed in a play, and it was certainly a period piece. But why was she there? That was what was worrying her. People had already asked that question and nobody had come up with an answer so far. Sarah decided to stay quiet and let events unfold, and perhaps she would understand things later. It was like one of those daft programmes with Jeremy Beadle when people got put into terrible situations to watch their reactions. Well, if it was something like that, she wished that someone would hurry up and come and tell her it was all a joke. She tried surreptitiously pinching herself, in case she was dreaming. That's what they did in all the best books. But she didn't wake up.

Lady Grace bustled herself into action, shouting for the maids to come and help her. Lord Grace again picked Sarah up and carried her up the stairs to a bedroom, with the maids bustling round, opening doors and making room for Lord Grace, and holding the candles so that he could see where he was going. It was obvious why it was called the Blue Room. The walls were covered with the lightest of blue paper and dark velvet curtains covered the windows, with elegant swags and tails in paler blue and cream. The bed was a four poster and had an elaborate patchwork quilt in different shades of blue and burgundy over the sheets and blankets. The room was hot and stuffy due to the large fire that was burning in the grate, and Sarah longed to ask them to open a window, but she remembered the doctor's instruction to have no draughts. She was put down onto the bed very gently and she turned to thank Lord Grace.

'Oh, please don't stand on ceremony, call me Josiah. Any house guest of ours is a friend.'

Sarah blushed. Was she a house guest? She couldn't remember how she got here, so she just smiled and said nothing.

'Now come along Josiah, this is no place for you. You can get acquainted with the young lady tomorrow, or when she is feeling better. Off you go, and ask Peggy to prepare a cup of hot tea for our patient. Sarah, you said your name was, dear, didn't you?'

'Er, yes, that's right. Sarah Evans.'

'Evans? Now would that be the Sheffield Evans that you come from?' quizzed Lady Grace.

'Er, no, I'm from Lancashire,' mumbled Sarah. 'We don't have any relatives in Sheffield.'

'Oh, listen to me,' said Lady Grace, 'I'm as bad as Josiah. We must let you sleep. Drink your tea up and then you can settle down for the night. We'll have a good talk in the morning.'

'Here's a spare nightgown, yer Ladyship,' said Myrtle, 'when she's finished 'er tea, I'll 'elp 'er inter it.'

'Oh thank you Myrtle, I'll leave her in your capable hands. Would you sleep in the dressing room tonight, so that if Miss Sarah needs anything you can help her? I'd feel easier myself then.'

'Yes, yer Ladyship, I thought as how yer would say that, so I've brought mi things along when I got the young miss's nighty.'

'Thank you Myrtle, I'll leave you alone now.' Lady Grace swept out of the room and Myrtle closed the door behind her.

'Now miss, could you gerr inter yer nighty, if yer please'.

'Oh, please call me Sarah,' she asked.

'Eh, I couldn't do that Miss, 'twouldnt be reight. 'Er Ladyship 'ud go mad if she heared me,' replied Myrtle, a little shocked.

'Well, just when we're on our own then, I'd like it ever so much. Especially if you are going to be my nurse.'

'Eh, I dunno wha' ter think. I've never heard the like from t' gentry.' Sarah laughed.

'But I'm not gentry. What ever gave you that idea?'

'Well, tha must be ter be stayin' 'ere,' Myrtle replied.

'Well, I'm not. So Sarah when we're on our own, then Myrtle?'

'If yer say so miss, but it ain't reight.'

'It's Sarah, when we're on our own.'

'Alright, miss, er I mean Sarah.' Sarah watched in amazement as Myrtle turned and looked over her shoulder, as if she were checking that nobody had heard her. 'Now you settle down ter sleep or else 'er Ladyship 'ull be after mi.'

'Could you just tell me where the bathroom is then Myrtle?'

Myrtle gawped at Sarah. 'Bathroom, Miss, what do you mean?' It was Sarah's turn to gawp. 'You know, toilet, pass water.'

Myrtle's face was suddenly wreathed in smiles. 'Oh, of course Miss, I forgot, the chair's i' the dressin' room. I'll just bring it in 'ere so tha' yer can use it i' the night. Just through 'ere.' Myrtle went into the dressing room and brought out an old-fashioned commode. Sarah started to laugh and then realised that if she wanted to go to the toilet that night, she had better get used to using the commode. Myrtle turned discreetly away and straightened the sheets whilst Sarah used the commode. Sarah climbed into the bed and Myrtle fussed round her, tucking the sheets in.

'Does tha' want a candle on yer table, wi' bein' in a strange place, like?' asked Myrtle. Sarah decided to play along with this charade, whatever it was.

'Yes please,' she replied as she snuggled down into the covers. Her head was still pounding and she decided that tomorrow was soon enough to call everyone's bluff and start telling her what they were playing at. Myrtle wished her goodnight and retired into the dressing room that had a small trundle bed made up for her. Sarah ached all over, yet sleep didn't come straight away. There had been too many confusing images crowding her brain, and her poor head ached very badly. She turned towards the pillow and breathed in the delicate fragrance of the lavender, and eventually she drifted into a restless sleep.

Chapter 7

She woke up suddenly in the dark, the candle having gone out. The room was very dark; the fire had burnt down and was shedding only a faint glow. The coals shuddered and hissed in the grate as the fire settled down. Sarah looked round for the light switch but, in the dim light, could not find one. She got slowly out of bed and felt her way along the panelled walls towards where she thought that the door was. Finding the doorframe, Sarah felt all around the edges for the light switch. There was none. 'Perhaps they have a cord light switch like they do in the bathroom,' Sarah mused to herself. She edged gingerly back to the bed and, kneeling onto the bed, waved her arms blindly around, trying to locate the pull cord, with no success. This was getting more absurd by the minute. She didn't hear the door to the dressing room opening and was shocked to see Myrtle standing near her. Sarah jumped and let out a shriek.

'Oh Myrtle, you startled me. I was trying to find the light.'
Myrtle looked at Sarah strangely, and then moved slowly to the
top of the bed and re-lit the candle.

'Is tha' what yer were lookin' fer, Miss?' said Myrtle
suspiciously, edging away from Sarah. 'I'll just go and get Mrs
'Ardcastle.'

'Who's Mrs Hardcastle?' asked Sarah.

'She's th' 'ousekeeper 'ere. I won't be long. Jus' stay there.'
Myrtle ran out of the room, leaving Sarah even more confused.
Whilst she waited, Sarah looked all round the room. There was
no sign of any electric lights or switches. Surely they hadn't
gone to the expense of hiding all the switches just for the ball.
She could hear sounds of voices coming along the hall. Myrtle
appeared to be telling someone that Sarah was acting strangely,
standing on the bed and waving her arms around. Mrs
Hardcastle seemed to be telling Myrtle off for being too
fanciful. Fanciful, mused Sarah, that was a word that you never
heard these days but, then, in the last few hours there seemed to
have been a lot of words and phrases that were not in common
usage or that she hadn't understood. Perhaps this was a bad
case of concussion. Or perhaps she was going mad, as Myrtle
seemed to be suggesting. Sarah sat demurely in the bed and
waited. Mrs Hardcastle followed Myrtle into the room, holding
a large candlestick in her hand. She stared for a long time at
Sarah and then turned to Myrtle.

'She seems alright to me, Myrtle, are you sure what you saw?'

'Yes, missus, I did, 'onest. I don' tell lies.'

'Sorry, Myrtle, you're right, you don't tell lies. You're an
honest lass. Well, you'd better watch her closely and don't let
her out of your sight. I'll tell her Ladyship what you saw, and
she can tell the doctor when he comes.' Mrs Hardcastle came
nearer the bed and spoke to Sarah in a slow voice.

'How are you feeling, Miss?'

'I'm better than I was, thank you, but my head is still very
sore.'

'I'm glad you're a little better. I'll tell Lady Grace. Do you
think that you could manage a little drink of beef tea? Cook is

famous for it. It is very beneficial in cases of brain fever or illness.'

'Thank you, that would be nice,' smiled Sarah, whilst gritting her teeth at the thought of beef tea, and thinking that she could murder a good hot cup of coffee.

'You go down and get Cook to prepare her some, Myrtle. Have your own breakfast whilst you are there, and I'll stay here.' Myrtle scurried out of the bedroom door, and Mrs Hardcastle started opening the curtains. 'Does the light hurt your eyes, Miss?'

'No, they seem to be all right so far. My head is still throbbing though. I need to go to the dressing room, though.' Mrs Hardcastle bustled back to the side of the bed and helped Sarah out of it. She stood up rather quickly and went dizzy, grasping hold of Mrs Hardcastle's arm. 'Oh, I'm sorry, I feel so peculiar and lightheaded.' Sarah fell back against the bed.

'Right, that's it. Back to bed young lady. I'll bring you a slipper pan. You had better stay in bed until the doctor sees you again.' Mrs Hardcastle walked across to the dressing room and returned with a white porcelain elongated dish. She pulled the bedclothes to one side and slipped the pan under Sarah. It was freezing. She tactfully moved away to the other side of the room so that Sarah could 'perform'. It was not easy, but she managed without spilling in the bed, thankfully.

'I've finished, thank you.' Mrs Hardcastle returned and moved the pan carefully from under her.

'We'll come and give you a wash later, and then change your sheets. You need to look your best for the doctor.' At this point, Myrtle returned with a tray set out with a pure white linen cloth, a single yellow rose in a silver single stem vase, a napkin rolled in a silver napkin ring, and a tall cup of steaming beef tea. The tray looked beautiful, and Sarah decided that she could get used to this life, before she remembered the mess she was in. She didn't even know what had happened last night. Sarah tried to show enthusiasm for it, but as she drank it she was pleasantly surprised. It was indeed good. When she had finished it, Mrs

Hardcastle returned with clean sheets, followed by Agnes with a bowl of water.

'Myrtle and Agnes will bathe you now and then you will feel better. The doctor may be here anytime. I'll see you later. Just tell them if you need anything else. Don't let her get a chill, you two,' she said. Then, with a smile, Mrs Hardcastle left the room, closing the door quietly behind her. Agnes started stripping the bed of the blankets and left only a sheet over Sarah.

'Now Miss, if yer just tek yer nightie off, an' then we'll wash yer,' said Agnes.

The bowl of water was placed on the bedside table and the two servants started to wash her. Sarah was quite embarrassed. She couldn't remember ever having been bathed by anyone before. She lay placidly whilst she was soaped and rinsed. A clean nightie was placed over her head and Sarah laughed at the voluminous size of it. She could have cut it in half and still had plenty of room. It was like those nighties that she had seen in the Past Times shop in York recently. Still, at least they seemed to have a plentiful supply of clean linen, which was just as well, as she didn't have anything with her. Her worries returned, and her stomach flipped over as she remembered. How had she got into this situation and, more importantly, how was she going to get out? She wondered how she could get her own clothes from the hotel. She decided that if this archaic doctor insisted that she stay in bed, then she would demand her own belongings. With that firm resolve, and the exhausting effort of being bathed, Sarah fell asleep almost as soon as they finished her bath.

Some time later, she woke to hear Mrs Hardcastle telling the doctor and Lady Grace about the strange happenings in the night. She kept her eyes shut, and pretended that she was still asleep. As they approached her bed, Myrtle jumped up from the low chair that she had been sitting on and curtsied to Lady Grace and the doctor, and stood by the window.

'Come here, Myrtle, tell the doctor what you saw,' commanded Lady Grace. Myrtle nervously told the doctor what she had seen.

The doctor gently touched Sarah's arm and Sarah opened her eyes suddenly as if she had still been asleep.

'Good morning young lady, and how are we feeling now, hum?'

'A little better, but I still have a lot of pain in my head. Could I have something for the pain?' The doctor looked at her again, for a long time.

'Yes, I'll mix you a draft. Perhaps if young William could be spared from the garden, I could take him back with me to the house and make one for her.'

'Certainly Doctor. Mrs Hardcastle, perhaps Myrtle could arrange that?' Myrtle scurried away.

'Do you know what day it is?' the doctor asked Sarah.

'Friday' replied Sarah but, on seeing the astonished reply on everyone's face, she suddenly realised that she had slept a night. 'Oh no, I mean Saturday.' A silence fell on the room.

'Now my dear,' said the doctor, 'can you tell me where you are?'

'Yes, I'm at Roding Hall.'

The doctor smiled and said, 'Yes that's correct,' and he smiled at all the people in the room. The tension in the room seemed to slowly ease.

'Is there anything you need, my dear?' asked Lady Grace. Here goes, thought Sarah. It's now or never.

'Well, I'd like my clothes from the hotel. I'd feel better in my own clothes. And really I'd like to be getting home. The others will be worrying about me. I don't want to be a burden to you all.'

'Nonsense,' said the doctor, 'you can't go home yet. Goodness, that would be sure to bring on a worse fever. You must reside here. Besides you won't need your clothes yet, because you have to stay in bed. But I'm sure Mrs Hardcastle can arrange that for you.' Sarah slumped back against her pillows. The thought of staying in bed was worrying, to say the least. She couldn't sort out what was going on from her bed. She would wait until everybody had gone and then try and see if she could get up without going dizzy again. Lady Grace led the doctor out of the room, as Sarah looked away from them. She couldn't stand the way that the doctor was staring at her. From what she had heard Mrs Hardcastle saying to him, he probably thought she was going strange. Sarah felt quite exhausted by all the ministrations from the servants and the doctor, and drifted back to sleep.

The door opening roused Sarah from her sleep. Myrtle was bringing the tray back in with a dish of soup and a cup of tea. There was also a small tumbler with some noxious looking substance in.

'Well Miss, here's some lunch fer yer. I 'ope that yer like it. Now sit thaysen up and I'll put this tray on yer knee.' Myrtle bustled round the bed arranging the pillows behind Sarah and placing the tray across her knee so that she could manage the meal.

'What's your real name, Myrtle?' Sarah asked.

'Wha' do yer mean, Miss? Myrtle is my real name. Do you mean my last name? It's Bracewell. I were named Myrtle after mi mam's sister what died i' childbirth.' Sarah made no comment and carried on sipping the soup. A little later, Sarah tried again.

'Who do you work for, Myrtle?' Poor Myrtle looked perplexed.

'Wha' d' yer mean, Miss? I works fer Lady Grace and 'is Lordship. Wha'ever do yer mean. I think yer goin' queer in th' 'ead again. Yet, yer were normal when t' doctor cum. Med me look a proper nelly. Think 'er Ladyship thought as 'ow I were goin' daft wi' yer,' Myrtle replied somewhat irritably.

'Oh, I didn't mean anything, Myrtle; I didn't mean to upset you. I just feel so confused. It's since I banged my head. Everything seems to have changed and I don't know where I am or where I've come from.' To her horror, Sarah burst into tears. Instantly Myrtle ran to the bedside and cuddled Sarah.

'There, there, mi love, don't tek on so. It'll be all right. I'll look after yer, never fear.' Sarah rested in the circle of Myrtle's arms, feeling better after her childish outbreak, and yet soothed by the tears. 'We'll find out where yer cum from, don't fret.

Now, can you finish this soup? It's lucky I caught it before it fell on t' floor. I would've caught it from Mrs 'Ardcastle. She goes mad if yer spill owt on t' polished floors. More than yer life's worth.'

'Is she a hard task master then, Myrtle?'

'Eh no, lass, mostly she's reight gradely, but she does 'ave 'igh standards. That's wha' she tells us, 'igh standards. Mind, I'm ever so grateful to her, if it weren't fer 'er I'd be in t' workhouse living on t' Parish. Mi mam died when I wer born an' mi dad couldn't cope wi' all of us. Especially me bein' a bairn, like. But Mrs 'Ardcastle wer reight good. She found out abaht mi dad and she told Lady Grace. She'd just lost 'er two little lasses and she were reight upset. She said as how she couldn't bear th' thought of a poor babby goin' on t' Parish, so she let Mrs 'Ardcastle pay a woman at 'ad lost 'er own babby to feed me, and when I were eight I come 'ere to work as a scullery maid. I were that grateful. I've gorra lovely little room in th' attic and I get loads o' food. I'm so 'appy 'ere. It's hard work, but I'm 'appy. And 'is Lordship don't try and mek yer do things, or keep touching yer. Like, yer know what I mean, like they do at Hollins Hall. A girl I knew got thrown out from there, 'cos she were 'aving a babby. It were young Master 'Ollins babby, but they called 'er a slut and a liar, and threw 'er out. Ooh, it were someat awful. She were only fourteen.' Myrtle stopped suddenly in mid sentence, her features twisted and saddened.

'Eh, I'm reight sorry, Miss, I didn't oughter be talkin' like this.'

'What happened to the girl?'

'She died. She went on th' Parish and she died of a broken 'eart. They sed that babby were too big ter gerr out, wi' 'er bein' so young like'. Sarah listened in stunned silence, her heart sinking. This was no acting. This was real. So why was she in some historical time warp? They already thought that she was acting strange so she could hardly ask what year it was, or they would probably have her committed to some mental asylum and she'd never get out. What on earth could she do? She must plan some strategy; to deviously find out what year she was in.

Chapter 8

A knock on the door startled her from her planning reverie. Myrtle went to the door and there was Lord Grace.

'May I come in and see Miss Woozy? Or is she still in that delicate condition?' Myrtle opened the door wider, looking to Sarah to ensure that this was alright.

'Oh do come in, I am so sorry to be such a trouble to you and your family, not to mention your staff. Whatever must you think of me?'

'Nonsense, it's not every day that someone falls into our life. I'm just intrigued as to how you got here. Can you remember nothing?'

'I remember arriving with a group of people, but I can't remember any of their names or where we came from. I'm really sorry, you must think I'm mad. I must have really banged my head to make me like this. Do sit down.' 'Oh gosh,' thought Sarah, 'here I am asking a Peer of the Realm to sit down in his own house.' She blushed at the audacious manner she had taken with him, but he didn't seem to notice and was laughing as he went over near the window to get a small chair. Thank goodness Myrtle had moved the commode, thought Sarah to herself.

Sarah looked closer at him whilst he was getting the chair. He was fairly tall, about 5 feet 10 inches she reckoned, and of a slim build. His hair was dark brown and worn long over the collar. A neat moustache covered his upper lip. He walked and talked rather effeminately, Sarah thought, as she weighed him up. When he had been talking, he had appeared to be posing a little, by placing one hand on his hip and the other hand waving around as he talked. 'Now what was the word that they used in historical novels,' Sarah mused to herself. 'Foppish, yes, that was it, he looked foppish. Gosh, she was starting to sound like a historical novel as well as appearing to be starring in one. If only she could get some of the royalties, she could retire and enjoy life.'

He was wearing a multi-coloured satin waistcoat of gold, cream, orange and yellow over breeches of a dark brown thicker material. He had a white silky blouse with long sleeves under the waistcoat, which had a long bow tied at the neck. She remembered her mother wearing a similar blouse when she was a little girl. The breeches were fastened with a ribbon under the knee, and he had cream stockings beneath the breeches. He had 'womanish' type shoes with silver buckles on. In fact, now she thought about it, it was a very similar outfit to the one that Joe was wearing last night. Her thought of Joe brought a feeling of severe anguish to Sarah, and she wondered when she would see him again, or if she ever would. Sarah was brought back from her reverie by Lord Grace's voice.

'It's a lovely day. A pity you're confined to bed. It would have been lovely to go for a drive today. But never mind, there'll be other days, and I dare not cross Griffiths, he wouldn't like it at all. Now, is there anything I can get for you seeing that I can't take you out in the fresh air? A book? Or would that hurt your head even more?' A sudden idea leapt into Sarah's mind.

'Perhaps it is a little too early for a book, but could I read a newspaper? That would be probably enough for now.' She was shocked when Lord Grace let out a raucous laugh, his face alight with interest and his eyes sparkling.

'A newspaper? Well, Miss Woozy, you never cease to amaze me. Whatever will you ask for next? Don't tell me that you are one of these so-called educated women who demand to be equal with men. Oh, I forsee that I am going to have great fun whilst you are in the house.'

'What do you mean, so-called educated. What's wrong with a woman being educated? They have got the same size brain as men, and they are equally capable as men, if only they were allowed to do things.'

'But that's precisely what I mean,' laughed Lord Grace, 'women can't do the same as men, they're too busy having babies and running the household. And of course they haven't got the same size brain as men, how can they, they are smaller.'

'Only because men feel threatened by women and won't let them do anything. But they let a woman sit on the throne of England, didn't they?' Sarah burst out, getting quite exasperated. A searing pain shot across her temple and she laid back exhausted against the pillows. Lord Grace instantly reverted to the stately courtier and said, 'I do apologise, Miss, I see that you are in pain. I'll leave you now. I urge you to have a good rest. I'll see that the paper is sent up later in the evening, to show no ill-will.' He made a mock bow and left the room. Sarah, although exhausted, felt a small measure of triumph. By looking at the newspaper, she would know what year it was without asking. Excited as she was by this turn of events, it didn't stop Sarah from falling straight into a deep sleep.

When she woke up, Sarah's head felt a little easier, but was still throbbing slightly. As she stirred, Myrtle appeared from the dressing room.

'Oh, Miss, yer awake, I 'ope I didn't wake yer up? I've bin ever so careful ter be quiet.'

'No, Myrtle, of course you didn't wake me up. It was time for me to wake up anyway. I'm sleeping my life away here.'

'Well, Mrs 'Ardcastle reckons tha' if tha's poorly, tha can sleep thassen better, so it won't 'arm yer.'

'I wonder if I could have some more of the medicine for my head. I'd be ever so grateful. And anyway, what happened to Sarah? I thought we agreed that you would call me Sarah when we were on our own.'

'Er, alright, Miss, I mean, Sarah. Eh, it dunt 'alf feel queer, callin' one o' th' gentry by their first name.'

'But I've told you, I'm not gentry, I'm just a normal wor . . . .' Sarah stopped mid-sentence. She had been going to say working girl. What could she say instead? But fortunately, Myrtle thought that the gap in conversation was due to the pain, as she set off at a run, shouting, 'I'll get yer medicine now, miss,' as she flew through the door. Sarah decided that she would have to be careful what she said, but it was going to be hard, as she wasn't a person who thought long and hard before she spoke. She was inclined to be a little impulsive. In fact a form teacher at school had once told her that she should think before she spoke. In no time at all, Myrtle could be heard rushing back along the polished floor on the corridor outside.

'Ere yer are Miss, now drink it down quick and then tha'll be feelin' better. Oh an' by the way, Lord Grace give me this ere paper fer yer. No wonder yer gerrin' 'eadache if yer reading stuff, eh, I don't know. I'll keep this ere paper 'til later, when yer feel better.'

'Oh, no, Myrtle, please, please, let me have the paper. I really want to look at it. I'm sure it will help my headache by taking my mind off my troubles.' Sarah put her hand out to Myrtle and, very slowly, Myrtle handed over the paper.

'Well, don't blame me if tha's worse. I'm goin' fer mi tea now. Cook just said to 'urry up. I wont be long,' she replied quite sullenly, as she went off back down the corridor.

Sarah ignored her as she grasped the paper and turned to the front page, looking eagerly for the date. There it was at the top in bold type. Sarah gasped as she read it. All her fears were well founded. The paper said 1825. She **was** in 1825. Her heart sank as the full realisation of what that meant dawned on her. The saga had gone on too long for it to be play-acting. In some unknown way, she had travelled through time. Myriads of thoughts flew through her head one after another. The first one was would she ever get back to 2001? And if so, how? What about her work? What about her family in Texas? What about the lovely two nephews that she had never seen? What about her friends? What about her house, her mortgage payments? And then worst of all, would she ever see Joe again? At this, she broke down and cried, sobbing long and hard for the things that she had lost.

As the sobs subsided, she began to start thinking more practically. Was there any way that she could get back to 2001? She desperately tried to think about any time travel films or books that she had ever seen or read. '20,000 Leagues Under the Sea' came first into her mind, but that was soon dismissed as she remembered that it was about travelling under the sea, rather than time. 'Doctor Who' then sprang into her mind, but he whipped about through time in his Tardis, and she didn't have one of those conveniently to hand. Her feverish mind remembered the film 'Back to the Future', but they had had a fancy car to travel through time and, if she remembered rightly, it was to do with electricity and the Town Hall clock. Sarah thought ruefully that she hadn't enough knowledge about electricity, and anyway, in 1825 it hadn't been invented! Besides, she hadn't got a flash car. A Ford Fiesta was hardly a flash car, but it got her around, and she loved it dearly. How she wished that she was driving it now, going to work, or to Phillip's. 'Oh goodness,' she suddenly thought to herself. 'Whatever will Philip and Victoria think of me when I don't turn up to do the patterns?' The dull ache of the headache was returning, so Sarah tried not to think about it any more. She would start making contingency plans tomorrow. Just at this point, Myrtle returned with a tray, again beautifully set out.

'Ere's some home-made soup, Miss, this'll mek yer feel better.'

'Oh thank you Myrtle, I'm ready for something to eat. Thanks for bringing me the paper. Have you had your tea? What did you have?'

'Well, Cook made a nice steak and kidney pie with mushrooms in, fair gradely it were. Oops, sorry, I reckon as 'ow yer wish yer could 'ave 'ad some an all.'

'Yes, it does sound good, although I still feel a little bit sickly and am probably safer with the soup. I know you've told me a little about yourself Myrtle, but tell me more.'

'There's norra lot more ter tell than I telled yer before. I lived wi' that woman 'til I come 'ere, an' I've worked 'ere ever since. Wha' do yer' want mi ter tell yer?'

'Well, what were your mum and dad's names, and have you any brothers and sisters? What year were you born? Which town did you live in? What did your parents do for work? Where did your grandparents live? Did you go to school?'

'Well I don't know some o' them. I were born i' Keighley in 1808, an' as I sed, mi mam died when I were borned. I think she were called Ethel, and mi dad were George. There were some more of us, but I never seen um, an' I don't know their names. It were just like, mi dad couldn't manage wi' mi bein' a babby, all th' bigger lasses had died, so there were no-one ter look after mi. I never went to no school, that's fer th' gentry and the like. There weren't any schools fer th' likes of us poor folk.' Myrtle said all this in a matter of fact tone, not bemoaning her lot. If anything, she was grateful for the way her life had turned out. Sarah reflected that life must have been very hard for 'poor folk' as Myrtle called them. With her keen interest in history, she knew about the facts and figures of poverty in the working class in the nineteenth century but, to actually see and talk to people who experienced it, it was a sobering thought.

'So you're seventeen now. What do you hope for your life?'

'Well, I'd like ter think that when I'm a lot older I could be like Mrs 'Ardcastle. She's luvly. And I'd be kind to kids from th' workhouse, too.'

'Don't you have a boyfriend?'

'We're norr allowed followers, but I think that William who does the garden is sweet on me. 'E blushes someat shameful if I talk ter 'im. An' he looks at me long an' 'ard when we're 'aving our meals, unless I look at 'im. An' then he blushes!' Myrtle giggled at the thoughts of William blushing, but then became sober again. 'Yer won't tell Mrs 'Ardcastle though, will yer, she'd go mad. We as ter 'ave permission to go courtin'.'

'Of course not, but do let me know if anything develops, I like a good romance,' replied Sarah laughing. Sarah reflected on how different Myrtle had been for those few minutes, when her harsh life had taken on a little excitement. Myrtle scurried away into the dressing room, when she heard footsteps approaching. Lady Grace entered the room, followed by her son. Sarah sat up in bed.

'Well, my dear, how are you? My son tells me that you have been asking for newspapers. That sounds a great improvement to me. Did you find anything to amuse you in there? I always find the fashion pages are vital, to know what is going on in London. It's so difficult to keep up with the trends here. Even making the arduous journey to Leeds or York is disappointing as they are still behind the London fashions. It just means one must go up to London regularly to see what is going on, and who is wearing what. I don't always buy my clothes there though. The prices are extortionate. I often draw sketches and take them into the local dressmaker in the village. I'll take you there when you are better. She is amazing, and can copy anything from a simple sketch, and saves lots of money. Which keeps my dear son happy, as he is always moaning about the allowances we all need for dressing. But look at him. I bet he spends far more than I do. He's always dressed in the latest dandified style.'

'Now Mama, don't tell all our secrets. Sarah doesn't want to hear about that. I bet you never even read the fashion pages, did you? The paper doesn't look any more ruffled than when I sent it up. Now what did you find interesting? The report from Parliament? The latest news of the war with France and Napoleon's offspring? The murder in Hyde Park?'

'Well, actually, I didn't get further than the front page. I seem to have only slept or taken drinks today. The time has gone so quickly. But I will look at it later. I am interested in what is going on in the world. I think all women should be,' replied Sarah spiritedly.

'There, Mama, didn't I tell you she was a modern woman. She really gave me a start earlier. I only laughed when she asked for the paper, and she started shouting at me about the poor lot of women.'

'Excuse me butting in, Lord Grace, but I don't remember shouting at you. I wouldn't be so rude to someone who has taken me in and looked after me.'

'A thousand pardons Miss Woozy, perhaps you merely raised your voice a shade, and I'm exaggerating. I must make so bold as to admit that I do that quite frequently. I need to tell you that before my dear Mama tells tales.'

'And rightly so, Josiah, you were the biggest storyteller in the nursery. I am sure that you did not shout, my dear. Do take no notice of my son; he is an inveterate tease, as I am sure you have noticed. Why listen to him, calling you Miss Woozy on such slight acquaintance. I do apologise for him. He's incorrigible. Where on earth did he get that name from anyway?'

'Well, that's probably my fault,' replied Sarah, 'when I came round, I said that I felt woozy. It's a family word that we use when we feel light-headed or dizzy. I take no offence, anyway.'

'Unfortunately, he will probably call you that for the rest of your life. Once he gives a person a new name, he sticks to it.' Sarah shuddered at the phrase 'rest of your life'. It was a little too close to home at this stage of the events.

'Oh, my dear, you are shivering. Myrtle, get another log on the fire and another blanket. Dr Griffiths says that it is crucial that she doesn't get a chill.' Lady Grace pulled the blankets up higher round Sarah's neck.

'I'm fine, honestly. I'm quite warm. I don't know what made me shiver. You're all so kind.' Sarah could feel the tears brimming up into her eyes again and Lady Grace saw them too.

'Come along Josiah, this is all too much for Sarah. We will let her rest and leave her to the care of Myrtle. And Josiah, you must not provoke her. I don't want her getting shivering attacks. It could harm her head. It's bad enough that she has concussion, without having you to deal with.' Lady Grace marched her son out of the door, his head bowed as with remorse. Sarah felt a little guilty that he had got the blame and felt badly about him being told off in front of her. But as he went through the door, he half turned and winked at her. Sarah managed to refrain from laughing until they had gone out the door, and then both she and Myrtle collapsed in giggles.

'Oh Miss, did yer see that? It's a good job tha' 'is muther didn't. I think 'e must be sweet on you.'

'Nonsense,' said Sarah, 'he's just a tease, like Lady Grace said. Although I think that all this excitement is getting to me. I'm feeling very tired. I think I'll settle down for the night, now.' Myrtle brought the commode back in, and a bowl of water for her to wash, and then Sarah quickly fell asleep.

Chapter 9

The sound of birdsong woke Sarah next morning. There hadn't been a sound from Myrtle this morning, and Sarah had no idea what time it was. She had left her modern watch behind prior to the dinner, and there was no clock in the room. She was pretty sure that clocks had been invented long before 1825, so perhaps she may be safe in asking for one. It would certainly make her time in bed easier if she knew what time it was. The house noises seemed less this morning, and then Sarah remembered that it was Sunday. Perhaps life was a little easier even in such a big house. She called for Myrtle, but there was no answer from the dressing room. Sarah gingerly wriggled to the edge of the bed and rested her feet on the floor. So far, so good. She stood up, holding on to the bedside table and carefully walked to the door and back. Great. Miss Woozy was definitely not woozy today!

Sarah decided to look outside the window, to see if she could see the birds that were singing so beautifully. She walked carefully round the edge of the bed and then held on to the chair before reaching the window. She had worked out that the bedroom was on the front of the house, overlooking the lake, from the tour that she had had on Friday night. Sarah looked out of the window and the sight that she saw left her cold. Fully expecting to see the housing estate, Sarah was shocked to see nothing but great lawns and avenues of trees, with not a house in sight, except for the Lodge house that she had seen on Friday. If she hadn't already accepted the fact that she was in 1825, then this was the proof. Gone was the housing estate, the dual carriageway, the Chinese takeaway and the other shops, and the street lamps. She could see for miles. But not the view that she wanted to see. Sarah sat down sadly on the chair by the window. How on earth was she going to get back to her own time? Sarah tried to remember what she had been doing before she fell. 'That was it,' she suddenly realised, 'I banged my head. If I bang my head again, I may go back to my own time.' She didn't fancy banging her head on purpose, but it was the only way she could think of. She moved to the stone fireplace and taking hold of it for support, she banged her head sharply against the fireplace. The pain was excruciating, but when she opened her eyes she was still in the same room, with an outlook of fields and not a housing estate. It had not worked. But now she had a very sore head. Gritting her teeth to stop herself crying out in pain, she walked quietly back to her bed and curled up tightly, overwhelmed with disappointment. Hearing Myrtle coming, she turned away from the door, and feigned sleep. She didn't think that she could face talking to anyone at the moment, even the kindly Myrtle. Myrtle quietly came into the room, and busied herself with her duties, cleaning out the fireplace, and dusting the furniture and generally tidying round the room. Sarah sensed Myrtle leaning over her, so gently appeared to be waking up, and smiled a good morning.

'Oh Miss, whatever 'ave yer done ter yer 'ead? You've gorra awful bruise comin' up on yer fore'ead. Looks jus' like yer've banged it.'

'Oh, I woke up in the night and lost my bearings and banged my head on the wooden headboard. Has a bruise come up?' Sarah asked innocently.

'I'll 'ave ter get Mrs 'Ardcastle ter come up an' 'ave a look. She'll know what ter put on.'

'Don't make a fuss, Myrtle, I'm sure she has more important things to do than this. By the way,' said Sarah trying to divert her, 'where were you earlier? I called for you and you weren't here.'

'It bein' Sunday, Miss, we ger an extra long break. Family go ter 10 o'clock Mass. We can go an all if we want ter, but most of us don't like the 'igh church service. Th' family are big Catholics, but it's only jus' gettin' safe ter admit yer a Catholic now. That's why there's no chapel in th' 'ouse like what there is i' sum big 'ouses. The family gave sum land ter build a new Catholic church down i' th' town. So while they're at church we mek the most of 'aving a nice long breakfast wi' out the bells upstairs ringin', and us 'avin' ter go an' answer 'em in th' middle o' our breakfast.'

'I'd love to get up and sit out for a little while today, do you think I could? I feel so much better.'

'I'll go and get yer breakfast and ask Mrs 'Ardcastle at same time.' Myrtle trundled off out of the bedroom and Sarah rested back against the pillows. She soon became aware of little girls' voices outside her door, but nobody came in. Sarah eventually called to them.

'Hello, who is there?' The giggling stopped instantly. Sarah called again. 'Do come in and see me, please.' A little head peeked round the doorframe.

'Are you Miss Woozy?' and then she collapsed into giggles and retreated back out of the door.

'Yes, I am Miss Woozy. Who are you?' This time two little faces appeared and they moved slowly into the room and then stopped, staring at Sarah. They both wore matching dark blue dresses with white starched pinafores over the top. They had little black lace up boots and their long hair was arranged in ringlets down their backs, tied with a dark blue and white striped ribbon. 'Well, who are you and how do you know that I'm called Miss Woozy?'

'I'm Elly and I'm 9, and this is Mary, but she's only 6. My name is really Eleanor, after Mama, but I am called Elly for short. And our big brother Josiah told us that that was your name. He said that we hadn't to come in because you were poorly, but we wanted to see you. Mama is having her breakfast with the others. So we sneaked away from the maids on the nursery floor, whilst they were making the beds. You won't tell on us, will you? We're always getting in trouble for things. We try to be good, but we get bored.' All this time, Mary had been hiding behind Elly, but now edged further out so that she could see Sarah.

'No, I won't tell on you. You've both got lovely names. By the way, my real name is Sarah. Your big brother gave me that name, when I fell, as I said that I felt woozy, and he had never heard the word.' The giggles started again.

'Woozy, Woozy,' they both started chanting, dancing around on the spot. They soon stopped when another girl walked into the room, demanding to know what was going on. She was much bigger than the other two and, although dressed in a similar gown to the others, she did not have a pinafore on, and her hair was swept up at the nape of her neck, in a sort of French pleat. She was a dainty blond girl.

'What are you two doing in our guest's room? What did Mama tell you? She is not to be disturbed as she is unwell. I'm sorry Miss, I have forgotten your name.'

'It's Miss Woozy,' blurted out Elly giggling, but she soon stopped.

'That's enough rudeness from you Elly, just wait till Mama finds out. You'll be for it.'

'Just wait till Mama finds out what, Anna?' All three girls gasped as their mother came into the room. 'And what are you three doing in here? Anna, you should know better. You heard what I said at breakfast time. Miss Sarah was not to be disturbed. Kindly tell me why you are all in here?' All three girls stared down at their feet, as if their very life depended on them knowing the colour of their boots. 'Well Anna, I'm waiting.'

'Please don't be cross, Lady Grace. They have been no trouble. I've really enjoyed having them here. They've really cheered me up. It wasn't Anna's fault. Elly and Mary peeped in earlier and I invited them in. Anna came in only to tell them to go back to the nursery and not to bother me, and then you came in yourself. They're such delightful girls; I'd hate them to be in trouble on my account. I'm sure they could aid my recovery.' Three pairs of grateful eyes looked up quickly at Sarah, then back down at the floor again. Even Lady Grace's face softened to hear her girls being called delightful.

'I'm sorry Anna; I thought you were the ring leader. I should have known it would be these two scamps. Off back to the nursery both of you.' The two girls scarpered quickly out of the door. Lady Grace turned to Anna.

'You may stay for a short time and see if there are any errands that we can do for Miss Sarah.'

'I've already asked Myrtle if I could get up today. I feel so much better.'

'Yes, Mrs Hardcastle mentioned it. I think that should be alright. Anna, perhaps you could help Myrtle and ease her work. You are very good at helping in a sickroom. Besides, it's Myrtle's turn for a Sunday off, Mrs Hardcastle tells me. I'm sure you could keep Miss Sarah occupied for some of the time. Agnes will stand in for Myrtle. I've told Myrtle she may have a little longer off work because of all the extra work she has had to do. She won't be back until tomorrow morning. Anyway, I've no time to stand chatting, I need to go now and discuss the next week's menus with Mrs Hardcastle, so I'll leave you two together.' Lady Grace walked briskly out of the room and Anna visibly relaxed.

'Thank you so much Miss Sarah, that was kind of you to defend us.'

'Is your Mama such a tyrant, then?

'Oh no, she's a lovely mama, but she is very strict about guests and not offending people and doing the right thing. Everything has to be considered as to whether it is the done thing. It becomes quite tedious when you are wanting to romp around the lawns with the little ones. 'Now Anna,' she mimicked her mother's voice, 'you have put your hair up. Please behave with a little decorum as befits your station in life. What will the servants think?' I tell you, I don't care what the servants think. They would probably like to romp round the lawns themselves, given half a chance. They probably have a miserable life anyway, having to work for us. Being at our beck and call all the time. It's ridiculous really, isn't it? All these people needed to look after one family. And yet in the town the poor women have to look after the little ones, the house, the husband and go out to work in the woollen mills as well. They haven't any servants. They are the servant.'

'Quite the little socialist, aren't you, Anna?'

'Socialist, I'm not sure what that word means.'

'Well, caring about the other people in life, realising that they have a raw deal and deserve better.'

'I'm sorry, have I been going on too much? Mama says that I talk far too provocatively, and it will hamper me when I go up to London for the Season and I'll never get a proposal. Men don't like girls to be too educated, or sticking up for the underdogs, Mama says.'

Sarah watched Anna as she spoke and saw the fire in her soul. She would have made a lovely Suffragette, thought Sarah, if she had lived a few decades later.

'And what do you think Anna?'

'I think women should be educated like men and be allowed to go to university and study things for the sake of studying them. Just to fill up the holes of knowledge that girls have. But Mama doesn't believe in girls getting an education. Says it spoils their marriage chances. That's all I hear nowadays. Marriage this, proposal that, Season the other. It's so wearisome.'

'I think the same as you, Anna. But I've already upset your brother by arguing that women should be educated.'

'Upset Josiah? Well, that is good news. You've quite made my day. You're so forward thinking. Did Josiah like what you were saying?'

'Er, no, not really. He said women didn't need educating to bring up babies and run a household, I'm afraid.'

'Huh, that is just what I would expect him to say. But he may take it from you. Please carry on telling him what you think, and together we may make a difference.'

'What would you like to do, if you could choose your own destiny, then Anna?'

'Promise you won't laugh if I tell you? I would like to be a doctor. There I've said it. You are the first person that I've ever said it to. Oh Sarah, you're not laughing. Then you approve of my idea?'

'I certainly do, but I don't think Josiah or any other of the males around here would agree. Why a doctor?'

'I really enjoy caring for the sick. Mama first took me to the poor side of town shortly after I put my hair up. She was preparing me for womanhood, she said, and for marriage is what she really meant. She envisages that I'll be a Lady of the Manor somewhere, and will have my beneficial and philanthropic duties to undertake. When my sister Cassandra was taken round with Mama on her 'duties', she hated it. She married the first man she danced with in London during the season. She was only sixteen. I would hate that. Although Cassy seems to like being married. It's probably because she can boss everybody around with no obstruction, because it is now her duty. She got short shrift when she bossed everyone round here, I can tell you.'

'How many sisters have you got, Anna?'

'Well, there were eight of us. Josiah is the eldest, and then there was Roger and James, but they died in infancy, before I was born. Then all Mama seemed to breed was girls. Oh, I do apologise, am I being too coarse?' Sarah shook her head, fastened by this young girl's hopes and fears, and also fascinated in hearing about the family who had so kindly taken her in. 'Then there was Isabelle. She's married to John and lives in Durham and has three children, no I mean two.' Anna quickly corrected herself. 'Then there's Cassy, then me, then Charlotte, she's 13, then Elly and Mary who you have already met. And Mama of course.'

'What about your father?' Anna's pretty face clouded over. 'He fell off his horse before Mary was born. He broke his neck. Mama was very upset, she loved him so much. They were very lovey-dovey together, just like a couple who couldn't wait to get married. We all loved him. He was a very good Papa. Many papa's hardly even talk to their children, but he used to say that we were his jewels and he used to cuddle us and spoil us. The shock of Papa's accident made Mama start with the baby early and Mary was very tiny. They thought that she may die, but as you saw, she survived. But Mama, knowing that it was to be her last child, was praying for a boy and was very disappointed it was a girl. We need the spare, you see.'

'I beg your pardon, the spare?'

'Yes, you know, the heir and the spare. If anything happens to Josiah,' at this Anna quickly crossed herself and said 'God Forbid' quietly under her breath, 'we don't have a 'spare' to inherit the title. It will pass to my cousin, and Mama is desperate to keep it in this family and not let it go to the cousins. That's why she is so desperate to get Josiah married. He needs an heir as well, or the title will still go to our cousin John.' Sarah was amazed at the way this young girl was talking, just as if they were talking about breeding livestock for the racing track. 'Mama is always putting on balls, or arranging for families with nice eligible young women to come and stay. She really encourages us to bring all our friends round. It's quite desperate really. He's thirty now. He should be thinking about getting a marriage arranged. He's very charming to all the ladies he meets, and they all fall head over heels in love with him, but up to now he hasn't fallen head over heels with anyone. It's quite frustrating. We keep getting hopeful, only to have our hopes dashed. My cousin Elisabeth in Durham and my cousin Emily in Northumberland both want to marry Josiah, but he still treats them like little sisters. It is really funny to watch them simpering when he comes in the room. Their voices go all husky and funny. But they don't sound nice at all. Just silly. And it's all a waste of time, because he has told me that he is not interested in them. My cousin John, that's Emily's brother, would like Emily to marry Josiah, so that they can keep the title in the family. Either that or Josiah dies without heir so that John will inherit anyway. '

Anna stopped in her flow and sat thinking quietly. Sarah was amazed by all that she had heard. Arranged marriages, they didn't bear thinking about. Although in multicultural Britain in 2001 she had read about arranged marriages still being carried out in the Moslem and occasionally the Jewish communities. But on reflection, she supposed that it was common in nineteenth century Britain, when money and estates were involved. Anna had started talking again and Sarah was roused from her thoughts when she heard what Anna was saying.

'Mama positively glowed when you came here. She thinks that you would make a nice bride for Josiah, because you are a bit long in the tooth, and would be grateful for any offer of marriage, and anyway, you're the first person that Josiah has ever taken a real interest in. Mama's quite hopeful.' Anna turned round to Sarah and found Sarah had a shocked expression on her face, her mouth wide open in amazement. 'Oh I'm so sorry Sarah, my tongue ran away with me. Please ignore everything that I said.' With that, she fled from the room, leaving Sarah gasping with amazement at what she had heard.

'So I'm a bit long in the tooth, am I?' she said to herself. 'Well I suppose she's right. To a fifteen year old, I must appear positively archaic.' Still, she had enjoyed talking to Anna, and would look forward to their talks again. She sat back against the pillows and thought about Josiah. He was very charming, but there was no spark there. Besides, she didn't intend staying in 1825. As soon as she could, she was going to try again to get back to the twenty first century, and Joe.

Chapter 10

There was a sound of footsteps in the polished hallway outside, and Sarah turned eagerly, expecting that Anna was returning. It was Agnes.

'Ello Miss, I've cum ter get yer up.'

'Why thanks, Agnes, that's brilliant news. I'm getting quite sore stuck in bed.'

'If yer tell us where yer clothes are Miss, I'll get 'em out and see if they need pressin' or owt'.

'Well, er, I'm not sure where my clothes are. I've only got the green dress, and that's not suitable for daytime.'

'P'raps they've shoved 'em in th' wash house. Never mind, I'll go and get some of Miss Cassy's clothes. She left 'em all behind when she got wed, and yer abaht 'er size. 'Er Ladyship keeps 'em ter give ter th' poor, but it's a bit daft, like, 'cos the poor could never wear some o' them posh things. But she 'ad sum nice day dresses. She never took 'em wi' 'er, cos she wanted all new for 'er weddin'. It cost 'er Ladyship a fortune. Well, I'll be off and find someat a bit like.'

With that, Agnes left the room, leaving Sarah amazed. What was the matter with everyone today? They were all giving out secrets and talking longer than they had done before. Perhaps they were beginning to see her as one of the family. Sarah didn't know whether to be pleased or sad about that. It was nice that they were accepting her, but if it was only for her marriageable values, she was not so happy. She so desperately wanted to marry, but definitely not Josiah, and not in 1825. If only she hadn't fallen into 1825. 'But,' she thought to herself, 'it's no good crying over spilt milk, I'm here for now, and I'll have to make the best of it.' Agnes arrived back into the bedroom with several garments over her arm.

'Mrs 'Ardcastle ses as 'ow yer can choose from this lot.' The bright array of dresses were dumped onto the bed, and Sarah and Agnes had a pleasant hour sorting through them.

Sarah picked out three dresses and some underclothes, laughing to herself at the size of the undergarments. 'It's a good job that I wasn't wearing a thong when I came here. They would have thought me a real hussy,' she thought to herself. But when she actually looked at the enormous undergarments that she was to wear, she was the one that was shocked. She had expected large bloomer-like pants, but they were worse. The undergarments consisted of two wide legs, tied together with strings. They came up to the top of the thighs, and that was it. There was no other part of the garment. No seat, no crotch. Just legs. She couldn't believe what she was seeing. Talk about draughty, there was nothing there. But then she thought of a benefit. At least she wouldn't have to remove them to go to the toilet! She dreaded to think what would happen during a menstrual period, but she would cross that bridge when she came to it.

Agnes guided Sarah into the dressing room and helped her to wash. They then dressed Sarah in the underclothes that they called drawers, then added fine white woollen stockings fastened up with garters, thick cotton underskirts, and a lemon cotton print dress. The material had green sprigs of flowers over it, and the dress was trimmed with matching green velvet under the bust and in a large bow at the front. The sleeves were puffed up and were also trimmed with the green velvet. The neckline was a lot higher than the green velvet had been, and Sarah could see why this was called a day dress, as it was much more circumspect than her previous one.

Sarah looked at herself in the long cheval mirror in the dressing room. She appeared to have lost weight, but this only enhanced the shape of her face, with the cheekbones showing more prominently than before. The feminine floaty style seemed to suit her, and she was pleased once again not to have landed in the crinoline era. Agnes sat her down and started to brush her hair quite vigorously. 'Is this 'ow yer own maid did yer 'air, Miss Sarah?' Agnes asked.

'Er, yes,' replied Sarah, thinking that Mel and her hairdressing staff would not be too pleased to be called servants. That was another factor. How on earth was she going to inform Mel that she wouldn't be keeping her regular Saturday appointment at the salon. Pretty hard when telephones had not been invented, especially ones that could ring through time.

'Yer've got luvly hair, Miss, such a bonny colour, if yer don't mind mi sayin'.'

'Thanks, Agnes. I always find it a trouble myself; it won't go where it should. It seems to have a mind of its own.'

'Still, I expects yer maid 'as got it down to a 'T' now.'

'Well, yes, I suppose she has,' replied Sarah, thinking that she had better change the subject before Agnes asked too many awkward questions. 'Where do you come from, Agnes?'

'From th' village. My ma an' dad 'ad thirteen kids, so they were that glad when I got this job. One less mouth ter feed, and more room in th' beds fer th' little uns.'

'How long have you been here, then?'

'Ten years. I were nobbut a little tiddler o' nine when I cum 'ere.' That made her nineteen, Sarah reflected. Already spent more of her life in service than she had spent at home. But like Myrtle, she was grateful for the good fortune that she had received. It made Sarah feel quite humble about her lot in life, both in 2001 and even in 1825. At least she had fallen into a 'gentry' home in her time travel, and was being treated like one of the gentry. With an awfully snobbish and uncharacteristic thought, Sarah was glad that she had landed 'upstairs' rather than 'downstairs'. She was shocked at her own thoughts and wasn't comfortable with them.

'I'll jus' go an' get yer tea Miss,' said Agnes, 'I won't be long.' Sarah felt strangely calmed by all the brushing that Agnes had done. She walked slowly over to the window and sat on the chair, looking out of the window. She could see a carriage drawing up the drive. It followed the curve of the drive and came to a gentle stop outside the front door. The footman jumped off the top of the carriage and opened the door, before handing Lady Grace out of the carriage. Lord Grace jumped out athletically from the other side of the carriage and rushed round to help his mother into the house. She couldn't see many men doing that in her own generation, and she decided that she was beginning to like this gentle way of life. As fast as she had thought these words, Sarah began to panic. She mustn't become complacent about being in 1825, she must get back to 2001. And, more importantly, to Joe.

She wondered again how she could achieve this. A sudden thought came into her head. If only she could get back into the kitchen where she first fell, then perhaps she could get back into her own time. The idea filled her with expectancy. She would wait patiently until she was allowed downstairs and would make an excuse to go to the kitchen. Agnes returned with her tea, and she was pleased to note that she had been promoted to eating a sandwich. This gave her great hopes. Perhaps tomorrow, she would progress to going downstairs. But first, she had to get the old-fashioned doctor on her side. He would probably keep her in bed for years just to boost his own bill! Some time later, Lady Grace and her son visited her in her room.

'And how is our patient feeling today?'

'Not very patient, I fear. I feel so much better, I would love to get up and come downstairs.'

'Whoa, not so fast, Miss Woozy, we must wait for Griffiths permission. He'll be here tomorrow. I must admit that you look better now that you are dressed.'

'Josiah,' said Lady Grace in shocked tones, 'what a thing to say to a young lady. Whatever must she think of us? How uncouth. Apologise immediately.' Lord Grace made a deep bow and begged Sarah to forgive him. Sarah merely laughed to see him so penitent.

'Apology accepted gratefully,' she replied still laughing. 'At least you are treating me like you treat your sisters and see me as one of the family now. I saw you coming back in the carriage earlier. Have you had a nice trip?'

'We went to my father's grave,' Lord Grace replied quietly.

'Oh, I am so sorry. I didn't mean to pry.'

'That is all right' said Lady Grace, a tight smile on her face, 'you weren't to know. It was his dearest wish to build our own chapel here at Roding Hall, but we only got as far as the plans. I do hope that we can indeed build the chapel, and once we have had it consecrated, we will apply to have my husband brought back here, so that he may forever rest in his beloved gardens, and I can visit him at my will. I'll leave you now my dear, I have things to attend to.' With that, Lady Grace turned and glided quietly out of the door. Lord Grace gave her a reassuring smile, and followed his mother. As they left Sarah heard Lord Grace reassuring his mother that the plans were well in hand, and would be carried out in the not too distant future.

Sarah felt a lump in her throat. Why had she said anything? 'Me and my big mouth,' she thought ruefully. It also reminded her of her own loss of her parents. She remembered having had feelings of relief when her parents had died together. Even though the loss was double for her and James to bear, at least their parents were together. They were the sort of couple who did everything together, and would have been lost without each other. Suddenly, Sarah felt weary. She made her way back to the dressing room and got ready for bed. Slowly, she walked across to her bed. She felt that she had made progress today. Certainly she had also made progress in her knowledge of the family that were so kindly looking after her, without even questioning where she had come from. That, decided Sarah, would have to wait. And she had better think up some good excuses as to where she had appeared from. Climbing into bed, she fell fast asleep, tired by the efforts of getting up and about for the first time. She didn't even hear Agnes come in and light the candle.

Chapter 11

Sarah woke suddenly in the night, hearing a noise that sounded like a child crying in pain. She sat up in bed and tried to work out where it was coming from, but it seemed to be a long way away. There were sounds of people moving about for a while, and then everything went quiet again. Sarah was mystified by the noise and shouted for Agnes, but there was no reply. Obviously the family felt that she was getting better, if they didn't keep a servant staying in the room nearby anymore. She tried to drift back to sleep, but she tossed and turned quite a while before she got off to sleep again. There were no further sounds and Sarah thought that perhaps she had been dreaming. When she next woke, it was a bright, sunny day, and the sun was shining through the open curtains. She could here someone humming in the dressing room. 'Agnes, is that you?' she shouted.

'No Miss, it's me, Myrtle, I didn't wek yer up did I?'

'Lovely to see you again Myrtle. No, you didn't wake me, did you have a nice day off?'

'It wer luvly Miss. Nowt ter do an' all day ter do it in. I 'ad a gradely time. Did yer sleep well last neight? I 'ear that yer were up and sittin' in th' chair. I were that amazed. I thought that yer'd be i' bed fer days yet.'

'Well, I did sleep well for most of the night, but I woke in the night to hear a child crying out in pain. Was one of the children ill? Perhaps Elly or Mary?'

Myrtle's face changed suddenly, and she turned and left the room saying that she would go and get Sarah's breakfast. Sarah mused over the sudden change in Myrtle, but decided that she would ask later. Myrtle wasn't long in returning with the breakfast, and said that Miss Charlotte had been ill in the night, and that must be who she had heard. Sarah laughed as she remembered the antics of the little girls yesterday.

'I've not met Miss Charlotte, but I had Elly and Mary in here yesterday. And Anna. I had a lovely time with them. Lady Grace was quite cross that they were with me, but I was glad. They cheered my day up. I do hope Miss Charlotte is soon well. I trust that it is not anything serious?'

'Er, no Miss, not serious,' Myrtle seemed to repeat the words after Sarah, and then turned away. It was obvious that Sarah was not going to get any more information from Myrtle on the subject of Miss Charlotte that day. After eating her breakfast, Sarah got washed and dressed and sat on the chair by the window. At mid morning, she saw a pony and trap coming up the drive. It was Dr Griffiths. 'Good,' thought Sarah to herself, 'perhaps I'll be given permission to get up and about a little now.' She waited for quite some time, but Dr Griffiths did not appear immediately. Perhaps he's seeing Charlotte or talking to Lady Grace. Or probably be having a small noggin with Lord Grace. Dr Griffiths red nose hinted that he was perhaps a little too fond of the spirits. At nearly lunchtime, Dr Griffiths arrived in the room, accompanied by Lady Grace.

'Well my dear, and how are we this morning?'

'Much better thank you,' Sarah replied. 'Will I be able to get up a little today?'

'Well now, I'll just have to take a look at you and then we'll see.' He smiled at Lady Grace in a patronising manner. It irritated Sarah no end, but she daren't say anything, and submitted to his ministrations. He felt her pulse, her forehead, moved her arms and legs, and pulling her eyelids down a little, looked in her eyes. He also felt at her head very carefully. 'What happened here, young lady?' he asked, pointing at the bruise on her forehead.

'Oh, I fell as I was getting out of the bed and banged my head. It was my fault. I wouldn't wait for Myrtle to return.'

'Hmm, I hope that this hasn't done any more damage to the brain. The brain is a tricky thing. One never knows how it is going to respond. You will need to be a lot more patient young Miss, heads do not mend overnight. But I can see that you are a lot better in some ways. Tell me, what date is it today, and where are you?'

'Er, er, it's 18th June 1825 and I'm at Roding Hall.' Sarah realised that the doctor was checking how her brain was recovering. This could be tricky, as she couldn't answer much more than she already had done.

'Very good. And where do you come from and how did you get here?'

'Er, well, I, er,'

'Yes, you were going to say,' prompted the doctor.

'I come from Read, near Clitheroe in Lancashire, and I came here with friends, but I can't remember any more.'

'Well, that is something. She can remember where she came from. I think that this blow to her head has caused further damage, and she may not recover fully. I think that we will have to wait and see if her full memory returns. But I am not hopeful. In these cases, the brain seems to forget certain things and remembers others. It could be a long time. I'm afraid that you are going to be inconvenienced for quite some time, Lady Grace. Have you contacted her family? Although perhaps that might not be a good idea, as they would want to move her to their house, and whilst she may get up now, and slowly take part in a normal life, I expressly forbid her to be moved. Certainly not an arduous journey such as over the Pennines. Or worse still the family may wish to move here until she is better, causing you even more inconvenience. You have enough on your hands at the moment.'

'Yes well, nothing that we can't manage between us, Doctor. Now let us go downstairs with Mrs Hardcastle and discuss how you want Sarah to be looked after, and what she may eat.' Sarah was amazed as Lady Grace almost marched the doctor out of the door. People were being strange this morning. It was as if they all knew something that they were keeping from Sarah. Her thoughts were disrupted at that moment by the arrival of Lord Grace.

'Good morning, Miss Woozy, and how are you this fine morning?'

'Well, I've had good news and bad news. Doctor Griffiths thinks that I am improved, but that full recovery may be a long time. The bad news is that I may be staying here quite a while longer yet.'

'Oh, that's not bad news. That is marvellous. I will look forward to watching you recover, and I hope that it is not too speedy a recovery so that I can delight in your company.' Sarah blushed at this fulsome speech, remembering what Anna had said the day before. Were they really considering her for the role as Lord Grace's wife? It didn't bear thinking about. To change the subject, Sarah asked how Charlotte was. Lord Grace stared at her.

'Charlotte? Why she's fine I think. Can't say I've seen her today.' Myrtle spoke suddenly.

'Beggin' yer pardon, sir, but Miss Charlotte were teken ill i' th' night. That's what Miss Sarah were on abaht.' The light suddenly seemed to dawn on Lord Grace.

'Oh yes, Charlotte. Yes, she probably was ill.' Myrtle seemed to be pulling a face at Lord Grace. 'I'll go an' find out fer yer, Miss, while 'is Lordships 'ere.' With that Myrtle shot through the door and down the stairs. 'Strange,' thought Sarah. 'Everybody is acting strangely today, unless I am getting better and noticing more things today.' Lord Grace pulled the divan lounger over by her chair. He was obviously going to have a long chat with her.

'So you live in Read'.

'Yes.'

'In Read Hall?'

Sarah laughed at the thought of the grandeur of Read Hall and her little modern mews house. 'No, a much smaller establishment, your Lordship.'

'Josiah. You keep forgetting.'

'Sorry, Josiah.'

'That's better. Now where were we? Oh yes, your home. Where is it exactly?'

'It's just further down the road from Read Hall.'

'And who is your father?'

'My parents are both dead. I live alone'.

'Alone, surely not alone, you mean, without parents. Perhaps you live with a brother?' Oh dear, this was tricky. How could she explain without scandalising his nineteenth century sensibilities?

'My brother James had moved to America before our parents were killed.'

'Indeed, I am so sorry. You shocked me so much by saying that you lived alone that I didn't commiserate with you on the loss of your parents. What happened to them? You say they were killed, rather than died. Were they murdered?'

'Oh no, not really murdered. They were killed in a car. . . .Sarah stopped mid sentence. She had been about to say a car crash. What could she say now? Fortunately Josiah jumped in.

'A carriage crash, oh how awful. Was it highwaymen?'

'No, two carriages collided in the fog. They were killed instantly.' Sarah hoped that that sounded feasible. She didn't like telling lies, but didn't see what else she could do in the circumstances. At least the fog part of it was true, Sarah reflected, but she didn't think that Josiah would understand the concept of 'motorway'.

'I am sorry Sarah. It must have been awful for you. Especially as your brother had gone to the New World. Did he not return to inherit the family home?' 'Oh my goodness' thought Sarah. 'How did she get out of this one?'

'Well, er, he has a wife and children out there, and a thriving business. Actually, the family home is no more. There were debts, and er . . .,'

'Sarah, I am so sorry. I have no right to pry. It must be really upsetting for you to have to go through this again. Accept my apologies.' Lord Grace sat with his head on his chest, obviously thinking deeply. Sarah was glad that she didn't have to make up any more lies for now. Perhaps she should change the subject.

Myrtle came back at that moment and reported that Mrs Hardcastle said that Miss Charlotte was doing very well, thank you very much. She had brought a tray with hot chocolate on for both of them. There were little macaroon biscuits as well. Sarah gratefully accepted hers, whilst Lord Grace simply took his cup, ignoring the biscuits, and barely acknowledging Myrtle, because he was so deep in his thoughts. As she was sipping her chocolate, Josiah suddenly spoke, without him looking up at all.

'So who do you live with? Are you married?'

'Oh no, I'm single. I have a housekeeper, a maid and a gardener and that is all I need. It's only a small house.' Josiah nodded at her answer. Sarah laughed to herself at saying she had a housekeeper and a gardener. Mrs Foote, her next door neighbour cleaned her house for her once a week, and Jim, the local gardener, cut her lawns and kept her tiny garden tidy. Josiah probably thought that by calling it a small house she meant a mere eight bedrooms, with four parlours, a library and goodness knows what else. She noticed that Josiah was looking at her strangely. She looked at him expectantly, thinking that he was going to speak, but he carried on staring. 'Goodness,' thought Sarah, 'he's probably deciding if he can still think about me as a possible bride if I'm only poor.' As if he were reading her thoughts, Josiah suddenly spoke.

'Is there anyone that you have an arrangement with?'

'No,' replied Sarah, trying not to laugh and sipping her chocolate as if her life depended on it.

'I find it hard to think why you are not married. You are pleasing to the eye. Have you had no suitors?' 'Oh yes,' thought Sarah, 'but the rat was married.' Strange, thought Sarah, she hadn't thought about Darren since she arrived here. But landing up in the nineteenth century was a bit of a drastic way to forget a boyfriend.

'Am I being too personal in my questions? Am I offending you?'

'Not at all. There was a suitor, but he changed his mind when I became impoverished.' 'Wow,' thought Sarah, 'I'm getting into this storytelling lark. I should write it down. I could make it into a novel. Mind you, I only hope that I can remember all the lies that I've been telling and don't put my foot in it.'

'What a cad. You were better off without him. Do you intend to go out to the New World and live with your brother?'

'I don't think so. I prefer England. I may visit someday, though. I have never seen my nephews. They were born over there'.

'How old are they?'

'One, both of them, they're twins,' she laughed.

'Twins in the family. Well, well. That saves a lot of time and bother. Two boys at one go, a pretty turn of affairs. I'm sure that your sister by marriage was grateful to have two at once. What do you think about having children? Would you like children?'

'Why yes, I think most women would want children, although some of my friends have said that they may not have any.'

'It's not up to them, really, is it? You have to take them as part of marriage. Babies happen in most marriages. But really, this is a most indelicate subject for an unmarried man to be discussing with an unmarried lady. Mind you, many of our friends would be scandalised that I was in your boudoir unchaperoned. It would ruin your reputation forever. No chance of marriage then. Well not to any one of worth or integrity. I do apologise.'

'Think nothing of it. I don't offend easily. And you don't look as though you are going to pounce on me and further ruin my reputation.' Josiah laughed loudly.

'That is true. And what is more, you are very forward thinking in your ideas. It is refreshing to talk with you. Most ladies only want to talk about fashion and who is marrying who, and how much people are worth. I know that I will have to marry eventually, but I must say, most of the young ladies of today leave me cold. They are so frivolous. Or perhaps I am growing old. The longer that I avoid marriage, the younger the available ladies are. But Mama is getting more insistent nowadays, so I'm going to have to give it some serious thought. I must be going now. I have an appointment with the architect who is drawing the plans for Papa's chapel. It's a lot further on than Mama thinks. The work planning is all ready and when Mama goes down to London for the season, I shall give the word to start building. Hopefully, it will all be finished when she gets back. But you must keep it a secret.'

'What must Miss Sarah keep a secret?' said Lady Grace as she entered the room. Both Josiah and Sarah froze. Josiah recovered first.

'I was just telling Miss Sarah that you were trying to marry me off, but I haven't to know about it, in case I run away from every available female that you manage to inveigle into our house for my perusal.' 'Well thought up,' thought Sarah approvingly, smiling at Josiah.

'Nonsense, I do nothing of the sort,' snorted Lady Grace. 'Come Josiah, the estate manager has arrived, and wishes to talk with you. I want to see if we can find out about Miss Sarah's family. I'm sure that they will be worried about her.' Josiah took his mother by the arm and quickly marched her out of the room saying, 'Let me tell you Mama, it is a very sad story and it hurts Miss Sarah to keep repeating it. Once I have told you, nobody else must ask her. It could undo all the good work that Griffiths is doing.' Sarah relaxed in the chair. That had been a close call. How perceptive Josiah had been in not only protecting her from his mother, but also from all their family. He really was a nice man. He would make someone a good husband.

Chapter 12

Myrtle returned with some clean clothes and bed linen for Sarah and told her that she was to be invited down to dinner that evening.

'Now where's yer evenin' dresses? Same place as rest o' yer stuff?'

'Yes,' said Sarah ruefully, 'I only have the green one. I don't suppose that will do, will it?'

'Well, Mrs 'Ardcastle 'as give it ter th' sewing girl, 'cos yer ripped it when yer fell. Seems as 'ow I'll 'ave ter go ter get some more of Miss Cassie's stuff. I won't be long.'

'Didn't Miss Cassy take her evening clothes either?'

'No Miss, not a one. Eh, she were a reight 'un, that 'un. 'Er Ladyship nearly tore 'er hair out. Mind, by th' time 'er got wed, I think they was all glad ter see back of 'er. At least yer are th' same size as Miss Cassy, that's a lucky thing. I'll see what I can find up there.' Myrtle hurried away again, leaving Sarah to ponder on her invitation to dine. She would have to be very vigilant in her speech, so that she didn't say the wrong thing and let her secret out. She had nearly done it with the car crash. It would be so easy. But they wouldn't worry about anything strange that she said, they would probably blame it on the head injury. That had been quite useful when Dr Griffiths had said that she could have variable memory loss. 'I don't remember' could become her favourite phrase for getting herself out of awkward situations.

Myrtle returned with another selection of gowns, but this time they were far more glamorous and expensive looking. No wonder Josiah worried about the trousseau budget, if she was leaving all these gowns behind. And as she was only sixteen when she married, they must have been reasonably new ones. Myrtle was asking her to select one for that evening. There were gowns of every hue. Some with frilly flounces and lace insets, and others that were a simple Empress style gown not unsimilar to the green one that she had worn on that fateful night. Sarah looked admiringly at them all. At the bottom of the pile, she saw a pale green shot silk gown. As she held it up, she saw that it was fitted to the waist, with a pointed 'V' shape panel going down into the skirt. The rest of the skirt was gently gathered, and had frills of a deeper green silk round the hem. The 'V' at the waist was matched by one at the neck, but a cream lace fichu was fastened across the 'V', to make it less revealing. The shoulders were puffed, with the sleeves caught into a tight band halfway down the top half of her arm. The rest of the sleeves were tight down to the wrist, finishing just above the wrist, with a cream frill. Sarah tried it on. As she slid the dress over her shoulders, and allowed Myrtle to help her, Sarah shivered with delight. The dress felt wonderfully cool and elegant. It fitted her perfectly.

'Well Miss,' gasped Myrtle as she turned slowly round to look in the mirror. 'Yer look a proper picture. Miss Cassy never wore this 'un, so yer'll be th' first. It fair suits yer Miss.' Pleased by what Myrtle was saying, Sarah finally looked in the mirror. A glow of pleasure flooded through her when she saw herself. The dress did indeed fit her perfectly. The colour was also a perfect foil for her colouring. Agnes entered the room, and she praised Sarah on her looks, too. Agnes had brought down some of Miss Cassy's shoes and accessories. Sarah noticed a lovely pair of pale green shoes, which nearly matched the colour of the dress.

'What about these?' she asked.

'Just perfect Miss,' replied Agnes.

'If I remembers rightly, there's a bag what goes wi' 'em. Yer know what she were fer wantin' all of 'er stuff matchin'. Even when she were a little 'un.'

'Drove 'er Ladyship wild,' added Myrtle. 'They spent loads on 'er comin' out clothes, and she were married that quick, she never wore 'alf of 'em. And then wanted new 'uns fer her weddin'. Eh, I don't know, yer could've fed a family o' eight fer a year on what were spent on 'er clothes. Anyroad, it's not fer me to say owt, beggin' yer pardon, Miss'. Myrtle looked downcast, even a little ashamed at her outburst. Sarah laughed.

'Well I'm glad that Miss Cassie was so greedy and selfish, because now I'm reaping the benefit, and have the choice of so many beautiful clothes.' Myrtle had been rummaging through the large container of bags and fripperies.

'Ere it is, Miss, it's so seemly. I'm sure yer'll like it.' The bag was indeed lovely. It was like a little drawstring purse, made of a stiffened brocade in the same colour as the dress. It had cream beads sewn into the shape of a flower, in the centre of the bag. Cream lace was fastened round the outer rim of the bag, and the handle was made of a twisted loop of the cream and green material. It had obviously been made to match the dress she was wearing.

'I'll gerra nice clean kerchief fer yer ter go i' th' bag' said Agnes as she scurried out of the door. Myrtle was still rooting in the container. She found some small artificial flowers in pale pink and cream.

'These'll do nicely fer yer 'air, Miss. Shall I do it now?' Sarah sat down at the dressing table and looked in the mirror. Myrtle swept her hair up into a type of chignon, and then wound the flowers down the back of the hair, saving one each for behind Sarah's ears. Sarah gaped at herself in the mirror. She looked totally different.

'Now all yer need is yer jewel that yer wore when yer come 'ere. I'll gerrit out o' th' drawer.' Myrtle went in to the dressing room, and came out shortly afterwards, but the choker was now a cream one to match the trimmings on the dress. The large emerald looked even darker against the paler choker. Sarah shivered as she let Myrtle fasten it round her neck.

'There, Miss, yer look as pretty as a picture. Now let me just see who tha' is at th' door.' It was Anna.

'Hello Myrtle, is Miss Sarah ready? I've come to escort her down to dinner.' Sarah moved towards the door, and was pleased when Anna smiled at her. 'You look lovely, Miss Sarah. You do suit green. I wish I had your colouring.'

'You wouldn't if you had it,' quipped Sarah, 'and you look lovely too. Lilac is such a lovely colour. It makes you look so dainty and ethereal. And do call me Sarah, you don't need to say Miss.' Anna looked slightly embarrassed.

'Although I have my hair up, it would be an impertinence to call an older lady by her first name.'

'Less of the older lady, young Anna. I'm not quite in my dotage yet,' laughed Sarah.

'Oh, I do apologise,' added Anna blushing beetroot red, 'you're not old at all, I feel that you are the same age as me, because you have such modern views. But Mama is such a martinet for manners.' Sarah took Anna's arm and led her through the door. 'Come on Anna, take me down to dinner, or else it will all be cold.'

The two girls walked slowly down the wide staircase, chatting companionably. As they turned into the dining room, Sarah stopped in her tracks, staring about her at the unfamiliar room. It was smaller than the one she had been in for the dinner on the Friday night, and seemed to be at a different angle all together.

'What's the matter, Miss Sarah' asked Anna, 'do you feel faint?'

'Just a little' replied Sarah. 'But I'm fine now.' She didn't want them putting her back on bed rest when she had only just regained her freedom. Lord Grace moved quickly towards her, and guided her to the chair next to him.

'Come Miss Woozy, can't have you falling again.' He sat her down; pushing the chair to the table himself, a job that she noticed was done by the servants for the rest of the family. He leaned over her hand as she settled herself in the chair, and quietly asked if she was really all right.

'Yes, I assure you, I'm fine.' Sarah felt slightly embarrassed by the extra attention that she was getting, as Josiah was still holding her hand. He seemed to stay in that poise for a while, and then released her hand. Sarah noticed that the whole room was in silence, even the servants. And they were all looking at her and Josiah. Sarah dropped her head into her lap, to save her blushes.

Lady Grace suddenly broke the spell by asking Williams to start serving the meal. It was as if there had been a frozen tableau, and somebody had flicked a switch. Everybody jerked into life and seemed to become very busy. Sarah gingerly looked up at Josiah, and noticed that he was looking at her with a tender expression. She looked away quickly. 'Goodness,' thought Sarah to herself. 'I feel like I am acting in a Victorian melodrama. Victorian,' she mused to herself. 'Am I in the Victorian era?' She couldn't remember when Queen Victoria came to the throne. She vaguely remembered that she died in either 1901 or 1902, but how long did she reign? Well it was no use asking anyone here. They already thought she was a little simple.

Then she remembered Joe telling them that the dining room had been altered. He had made a quip about not being able to change it back just for the one night. He had also said that the old dining room had been awful for the servants as they had a long way to carry all the food from the kitchen. So this must be the old dining room. She was startled from her reverie by Anna.

'Miss Sarah, Mama is speaking to you.' Sarah looked up and apologised.

'I was just saying, Sarah, we haven't invited any guests tonight so that you could acclimatise yourself to our ways. We didn't want to discomfort you.'

'That is so thoughtful of you, Lady Grace, thank you.' Everybody started to drink the soup that the servants had served. It was a thin French onion soup. Sarah was relieved, as she knew that she wouldn't be able to eat a great deal after having eaten so little over the last few days. Following the soup was a substantial beefsteak pudding, which was brought to the table still wrapped in a white cloth. Sarah had never tasted food like it. It was so rich and tasty. Fortunately she had only asked for a small portion and took only small amounts of the vegetables and potatoes. The gravy was like she had never tasted before. Certainly beat the instant variety that she used herself. For the last course, pyramid creams were brought out. These seemed to be a concoction of wine, cream, candied peel and jelly, served in high fluted glass dishes. It was very light but Sarah could not finish it.

It was the largest meal she had eaten for days. As well as the pyramid creams, there were large displays of fresh fruit, and small dishes of bonbons and other sweets. During lunch, Lady Grace had commented that this was only a light meal, taking into account that Sarah had been ill, and also there were no guests present. Sarah smiled at this, thinking that she wouldn't like to see a sumptuous banquet in this house, if this was a light one. The table would probably groan under the weight of the food. Sarah could imagine that she would gain a lot of weight if she stayed around for any length of time. Not that she intended to stay, but she would work on that later.

The meal seemed to go on forever, the different wine glasses being filled up. Sarah was considerably wilting. She could no longer eat anything and certainly dare not drink anymore. She wondered how she could get away from the heavy warm atmosphere. The numerous candles alone seemed to add to the heaviness of the room. It was Anna who came to her rescue.

'Shall we take a little air, Miss Sarah, you look a trifle warm.' Sarah replied in the affirmative and rose to her feet. Lady Grace was instantly roused into action.

'Williams, get Myrtle to come and take Miss Sarah upstairs. She's a trifle overcome by the heat.' Williams bowed and left the room. Myrtle soon arrived looking flustered at being called into the dining room whilst the family was at table.

'Take Miss Sarah upstairs and stay with her,' commanded Lady Grace. Myrtle merely curtsied to Lady Grace and hurried Sarah out of the door, followed by Anna. 'I don't remember asking you to go, Anna, remember your place, please.' Lady Grace's voice had sailed through the air, imperiously.

'Sorry Mama' she replied as she sank back into her chair. Sarah was stunned at this remark, but felt so weary that she ignored it and went upstairs with Myrtle. She soon fell into bed and was very quickly asleep, despite all the disturbing images that had occurred during the dinner.

Chapter 13

The sound of the curtains opening woke Sarah next morning. She stretched in her bed and shouted good morning to Myrtle. Myrtle bustled around tweeking the curtains and the drapes around the room, and Sarah lay watching her, luxuriating in the comfortable bed.

'You are up early today Myrtle,' commented Sarah. Myrtle laughed.

'I am Miss, but yer not yersel'. It's past ten o' clock.'

'Ten! I don't believe it. Let me see a clock.'

'Yer timepiece is o'er by the winder, 'aven't yer sin it yet?'

'Er, oh yes, of course, timepiece,' muttered Sarah. Sarah looked across to the clock and it was indeed quarter past ten.

'Miss Anna 'as bin in ter see if yer were awake a coupla times. She's a reight early bird that one. Allus gerrin' up early and playin' outside when she were little. Eh, they'll 'ave sum trouble wi' 'er if they tries ter marry 'er off against 'er will.'

'Are they likely to?'

'Aye, they will an' all. 'Specially if she keeps upsetting 'er Ladyship.' Sarah reflected on this to herself, feeling sorry for Anna's lot. Certainly a girl born before her time. As she was thinking about her, Anna appeared.

'How are you Miss Sarah? I thought I'd call and ask whilst Mama was busy with Hardcastle. Once they get together, they spend ages planning every little detail of every meal. It's quite a relief when Mama goes away. Hardcastle just gets on with the job and the whole place runs just as well, and we all get fed just as well. But I couldn't say that in front of Mama. She'd be mortified. Oh, that's a carriage coming up the drive. I bet it's Doctor Griffiths.' Anna ran to the window, opened it and leaned out. 'Oh, it's my uncle's carriage. Oh goody. I hope that he has brought my cousins Jessica and Rachel to stay. We get on so well together. Oh, that's strange, it's just Thorndyke, that's their man,' she shouted back to Sarah by way of explanation. 'I wonder why he has come alone, and yet has brought the carriage? Why didn't he come on horseback? Very strange.'

Anna prattled on to herself, but the curiosity got the better of Sarah and she joined Anna at the window. A knock at the door alerted both their eyes away from the window. It was Mrs Hardcastle.

'There you are Miss Anna, your Mama is looking for you. She wishes to speak with you this instant.' Anna rushed out of the door, closely followed by Mrs Hardcastle. Obviously something was astir, but nobody was saying anything. Myrtle looked agitated.

'Do you want to go and see what is happening, Myrtle, you look worried?'

'Oh, thanks, Miss, I'll see if Mrs 'Ardcastle needs anything doin'.' With that, Myrtle hurriedly left the room. Sarah walked back over to the window and picked up a book that she had been looking at. It was an illustrated book of birds, which had been drawn by a lady. They were really lifelike and Sarah was amazed at the exquisite detail. In her own time, she would have thought that they were photographs; they were so perfect. She spent quite some time looking at them, and deciding that the robin was her favourite, with the delicate browns of his body making a stark contrast to the red breast, from which he got his name.

Sarah could hear people hurrying and scurrying about outside the room, but did not like to go out and find out what was happening. She was alone for a long time. Eventually, she could hear something happening outside the front door and, unable to contain her curiosity anymore, Sarah peered out of the window. Josiah was handing his mother into the carriage, and patting her hand, as if in sympathy. Anna was also fussing round, and appeared to be getting lots of instructions from Lady Grace. Many boxes and bags were being carried into the carriage by the servants.

Eventually, a young girl was also helped into the carriage. Sarah didn't recognise her. This must be Charlotte, as she seemed to be younger than Anna, yet much older than Elly. She must be feeling better for her to be going on a trip with her mother. Unless her mother felt that she was too ill to be left.

Sarah wondered where Lady Grace was going. It was obviously not just into the village judging by the bags and boxes. It was more than a family of six would take on a fortnight's holiday, all for one lady and her daughter. Thorndyke climbed up to the front of the carriage, and picked up the reins.

Anna, Josiah and Mrs Hardcastle waved the carriage off, and appeared to stand a long time watching. It was Mrs Hardcastle who moved first. As they moved away, Sarah failed to hear what Mrs Hardcastle was saying, but they all looked quite sad. Sarah felt uncomfortable, but still didn't feel that she should intrude. Hearing footsteps outside on the polished floor, Sarah quickly sat down and pretended to be avidly reading the book of bird pictures. It was Josiah. He seemed agitated and not his usual carefree charming self.

'Sarah, I'm sorry that we have neglected you this morning. My uncle's man, Thorndyke, came to say that my aunt is very ill, and wished her sister to be there with her. What could Mama do, but go and help? She's taken Charlotte with her, as she will be quite a help with my auntie's little ones. They live a long way away up in Durham, so Mama could waste no time. She said that I must come and speak with you immediately and apologise for not explaining herself. She is so sorry for treating a guest in such a way, but she needed to get ready and go quickly. It really is a serious illness. She was most perturbed at what you would think of her.' Sarah marvelled at the graciousness of this lady who, having received news of her sister's serious illness, had time to worry about an uninvited guest, who had landed themselves on the family. 'Tell me you forgive her, put her and my mind at rest, please do,' Josiah urged with a forlorn expression on his face.

'There is nothing to forgive. It is I who am a burden to you.'

'Not at all, you are very gracious. Mama was worried that you would think it indecent that she had left me here with you, almost unchaperoned, and begs you not to think that this will compromise your reputation. She has left Anna with you, as you both seem to get on well. She has also decided that she will introduce you as Anna's companion, so that there can be no hint of indecency.' Sarah thought of all the servants that were around the house and laughed to herself. She was not exactly alone with him. How could her reputation be besmirched by being under the same roof as an unmarried man, amongst all these servants? If it was under the same quilt cover she could understand, but then, morality was very different in those days. She suddenly thought of Darren. It was a bit too late to worry about her reputation anyway, she thought. Well and truly besmirched by that rat.

'I quite understand the problem that Lady Grace was facing. She had no need to worry about me at this time. She did right to hurry off to her sister's house. What is the matter with her?' Josiah looked uncomfortable.

'Well, er, er, it's a, er, delicate matter,' he stuttered, blushing. 'I must go and see to the household if there is nothing else you require?' Without waiting for an answer, Josiah hurried out of the room as he was speaking, almost colliding with Anna.

'Oh, Josiah, stop being quaint. Aunt Marguerite is with child, and is very ill because of that. She's probably getting too old for childbearing, but she just carries on, like most women. Like Mama would have done if Papa hadn't died. I wouldn't keep having more children. They just die and then break your heart.' She stopped abruptly at the end of the sentence, and her eyes filled up. Josiah moved across to Anna and cradled her in his arms, stroking her forehead and soothing her. For a few moments, Sarah was forgotten as brother and sister became engrossed in each other's cares.

'There, sweet Anna, don't distress yourself, I know how it hurts you when a baby dies. You've always been the same.' He turned to Sarah. 'When Mama lost her last child, the one between Elly and Mary, Anna was distraught. Mama had been ill after the birthing, and Anna was allowed to help the nurse with the care of the baby. Cassy wasn't interested at all, even though she should have been the one to help. But Anna has always been far more caring than Cassy. Anyway, enough of our family failings, what must you think of us? Now Anna, go and clean yourself up, and then perhaps you could ask Myrtle to bring you and Miss Sarah a cup of chocolate up.' Anna sniffed and dabbed her eyes daintily on her kerchief, and then brightened up considerably.

'There, she always cheers up if you mention chocolate, Sarah. You should remember that for the future.' As if by magic, Myrtle appeared in the door. 'Oh Myrtle, please could you bring Miss Sarah and Miss Anna a cup of chocolate each, in fact, no, make that three, I shall share their morning repast with them.'

'Beggin' yer pardon, yer Lordship, yer can't 'ave a chocolate, 'cos Mr Taylor th' architect is waitin' fer yer, in th' library,' Myrtle burst out, all in one breath, and curtsying at the same time.

'Couldn't be better timed, with Mama being away. Thank you Myrtle, could you go and bring two chocolates for in here, and a tray of tea for myself and Taylor. I don't think that he will want chocolate. He'd probably prefer a whisky but it's too early in the day.' With that, Josiah left the room and his feet could be heard jumping down the stairs in great leaps.

'Well, he looked happy. Is this Mr Hartley a good friend?'

'Oh no, he's just a tradesman,' replied Anna airily, 'but he will have brought the plans for the chapel. Now Mama is away, Josiah will probably want to get on with the work immediately. If he waits until we go to London for the Season, the ground will be either too wet or too hard. Although it is sad that Aunt Marguerite is ill, it is fortuitous for Josiah's plans.' Myrtle returned to the room without the chocolate, and asked the two girls if they would be so kind as to go to His Lordship in the library and have their drinks there, as he wanted them to see the plans. The two looked at each other, shrugged, and then agreed. 'This is a rare honour, you know, if Mama was here, she wouldn't have liked this, but Josiah is probably so excited that he wants someone else there to see his handiwork.'

'I thought the architect would have drawn up the plans?'

'Well, yes, the technical part, but Josiah gave him so many sketches, maps and ideas, that Taylor will have been very limited in what he could achieve,' replied Anna chuckling as they went down the stairs. They arrived at the library and Anna knocked at the door. It was opened by Agnes, who then went back to pouring tea for the men. Two large cups of chocolate were also on the tray.

'Ah Anna, and Miss Sarah. Do come in. Taylor, this is Miss Sarah Evans of Read, near Clitheroe, she came to visit with us for a while, but has agreed to stay and be Miss Anna's companion.' The man introduced as Taylor was a short plump man, probably in his forties, with receding hair. He was dressed in sober clothes, and his hair was shorter than the other men that Sarah had seen. He was leaning over a table holding a paper out on to the table, but let go as he stood up, and appeared to be quietly appraising Sarah.

'Pleased to meet you, Mr Taylor,' Sarah smiled.

'Likewise Miss Evans, I'm sure,' said Mr Taylor. He had a fairly high voice. As he bowed rather low over Sarah's hand, it was all she could do not to laugh.

'Hello, Taylor, have you got the plans then?' said Anna cheekily butting in to the conversation.

'Ah Miss Anna, lovely as ever. Here, let me show you the plans.' He spread them out over the table, but once he started explaining them, his voice took on a note of excitement. He explained how at first, he thought that he would have problems converting His Lordship's ideas into reality, but he had managed to incorporate them all. The chapel was to be built beyond the lawned area at the back of the house. There was a clump of trees, almost out of sight, which would shelter the chapel from the house. It would be very private, but there were already paths that lead down to where the chapel would be built. Sarah could see that both Anna and Josiah were thrilled with the plans.

'How soon could the builders start, Taylor?' asked Josiah.

'Well, they were a little hard pressed to give us a starting date, but I explained that it was for Her Ladyship and they agreed to start immediately'.

'So they should,' said Josiah, with more than a touch of arrogance, 'if they want to continue working round here.' Sarah started to smile, and then realised that Josiah was in earnest, not in jest. This attitude didn't match up with the gentle man that she was coming to know. And yet, she supposed that the gulf between gentry and workers would be far wider than it was today, or in her day, as she sadly reminded herself. And they called him Taylor, not Mr or his first name. Sarah was not comfortable with that, but remained silent. After all, she was the guest. 'Please send Heap round to see me in the morning and we can negotiate the price. I suppose he and his workers will want accommodation with coming from Harrogate?' Mr Taylor nodded. 'Fine, I'll see Williams about a cottage. There is one free at the moment. They can stay there, and eat in the kitchen. I'm very pleased with your work, Taylor. You have exactly drawn the ideas that I had in my mind. I shall recommend you to my friends.' Mr Taylor smiled his approval and thanked Josiah very profusely, rather overdone in Sarah's opinion. But she supposed that a recommendation from the gentry would set a man's reputation up for life.

They did seem to be decent plans. The chapel was fairly plain and rather small, but that was what the family wanted. They had decided to keep the chapel plain, following the devastation of Catholic churches that had taken place previously. There was enough room for forty people and no more, to retain a sense of intimacy. A garden was planned to surround the chapel so that a graveyard could be built. Mr Taylor was now leaving and he again bowed over Sarah's hands, and politely bowed to Anna, without touching her hand. Sarah wondered about that, but as she was introduced as the companion, perhaps she was allowed a handclasp, whereas the daughter of the house would not. She had a lot to learn about nineteenth century etiquette!

Chapter 14

The next day, the workmen arrived and took up residence in the cottage on the outskirts of the estate. Sarah was amazed how they had just dropped everything and moved in. The work was painstakingly slow, with no modern tools, but even so, Sarah watched with quiet admiration as the building took shape. She had received a letter from Lady Grace the next day, asking forgiveness for leaving her without explanations. Sarah had decided to reply, but when a quill pen and a bottle of ink was brought to her, she suggested that Anna should write the letter for her, feigning a sore finger. Secretly in her room, Sarah practised writing with the quill pen, but her progress was very slow and her writing was barely legible.

As the weeks passed, Sarah got more used to the way of life, often being caught out by not knowing the answer to things, or nearly saying the wrong thing, that she wouldn't have been able to explain. Sometimes, Dr Griffiths visited her, and was still quite satisfied with her progress, and accepted her selective memory loss, always nodding his head, and saying 'blows to the head are a difficult matter to treat, and worse to predict. Only time will tell.' It seemed to Sarah that she had all the time in the world, unfortunately. Never a day passed when she didn't think about Joe and miss him, which was incredible to think that she had only met him that fateful night. If only she could get back to her own time, she said to herself for the millionth time. As the days went by, the news from Lady Grace was not good. Her sister had lost the baby, and was in a very weakened state. The doctors feared for her life, as she was not responding to treatment and it had been necessary to bleed her. Sarah was horrified to hear this, knowing that after childbirth, the last thing any woman needed was bleeding, but of course, she couldn't say anything. She knew that withdrawing a large amount of blood from the vein was a very important part of managing care of patients in earlier times, but all it ever did usually was hasten the patient's death. But often, it was the only thing that the doctors could think of to try and relieve their patient's symptoms, and she knew that it had remained popular well into Victorian times.

The family and servants seemed to be allowing her to fend for herself more nowadays, so Sarah planned a trip to the kitchens, to see if banging her head in the same place in the kitchen would take her back to her own time. She sneaked down one day when Josiah was out supervising the builders, or more realistically, getting under their feet. He was an exacting master, and wanted continual updates on their progress. Anna was with her pianoforte master, and the little ones were upstairs with the servants. By now, she knew that the kitchen staff usually had a sleep after lunch, and she knew that Myrtle and Agnes had gone into the town for some thread and buttons, the market being on that day. She quietly went down to the kitchen and banged her head hard on the stone wall at the bottom of the steps. The pain was excruciating and made her close her eyes and wince. She waited until the pain subsided a little, and then looked around her.

There was the sound of snoring still coming from Cook. The cone of sugar was still on the table. The open fire had a piece of meat dangling over the spit. The big copper warming pans were hung by the side of the fire. She was still in 1825. Bitter tears flooded her eyes, the pain from her head overwhelming her. She ran up the stairs to her bedroom, shutting the door none too gently. She flung herself onto the bed and sobbed uncontrollably. That had been her last hope that had sustained her through the last few weeks. Now there was no hope. She was stuck in 1825 for the rest of her life. And she had better get used to it. She sobbed for a long time, mourning the loss of her life, her freedom, her home, her friends, her work, and most of all, oh, yes, most of all, Joe. Such a precious new relationship that had so much promise, and now it was all gone to nothing.

When Myrtle came to call her down for dinner that evening, she could truthfully say that she had a headache and did not want to be disturbed. She hid the bruise on her head away from Myrtle, hoping that it would be less obvious in the morning.

She slept fitfully, and when she woke, her head was still sore, and the bruise was livid across her temple.

Anna was the first to visit her that morning and exclaimed at the bruise. Sarah told her that she had slipped and banged herself and insisted that it was worse than it looked. Anna was worried that Sarah may not want to go out today because of the bruise, but Sarah insisted that she would be all right.

'Find me a bonnet with a big brim and I'll be all right, really', she reassured Anna. Anna was behaving quite motherly towards Sarah in her mother's absence, which was quite amusing as Sarah was twice Anna's age. There was no way that Sarah would miss today's outing as it was going to be the first time out for Sarah in a carriage. Josiah had promised to take them to Leeds in the carriage to look at materials for the forthcoming trip to London for the Season. Anna was secretly hoping that her mother would be detained in Durham a little longer, then she would have an excuse to miss the Season altogether.

Sarah asked if this was likely to happen, but Anna mournfully replied that some other elderly female would take her instead if her mother couldn't get home. She didn't want to be presented to King George anyway. There always seemed to be a lot of goings on in London at Court, and she didn't want to be part of it. It was just a lot of fuss and bother. Although, she must be honest, she quite liked the idea of having lots of new frocks and accessories. She was dreading all the other mothers staring at her, never mind the young men. And the not so young, she laughingly added, they're even worse.

'Perhaps you will find a suitor, Anna. I'm sure all the men will be seeking you out'
Sarah teased Anna.

'You might get one yourself,' she teased back. 'Red hair like yours is all the fashion at the moment. And talking of suitors, I saw Taylor looking very closely at you. Perhaps you have already got a beau.'

'I hope not, he's not my type.'

'What do you mean by 'not your type?'

'You know, I don't fancy him.'

'Fancy him? What does that mean. You Lancastrians do have some funny phrases. No wonder we went to war with you. We couldn't understand what you were saying. Anyway, stop changing the subject. What do you think about Taylor? He's not really suitable for a lady of your birth, but it may be amusing, all the same.'

'It would not be amusing, young lady. I don't wish him to be my suitor. He's too old and I don't find him attractive.'

'What has that got to do with it? If the marriage is suitable, there is no discussion about age or liking. You just have to accept it.'

'Not where I come from,' said Sarah laughing.

'I wish I came from where you do then,' replied Anna, a little sadly.

'So do I, Anna. I think you would like where I come from.'

'Perhaps we could go one day. I'd like that.'

'If possible, I'll take you one day.'

'Good. Well if you don't like Taylor, what do you think about Josiah as a suitor?'

'I haven't thought about Josiah as a suitor. Why should I? I'm just a guest in your house. An uninvited one at that.'

'Well, I think Mama would like you to think about him. I've told you, she's getting desperate.' The conversation was leading into dangerous areas, and Sarah desperately thought of something to say to change the subject.

'Well, your Mama is not here at present. She has more serious things to think about. I wonder how your Aunt Marguerite is now.'

'The last letter said that she is slowly getting better, but it is taking time. I miss Mama, and Charlotte too.'

'I hope Miss Charlotte is better as well. She was unwell before she went away.'

'Yes, she is well thank you. Just a temporary illness.' Josiah prevented any further conversation by entering the door. He was dressed for outdoors.

'Come along you two, the day will be over before we get started.' Sarah blushed, remembering the conversation that they had just been having, and hoped that Josiah hadn't heard any of it. She busied herself with arranging the large bonnet that Anna had brought her. As she looked in the mirror, she saw that Josiah was closely watching her, and the blush returned.

'What is that large bruise on the side of your forehead, Sarah?' Sarah had completely forgotten about the bruise.

'I banged it on the fireplace,' she said quickly.

'Again?' he asked, raising one eyebrow quizzically. 'You are a careless girl. I can see that we are going to have to take more care of you, or you will be running away and saying that we have been cruel to you. Come, I had better take you by the hand and escort you down the stairs, so that you don't fall again. Are you ready Anna?' With that, Josiah took Sarah's hand and drew it through the loop of his elbow, retaining hold of her hand against his arm. He squeezed it gently and looked tenderly into her face.

'Are you sure that you feel up to this trip out? I wouldn't have suggested it if I had known about the bruise. I don't know what Griffiths will say if you damage yourself anymore. I'm sure he will blame me.'

'Please, let's go out. Anna and I have so looked forward to it. I'll take all the blame, and tell Doctor Griffiths that you have been very solicitous in your care of me.' Josiah appeared satisfied at this, and led Sarah down the stairs. As she passed Anna, she noticed the girl smirking and nodding her head. Sarah glared back at her, as much as she could, but was aware of Josiah watching her every move. But as they went into the hallway, it was not only Josiah's eyes that were on her. Elly and Mary were all wrapped up ready for a walk with Jenny, their maid, and Mrs Hardcastle was with them. Four pairs of eyes stared as Josiah led Sarah into the carriage, which was waiting outside. Sarah could just imagine the gossip that would go on in the kitchen as soon as they had gone. Josiah helped first Sarah, then Anna into the carriage. Once they were settled, he wrapped a heavy blanket round the two of them, and fussed around them like a mother hen.

'Oh Josiah, stop fussing.   You're worse than a nanny' said Anna. Josiah took the reins as he swung himself into the driving seat of the carriage and, clicking at the horses, they slowly set off. The drive was like a nightmare to Sarah. It was cold, and very bumpy. The carriage seemed to have no springs, and the journey was very slow. The roads were deeply rutted and the carriage often lurched as they went into a puddle that was deeper than it appeared. Occasionally, another carriage came past, and both carriages had to stop to ensure that they could both get through.

They passed one or two small hamlets on their way, and an occasional large house like Roding Hall, or bigger. Anna kept up a running commentary on the owners of the big houses that they saw, and went into great details about each house. It hardly diverted Sarah who had never been so uncomfortable in all her life. Eventually, after what felt like hours and hours, they saw a town on the horizon. Gradually, houses appeared. Single ones at first, then a few together. They were small poor-looking houses on the whole. The carriage stopped at a tollgate, and the driver handed over the requisite coins, before the toll keeper would open the gate. Small children stood at the door of the tollhouse, staring at the carriage and its occupants. Once they had passed the tollhouse, the houses became more densely packed and churches and shops appeared on the tree-lined roads. The roads, if they could be called such, thought Sarah, became more solid and less rutted.

Soon they were in the city. They passed through a very poor part of the city, where filthy children played almost naked in the streets. The smell was indescribable, as raw sewage was thrown into the open road. A stream of refuse was trickling down by the side of the road. Sarah felt her mouth gagging. The journey had shaken her up enough, without this obnoxious smell. She held her hanky to her lips and inhaled deeply at the lavender perfume that was on it. Now she knew why Anna had given it to her before they set off.

One particular woman took Sarah's eye. She was fairly young and heavily pregnant. Two or three small children were hanging round her ankles, and the mother looked weary worn and old before her years, worn out by constant childbearing and poverty. Later on, she saw a small child begging in the street, with only one arm. Sarah was overcome by the sight of this poor child, and commented to Anna that they should give her something. She was shocked by Anna's response, as she said that the family had probably chopped the girl's arm off to get sympathy, so that they would get more money. By now, they were nearing the city centre and Sarah could see more respectable shops and carriages. They alighted at a market square, outside an old coaching inn. Josiah gave the reins of the horses to the ostler, and helped the girls to alight. The interior of the inn was dark and dingy, but they had been taken to a private room at the back of the inn. It was much brighter and better furnished than the rest of the inn, and Josiah explained that this was especially for ladies who were travelling. The staff bustled round the visitors, bowing and curtseying at every turn. They called Josiah Lord Grace, so it was obvious that he was well known here. The landlord's wife brought in a tray of tea, a much welcome sight to Sarah. By now, Sarah would have given anything to sit in a corner and rest, letting her mind absorb all the images that she had seen. But there was no chance of that. Before they could hardly finish their tea, Anna was up and dragging Sarah to her feet.

'Come on, it is late enough as it is. We must get to the shops, or they will all be shutting. Are you coming with us, Josiah, or have you business?'

'What, come round the shops with you two? No thank you. It would be too tedious for words, waiting whilst you selected your fripperies. The two of you will be quite safe together. You do not need a chaperone. No, I have business to see to. I'll meet you here, back at the inn at four of the clock. And don't be late. We need to get home before dark if we are to be safe.' With that, Josiah set off at a brisk pace down a side street, just off the main market square.

Chapter 15

Anna also set off at a great pace. Sarah could hardly keep up with her. She was trying to keep one eye on the rutted pavements and one eye on the parasols that were waving about in front of her. Anna seemed to have no such difficulty. She only stopped to exclaim at some shop window, to comment on the shape of this bonnet or the colour of that dress material. Sarah had never seen Anna so excited. It seemed to light up her whole face.

'Do we need to get any food whilst we are here?' asked Sarah.

'Food? Whatever for? Mrs Hardcastle sees to all that. Why ever should we be worrying about food? That's what we have a housekeeper for. Really Sarah, you do have some funny ideas.'

Sarah remained silent, desperately trying to think of a suitable answer.

'Well, I quite like looking at food whilst I'm out shopping. Otherwise, how would you know when there is some new item to be had?'

'You would just ask Hardcastle, of course. She will see that anything you wish for is ordered. Is there something particular that you have thought of, or seen? Is that the problem? Don't be shy, I can order it if you want it. We're just here today to spend on ourselves.' Sarah thought that for all Anna was very socially minded, she could still treat servants like a possession at times. Her thoughts were interrupted by Anna.

'Now stop worrying about food and tell me what you are thinking of buying. If it is too big, we can tell Josiah and he will arrange for it to be delivered '

'Er, I'm not thinking of buying anything today' Sarah said quietly. Anna's head turned suddenly in surprise.

'Why ever not? This could be the last chance for quite some time. We need to get things to decorate ourselves up ready for the London Season. You know, trinkets, accessories, gloves, kerchiefs, feathers and furbelows.' Sarah wondered how to tell

Anna that she had no money. She decided that honesty was the best policy.

'I have no money, Anna.'

Anna gaped at Sarah in disbelief. 'No money,' she repeated.

'No. I'm sorry, I did not bring any money with me.'

'Don't worry about that. We don't really pay. We tell them to send us an account to Josiah, and he pays. Don't you do that where you live?'

'I can't let Josiah pay for my shopping. It is enough that he is housing me and feeding me.'

'Nonsense Sarah. What else could he do? Aren't we told to look after orphans and widows in the Good Book? Surely we are only doing what our Lord instructed us to do.' Sarah felt very humbled by this pretty speech and wasn't sure how to respond. Eventually she simply said thank you in a very quiet voice.

'Think nothing of it, Sarah. I'm cross now that Josiah didn't ensure that you had your own allowance to spend, like he gives all of us girls. I shall admonish him immediately that we see him.'

'Oh, please don't. I feel terrible about it. I'm not one of your sisters and he shouldn't have to support me.'

'That's enough for now, come and look at these gorgeous lilac dancing slippers in this window. Shall we go in and look at them? We'll need several pairs of dancing slippers for the Season and I've seen some lovely lilac material which will just match up with these slippers.' Anna almost dragged Sarah through the door. A tiny lady with a mass of black hair scraped back under a bonnet came towards them and curtseyed deeply.

'Good morning your Ladyship, and thank you for entering my humble shop. How may I help you?'

'We would like to look at those lilac slippers in the window, and see what other colours you have for dancing slippers, please.' The little lady led Sarah and Anna to a deep settee and asked them to be seated. She called out to an unseen girl in the back of the shop, asking that she bring the visitors some wine and biscuits, and to tell Mr Pollard that Miss Anna Grace was here. She then hurried to the window and brought the slippers out to the waiting girls. A small girl scurried into the shop at that point, carrying a small table and placed it in front of the settee. She scurried back out to the back of the shop again and returned more sedately with a tray bearing two glasses of wine and a plate of Madeira biscuits. Sarah sat and stared at this little gesture. It reminded her of one of her favourite shoe shops called the Last Trading Post near where she lived. As she entered, they always asked if Madam would like a coffee whilst she was browsing. She loved that. It was probably why she kept going back and buying even more shoes. But obviously, she was in good company with Anna, as Anna seemed to be inspecting every hue of material in the shop.

A tall elderly man came into the shop, carrying a last.

'Good Morning Miss Grace. I trust that you are well? And your family?'

'We are well, thank you.'

'Her Ladyship is not with you then?'

'Indeed no, Mr Pollard. Mama is staying with her sister in Durham.'

'A lovely part of the country. We went there once ourselves, but a long way, nonetheless.'

'It is. Josiah has brought us in today. Do you wish to check my last? I'm sure that I will have grown since the last visit.' Sarah expected the man to measure Anna himself, but his wife did the measuring, using chalk on a piece of felt.

'Could you measure my companion, Miss Evans, too. She has ended up staying with us for longer than she intended, and has not brought many shoes with her. She needs stout boots and some day shoes as well as dancing slippers.'

'Certainly, my wife will just measure you, Miss Evans.' With the measuring done, Anna rose.

'Thank you Pollard, Mrs Pollard. When will you be coming to Roding Hall then?'

'I'll come on Tuesday next, if that is convenient.'

'Certainly. I'll inform Josiah, in case he needs any new shoes.'

'I'll also bring all the family and servants' lasts so that I can complete the whole family needs whilst I am there.'

'Excellent. We'll see you next week, then. Goodbye.'

'Goodbye, and thank you for honouring our shop with your custom. And you, Miss Evans. Goodbye.'

Anna led the way out of the shop and strode off again. Sarah was mystified. She had been in a shoe shop, been measured, but not tried a single pair of shoes on. It appeared that the shoemaker would come to the house and make the shoes there and then. A queer way of working and no mistake. Come back Last Trading Post, Sarah thought to herself. Half the fun of buying shoes is trying them on, and parading round the shop. And then finding out that there is a handbag to match. I wonder what would happen if she didn't like the shoes once Mr Pollard had made them for her? She wouldn't dare admit it, anyway. By now, Anna was in front of a shop that had haberdashery on the sign. She was sighing over the goods in the window and telling Sarah to hurry up.

'Do look at these delightful fans and hair dressings. Aren't they pretty? I must have some. What do you think? Look, the purple fan and gloves to match. Wouldn't they look well with the lilac shoes?' Sarah agreed, and then followed Anna into the shop. Here, many accessories were pored over in great detail, and tried against themselves. Anna bought several fans, little handbags, feathers and ribbons for her hair. She then ordered the shopkeeper to take them to the Inn by four of the clock. Sarah and Anna then left the shop. Sarah reflected that she could get used to shopping like this. No money changed hands, you didn't have to carry anything, and everybody was jumping to give you good service. Not quite like some of the shops in the big towns that Sarah was used to. Sometimes, you almost apologised that the girls were having to serve you, as it interfered with their conversation about last night's evening out on the town. And it certainly beat staggering out of Tesco with your arms full. There followed more shops, and an amazing amount of fripperies were ordered. Sarah wondered how it would all fit into the carriage.

Anna was true to her word and arrived back at the Inn by four. Josiah was sitting talking earnestly to another young wealthy looking man in the private parlour. They stopped talking suddenly when they realised that the girls had arrived. Josiah and his companion jumped up.

'Miss Anna, how delightful to meet you again. And who is your delightful companion? Do introduce me.' Anna smiled at the man and turned to Sarah.

'May I present Lord De Vere. Lord De Vere, Miss Sarah Evans, from Read, in Lancashire.'

'Charmed to meet you, Miss Evans,' he drawled, bowing low over his hand. 'Josiah and I were up at Oxford together. We nearly got sent down together as well, but that's another story, and not fit for the delicate ears of such young and beautiful ladies like you.'

'Hello, your Lordship,' replied Sarah.

'Oh, call me Rolly. Everyone else does. I was just telling Josiah that I saw Miss Cassy in town whilst I was in London. She's having such a marvellous time. Her new house is completed and they moved in last week. But I'm sure you know about that.'

'We've heard of little else in her letters of late,' laughed Anna. 'To hear Cassy, there hasn't been a house that has ever been built that is as elegant as hers, or with as many rooms as hers, or with such beautiful furniture, or biddable servants. We can't wait to go and see it when we go down for the Season. But how are your family, Rolly? I've not seen your dear wife for such an age. I'm sure that you are overdue a visit. Aren't they Josiah? Try and persuade him.'

'My wife is tolerably well. The children are growing well. Young Adelaide is ten years now, and young Roland is coming up to eight. He'll be off to Eton shortly. Genevieve has taken the children up to her mother's in Westmoreland. The children love the scenery up there. They go a little wild up there, too. They are terrible to manage when they come back. But they are children, after all. Eton will soon knock any skittishness out of Roland, anyway. Like father, like son, I suppose.'

'Well, I'm sorry to have to say it, but we will have to be going. We have a long journey before us, and Miss Evans has been ill.

I don't want her to get cold from the bad humours that are around in the night air. I'll say goodbye for now, Rolly. I'll get my mother to invite you as soon as she gets home.' The farewells were said, and the trio got into their carriage, ready for the journey home. Despite the discomfort, Sarah soon fell asleep in the carriage and only woke up when they arrived home. As she woke up, she heard Josiah worrying that the whole expedition had been too much for Sarah and, if anything happened to her, his mother would never forgive him. Sarah sat up and reassured them that it would take more than a shopping expedition to make her ill, at which they all laughed. Sarah was soon to bed that night. It had been a tiring day, but she had enjoyed it, nonetheless, and looked forward to the purchases being unpacked tomorrow.

Chapter 16

Sarah woke in the night to hear a child moaning in pain. In her bemused state, she thought that it was probably Charlotte again. Then she remembered that Charlotte was in Durham. This time, the crying did not cease but became worse, preventing Sarah from returning to sleep. Sarah decided to investigate. She got a candle and went towards the sound of the crying. It appeared to be up in the nursery, but when she got near to Elly and Mary's rooms, all was quiet. A low moan was heard again, and she realised that the sound was coming from another flight of stairs, at the far end of the nursery corridor. Walking quietly towards the steps, she slowly walked up the stairs, wondering what on earth she would find. Being of a literary nature, her mind turned to the mad wife that Rochester had hidden up in the attic in Jane Eyre. She only hoped that if it was a mad creature, that she wouldn't attack her. As Sarah opened the door gently, the door was flung out of her hands and a wild apparition filled the doorway. A young girl, dressed as a servant, with hair all falling out of a bun stood transfixed, staring at Sarah, as Sarah stared at her.

'Who are yer?' asked the wild woman.

'I'm Sarah Evans; I'm Miss Anna's companion. Who are you?'

'Meg. I look after Bella.'

'Who is Bella?' The girl started to look frightened, and looked beyond Sarah, as if looking for another person who would help her out of this crisis. Whilst she was distracted, Sarah slipped past her and entered the room. It was a small ante-room, leading into another dimly lit room. A low moaning was coming from the room. Sarah entered the room gingerly, her heart pounding, wondering what she was going to find. Suddenly a child reared up in the bed and screamed. A shrill, unearthly, blood-curdling scream. Sarah froze. Transfixed to the spot. She stared at the child. The child stared back.

'Who are you?' the child said in an imperious voice.

'I'm Sarah, Miss Anna's companion,' Sarah repeated. 'And who are you, may I ask?'

'I'm Bella, but my real name is Isabella, after my Mama.' The young maid, Meg, had arrived in the room by this time, and was staring open mouthed at Sarah and Bella.

'Yer didn't outer be in 'ere, miss, even if yer are Miss Anna's companion. Mrs 'Ardcastle'll go mad. She'll get me discharged,' the girl gasped breathlessly.

'Discharged? What do you mean?'

'Well, she gie us th' job, and she can sack mi when it suits 'er. An' mi mam ud belt me if she knows I've lost mi place 'ere. It's a good job this, even if I never gerrout much', she sniffed loudly as she finished the tale, hanging her head down before Sarah.

'Why do you not get out much, Meg?'

'Cos of 'er', she said pointing at Bella. 'I've ter keep 'er up 'ere and not let 'er out o' mi sight. It's a 'ard job, choose how, 'cos she can be a right madam when she chooses. She leads me a merry dance.'

'Stop telling tales, Meg. You ask for all the trouble you get, and you'll be in even deeper trouble when Mrs Hardcastle finds

out you've let her up here, without Grandmama's permission.'
At this, Meg burst into tears. Sarah felt moved to comfort her.
She slipped her arm round Meg and a torrent of tears burst from
her. She sobbed and sobbed against Sarah's shoulder. Sarah
tried to calm her down, but Bella kept interrupting.

'Shut up, Meg, you big softy, or I'll tell Mrs Hardcastle about
you.'

'Bella, I think that is enough. Poor Meg tries her best from
what I can see, now just leave her alone whilst I calm her
down.' The speech itself was enough to calm Meg down as she
stared at Sarah.

'Why Miss, th' gentry 'as never stuck up fer mi before, like.'

'I'm not gentry,' Sarah snapped. 'I'm just an ordinary person,
why I'm a working girl just like you, because I am Miss Anna's
companion.' The sobs subsided and ended up as hiccoughs.

'Now tell me what is going on in here, I don't understand the
situation.'

'Well, I have to live up here away from everyone, because I'm
a cripple and people won't like to look at me. I'll probably die
soon, and then everyone will feel sorry for me, and be sad that
they were cruel to me.'

'Are they cruel to you, Bella?'

'Miss Bella to you, if you're a hired hand like you say you
are'. Sarah was taken aback at the tone of the child, who
couldn't be much more than six or seven years old. 'And yes, of
course they are cruel to me. They keep me locked up here don't
they? Isn't that cruel? My sisters never come to see me, or my
Mama and Papa. My Grandmama rarely visits me, and then only
with the doctor, to see what he is ordering. It's so lonely with
only Meg for company and sometimes Agnes, when Meg goes
away. There's only Anna that ever comes to see me.' 'Anna,
again,' thought Sarah, 'always the caring one of the family.'

'Don't you have any schooling?'

'What's the point, I'm going to die. I just look at picture
books. But I get so bored.' She threw herself back on the bed.
Sarah stood staring at her, and noticed that her legs were thin
and emaciated, her feet twisting at the ankles.

'Go on, stare, like they all do.'

'I'm not staring; I'm just looking at your legs. I know a little boy like you, and he is not kept in an attic. I help him; I do exercises with him to help his legs grow strong. The exercises are called patterns'. It was Bella's turn to stare, as she took in what Sarah had said. Sarah thought to herself that this was all becoming too familiar. Perhaps she was entering into novels now, as well as time travelling. She had definitely entered a film set, if not the book of the Secret Garden. Although the child was a boy in the Secret Garden, there were a lot of similarities. It had been her favourite book as a young girl, and she wondered if she could be like young Mary Lennox and help this child, who was mistakenly locked away and warned that she would always be a cripple. And, as if that was not enough, she appeared to be aware that she may die young.

'Is the little boy you know going to die?'

'Certainly not. He's very healthy. It's just that his muscles won't work very well and he wobbles a bit when he walks.'

'He can walk?' Bella asked with a look of wonderment on her face. 'Could you help me to walk, too?'

'I'll try of course, but it won't be easy, as you haven't been exercising up to now.'

'But why isn't he in an attic. Don't people think he's a freak like me? Aren't they afraid to see anyone who is a freak where you live? They are very frightened round here. Mama says it could spoil my sister's marriage chances if they know about me.'

'How old are you?'

'I'm six and a half. Why?'

'You sound like an old woman to me,' Sarah laughed.

'I don't think that is funny.'

'I'm sorry, but you are so serious, and miserable about yourself.'

'Wouldn't you be if you were stuck up here all the time?'

'Yes, I probably would. We'll have to see what we can do.'

'Oh, start now. Help me.'

'I certainly won't. It's the middle of the night and I want my sleep. So settle down in that bed, and I don't want to hear another word out of you until morning.'

'But . .'

'I said not a peep. If you aren't a good girl, I won't come and see you again, neither will I help you. So goodnight for now.' Sarah turned quickly and left the room. As she turned to close the door, she saw that Bella was settling down in her bed, apparently subdued. Sarah smiled to herself. It's probably the first time that she has ever been subdued in her whole life. 'What a madam,' thought Sarah, as she walked down the stairs. 'I feel quite exhausted.' What had she let herself in for? What if she couldn't help Bella? What if the family were cross with her for interfering? What if they sent her back? Sarah stopped at that and laughed at herself. She sounded like one of the servants, frightened of losing her place. But her situation was even worse than the servants, because most of them at least had a home to go to, and she had nothing. Well, not in 1825 anyway. Depression descended on Sarah again, as she thought for the millionth time about how she could get back to 2001, and Joe. Sarah climbed into bed and blew her candle out. She watched the smouldering wick in the dark, as she drifted into sleep.

Anna entered Sarah's room with a knock next morning.

'Good morning, Sarah. Let's go out for a drive today. Come on lazy bones lie-a-bed.' Sarah stretched sleepily in her bed.

'I'm tired because I was up in the night. And you have some questions to answer, young lady.'

'What about, Sarah, you sound quite vicious this morning.'

'And so I might be. I was awake in the night and heard crying. I followed the sound, knowing that it couldn't be Charlotte this time, and met Bella and Meg.' Anna's head drooped onto her chest and she stayed silent.

'I thought we were friends. Why couldn't you tell me about Bella?'

'Well, it's the embarrassment of having a cripple in the family. Cripples have to be hidden away as you know, or people will think that there is insanity in your family. It will spoil your marriage chances for the rest of the family.'

'Oh I know all that all right. Bella told me. What are you doing telling a child things like that and laying all the guilt on her? Besides that, she has a miserable existence, stuck up there all day. I couldn't believe my eyes.'

'Well it is so important for Josiah to marry well, that we don't want it to get out that we have tainted blood.'

'Humph, what a load of rubbish. Tainted blood indeed. What was her mother's labour like?'

'Long, hard, and they feared for her and the child's life for a long time.'

'Precisely. And those are all the ingredients for producing a cripple.' Sarah winced at hearing herself using that word, but she knew that it was the only one that Anna would understand.

'You're so knowledgeable, Sarah. How do you know all this?'

'Because a doctor near where I come from has studied these diseases, and the little boy I know has made steady progress with the exercises that he has been taught.'

'But don't the people fear him and ridicule him because he is a cripple? And object to him being seen in public?'

'Not at all. They value him for what he is. It is only his legs that don't work. Not the rest of him. His brain is normal.'

'Hum, you could be right. Bella is so bright. It's just a shame that she looks the way she is. At least we haven't put her in an asylum like most people do.'

'I should think not. But she is stuck up there all day on her own, with nothing to do. No wonder she gets cross with Meg. Meg must have a poor existence as well.'

'She gets extra money for her duties. She is well paid.'

'But she is only a young girl herself. How old is she?'

'I'm not sure, about fifteen I think, like me.'

'Would you like to live up there alone?' Anna's head drooped low.

'No, I wouldn't,' a little voice replied.

'Well let me help her, then. I know I can.'

'I don't know what Mama and Josiah are going to think.'

'We'll worry about that when we have to,' Sarah said firmly. 'Come, there is no time to waste.'

'Oh Sarah, let us break our fast first,'

'All right then, we can plan our campaign over breakfast.'

.

Chapter 17

The two girls ate only a small breakfast at a very leisurely pace, due to the fact that they talked incessantly during the meal. Sarah explained all about the patterns and how the constant exercises strengthened the limbs. Anna was fascinated by all that Sarah was telling her. It was as if the new knowledge was just the sort of information that she craved, in her attempt to understand and increase her medical knowledge. Anna asked if Sarah thought that she could do the patterns herself. Sarah replied in the affirmative, but reminded her that it was hard work and couldn't be just carried out now and then, when Anna had time to spare from her other duties. It would be a long term commitment. And she would need help. She couldn't do it all on her own.

'Firstly, we must explain everything to Meg, so that she can help you with the exercises. We may even need to employ some extra help. It can be very tiring.'

'I'll have to talk to Josiah, then. I'm sure he will help us. I know he is embarrassed that Bella is kept hidden.'

'You'll tell Josiah what? What are you up to now, Anna? I suppose that whatever it is, it is going to cost me money.'

'Josiah, when did you get back? We thought you were out for a ride.'

'Well, I went over Thurcross Moor, but Jet slipped and threw a shoe. She was limping quite badly, so I walked her into Thurcross Manor, and saw Jed Butler. His man has taken care of Jet, and they will bed her down, and get the farrier out to her.

I borrowed Jed's Thunder to get home. Now stop diverting me, and tell me what you were talking about.'

'You'll never believe what Sarah has been telling me, it's amazing. Just listen.'

'Oh, I probably will believe what Miss Sarah says. Everything she says appears to be amazing. She is definitely a modern woman. So what now, Miss Woozy?' Sarah proceeded to tell Josiah about finding Bella. His eyes narrowed when she mentioned Bella, but they widened again in disbelief as she continued her story.

'I knew it! It is going to cost me money. And a great deal of it by the sound of it.' He walked over to the bell pull and leaned against the mantelpiece whilst he waited for a servant to answer. It was Agnes.

'Yes, M'lud, did yer ring?'

'Ah Agnes, could you ask Cook to bring me some fresh coffee and bacon, and then I want you to go up to stay with Bella, whilst Meg comes down here. I want to have words with her. And get Mrs Hardcastle too.' Agnes gasped when he mentioned Miss Bella, as all the servants were sworn to secrecy where Miss Bella was concerned.

'Yes, Sir, I'll go immediately.' Looking worried, Agnes ran out of the room. Sarah could imagine her going to the kitchen and telling all the staff what had happened, and that his Lordship wanted to have words with Meg and Mrs Hardcastle. Meg appeared shortly after Mrs Hardcastle, and there were signs of tears on Meg's face.

'I'm sorry Sir, tha' the young lady found out 'bout Miss Bella. I won't have ter leave wilt I? Only mi mum is badly an' they need mi money ter 'elp yer see.'

'Silence girl, you will not be leaving. And I'll tell you why not. I'm glad that Miss Sarah found Bella, but things are going to change.' Josiah explained the situation to them both, and that they would be taught to do the exercises by Miss Sarah.

'We'll need more staff, Hardcastle, have you any ideas. Perhaps two young girls would be enough, to see how it goes.'

'Please, Sir, I . .'

'Silence Meg,' roared Mrs Hardcastle. 'Speak when you're spoken to. Do not address Lord Grace so directly without being asked.'

'Hardcastle, it is alright, let her speak.'

'I, er I er,' said Meg visibly trembling, 'I've gorra sister what's thirteen an' an 'alf, and she's seekin' a situation. She's only small, but she does as she's told, choose how,' Meg gabbled all in one breath.

'Perhaps you could see her, Hardcastle. You may go now Meg.'

'Certainly Sir, and I will ask around. I think Agnes has a younger sister too who is old enough for work now. She's just gone twelve, Agnes was saying.'

'Good, see them both, and employ them both if you think that they are suitable. I'll leave that up to you with Mama being away. That will be all Hardcastle.'

Josiah waited until Mrs Hardcastle had left the room, and then turned to the two girls.

'Well, will that satisfy you both?' he asked quizzically.

'Oh yes,' sighed Sarah, 'that will be wonderful. I'll do my very best with the girls.'

'I'm off now to see the progress on Mama's chapel. I'll see you at dinner tonight.' With that he strode out of the room. Anna and Sarah smiled at each other and then both rose together and went upstairs to see Bella.

They climbed up to the hidden room, up near the top of the house, pausing for breath at the turn of the stairs. Once in the room, they found Meg and Bella merrily hugging each other and laughing together.

'Well, you've worked a miracle already Sarah, I've never seen Bella so happy. Nor Meg for that matter. It's the most exciting thing that has happened for ages.' Sarah smiled, but reflected ruefully how poor their lives must be if this was the most exciting event lately. Sarah started to show Meg and Anna how to do the patterns, and then let them both have a turn. At first, Bella screamed and cried, and was cross at Sarah, but she explained that it would hurt for a little while, because her muscles had not been used for a long time.

'That is enough for today. We mustn't do too much at first, or else it will be too painful for Bella. Now go and ask Mrs Hardcastle if we can have some kind of salve for soothing sore joints and muscles.' Meg shot off down the stairs and was soon back empty handed.

'Mrs 'Ardcastle's cumin up 'ersel,' gasped Meg, 'she wants ter see what's goin' on.'

Mrs Hardcastle came shortly afterwards, with some ointment in an old blue glass bottle.

'This has a lavender base, so should be good for healing. We'll try this first.' Bella allowed Mrs Hardcastle to spread the ointment on to her legs. She was very quiet whilst it was being done, and Mrs Hardcastle kept looking at her. 'I've never seen her so quiet, no I haven't. I think this could be a good thing, Miss Sarah, even if it only wears her out. It will make Meg's life a lot easier. None of these disturbances in the night. By the way girl, I've sent a message to yours and Agnes' mums. Told them to have your sisters here for an interview tomorrow. Will you attend with me, Miss Sarah? With Lord Grace telling me to arrange it, and her Ladyship being away, I feel it would be better if you were there. Then you could tell whether the children would be any use for these exercise things.'

'Good idea, Mrs Hardcastle, I'd love to be there.'

'Right then Miss, I've told the girls two o' clock of the afternoon, in my room.'

'I'll be there'.

'It is time for your luncheon now. Please come down as soon as possible. Agnes is waiting to serve. I don't want what is going on here to disturb the whole household, especially when it may all come to nothing. I don't want all the blame for the household falling apart and new staff being taken on to fall on my shoulders. Her Ladyship can be very cross if things are not run smoothly. She takes great pride in that, and I've never let her down yet. I run a good, orderly household here.'

'Yes, yes,' said Anna, 'don't worry. Lord Grace has approved everything, Hardcastle, he will back you up.' Mrs Hardcastle swept out of the room, leaving Anna and Sarah pulling faces at each other.

'Come on Sarah, we'd better go to the dining room or we will be in trouble with Agnes and Cook as well!!' laughed Anna. The girls ran down the stairs together, in great spirits.

After luncheon, they spent some more time with Meg and Bella, leaving both of the young girls in the attic happier than they had ever been in their lives. Miss Bella even asked for second helpings of her meal, Meg told the astonished staff when she went down for her tea. And that had never happened before. She ate hardly anything usually.

The day and night passed quickly, without any further events. It was soon two o' clock, and Sarah made her way up to the housekeeper's room. She was invited in and made welcome, and given a cup of tea. Mrs Hardcastle served it from delicate china cups with a matching teapot, sugar bowl and milk set. Sarah gazed at the lovely quality of the china.

'I got this from my last post,' she suddenly said quite sharply.

'Yes, I was just admiring it, it's beautiful.' Sarah replied.

'Yes, they thought a lot about me,' Mrs Hardcastle still seemed to be justifying why she had such beautiful crockery.

'I know it would have been richly deserved. I've never seen so organised a housekeeper. I really admire how you work and keep the staff up to scratch,' Sarah smiled warmly. Well at least it wasn't a lie. She was the only housekeeper she had ever met, so she was easily the best. It seemed to strike the right note with Mrs Hardcastle who visibly relaxed. They sipped their tea for a while, and then there was a knock at the door.

'Come in,' shouted Mrs Hardcastle. There appeared to be a scuffling behind the door, and then it opened slowly. Two small children were pushed through the door, followed by a poorly dressed woman, who made the children curtsey to Mrs Hardcastle.

'Come, in, come in. Don't waste time. Where is the other mother?'

'Beggin' yer pardon, Missus, 'ers too badly. She can't walk now.'

'What's wrong with her? Is it the phthisis? I don't want anybody working here who has got it in the family. We've enough things in this family without anything else.'

Sarah wondered what this dread disease could be, but decided that she had better not ask. But the poor absent mother appeared to be worn down by constant childbearing and had suffered some kind of a seizure during the last birth, and not the mystery disease. Mrs Hardcastle proceeded with her interview of the mother, and inspected the girls, looking at their hair for lice, their teeth, and their hands. Sarah stared with disbelief at the whole proceedings. Mrs Hardcastle asked them their name and how old they were, and whether they said their prayers. She asked the mother if they were strong and biddable, and the woman agreed readily. She appeared as nervous as the little girls, whom Sarah thought should still be at home playing with their dollies, rather than being interviewed for a job. She was so busy with her thoughts that she didn't hear when Mrs Hardcastle asked her a question. She had to ask again, and was obviously not pleased.

'Oh, er, no, I've no further questions, I think that you have asked everything Mrs Hardcastle,' stammered Sarah.

Mrs Hardcastle told the mother that they would both be employed. They were to go to the dressmakers in town and be measured for their uniforms. The cost of them would be deducted from their first year's salary. They could start the following day, and should bring their best clothes with them. Sarah thought that they probably had their best clothes on today, and they were pretty shabby by any standards, and definitely handed down. But the mother appeared ecstatic, and was fulsome in her thanks to Mrs Hardcastle.

'They'll be good girls, I promise yer' she said, but was cut short by Mrs Hardcastle, who showed all three to the door.

'Well they look biddable enough, but you never know.'

'What's phthisis, Mrs Hardcastle? I've not heard that word before.'

'Not heard of it? Why it's the lung disease. That new fangled young partner of Doctor Griffiths calls it the consumption or something. But he's from your side of the Pennines, and you seem to have funny words for everything over there, anyway.' Light dawned for Sarah. They were talking about tuberculosis. Consumption she did understand. But Mrs Hardcastle was talking again.

'We'll wait and see, and if they don't suit, they'll have to go. Still, they've both got a sister here, so they won't be terribly homesick like they usually are. Thank you for being here Sarah. You may go now'. Sarah felt like a naughty schoolgirl being dismissed from the head teacher's study, so she bowed her head and left the room.

The days passed, and the young girls learnt their patterns with Sarah and Bella. Sarah suggested that Bella was moved down into the main nursery, so that she would have company, and then all the maids could sleep up in the top attic, and just one of them could sleep in the nursery with the other children as well as Bella. That would give them a good night's sleep three nights out of each four. Mrs Hardcastle thought that this was a bit too risky, but eventually she was persuaded when Josiah approved the idea with Sarah.

Once Bella was established downstairs in the main nursery, she dramatically improved, both in behaviour, temperament and appetite. She changed from looking like a pale, fragile child, to a much healthier being. But Sarah was concerned that she never got outside. She waited until Mrs Hardcastle had gone to the village for supplies and Josiah was out riding. She slipped up to the nursery, and borrowing a coat of Elly's, she wrapped Bella up and took her downstairs, and out into the garden. She had been shocked when she had asked for Bella's coat, to be told that she had never had one, as she had never been outside. The maids all watched Sarah and Bella, and were visibly worried about what was going on. Always, there was the threat of unemployment if they didn't meet the standards.

They had no need to worry. Bella took to the outside like she had been there all her life. Her cheeks glowed and, although she wasn't able to walk yet, she bounced up and down in the chair that Williams had put out for her. Sarah had to be quite stern when it was time for her to go back inside. The only way she could get her back in was to promise that she could come out again every day. It was on the third day that Mrs Hardcastle caught Sarah and Bella outside. Her rage was indescribable, all related to what her Ladyship would say when she found out, and she would get the sack. And if she did, then she would make sure Sarah got the sack as well. By now, Sarah was cross herself, and told Mrs Hardcastle that it would be difficult to get the sack, when she wasn't being paid for what she was doing. Mrs Hardcastle stared at her disbelievingly, then swept back inside.

'Oh well,' thought Sarah, 'that's one enemy I've made now.' For the next few days she studiously avoided meeting her when she could, and gradually Mrs Hardcastle started to be more civil to her.

Chapter 18

Sarah's next plan was to bring Bella downstairs for a meal. She got the children to tell Josiah that they had a surprise for him at Wednesday luncheon. He was obviously intrigued, but they wouldn't tell him anything. Wednesday luncheon arrived, and Josiah made a great play of getting dressed up in his new cream brocade waistcoat, with matching pantaloons and a very frilly shirt. He looked as if he was dining in high society. Sarah and Anna sat on either side of him at the small dining table that they used during the day. They heard the girls giggling from afar, as they came down the stairs. Elly came in first, followed by Mary, and they made a curtsey to their brother. Then in the rear of the procession was Williams, carrying Bella, with a very worried look on his face. As soon as he realised who Williams was carrying, Josiah jumped up out of his chair and stared at Williams and Bella.

'What in heavens name is going on here? Who told you to bring the girl in here, Williams?' Josiah looked angry. Williams started to stutter and went pale.

'Come on, man, what is going on?' Sarah stood up and spoke in a very quiet voice.

'I told him to bring her down.' There was a long silence, during which Josiah was obviously trying to keep his temper under control.

'Why? What gave you the right to interfere with my family affairs?'

'I did it for the child. After I found her, I knew that I could help her. She is dramatically improved, as you can see.' At this point Bella burst into tears, sobbing loudly.

'But what is the point, she is a cripple, an imbecile. You have wasted your time.'

Anna cut in. 'Pas devant les enfants, Josiah.' Josiah appeared to recollect himself.

'Williams, take the children back to the nursery. I will talk to Miss Anna and Miss Sarah alone.' The children all left with Williams, but not before Williams glared at Sarah, as if to blame her for getting him into trouble with his Lordship.

When the door closed, Josiah started to speak to the two girls saying that although he approved of them helping Bella to be better, there was a limit to what she should be allowed to do. Sarah sat with her head down, very troubled by what he was saying, and not knowing how to answer him. She had no need. A fiery Anna spoke up in Sarah's defence and went much further. She accused Josiah of being a hypocrite. He pretended to be so modern in all his ideas, but was very backward when it came to Bella. He argued that it was his mother's wishes, and he didn't like to go against her wishes.

Anna asked what harm it could do, and said not to say it would spoil his marriage chances, because as far as she could see, he would never marry, because he was far too particular, and would never find someone to marry. She stopped dead after this outburst and ran from the room. There was a stunned silence, and Sarah kept her head well down on her chest, fearful at what would happen next. The silence seemed to go on forever. And then she heard a funny noise and looked up at Josiah. She was surprised to see him stifling his laughter.

'That girl will be the death of me,' he roared, and then started to laugh uproariously. At first Sarah continued staring at Josiah, not sure what to say. She waited until he had stopped laughing, and then said that she agreed with all that Anna had said.

'So you think I'm too particular to marry as well, do you?' he asked with a roguish smile.

'Er, no, I didn't mean that part,' said Sarah blushing furiously, 'I meant about being backward about Bella. It's too late to stop now. She has improved so much, and all the children took great delight in planning the little surprise for you. They expected you to clap and applaud the improvement that Bella has made, not to be cross.' Josiah sat very thoughtfully for a few minutes, as if wrestling with his own conscience. Without looking up at Sarah, he spoke in a quiet voice.

'What do you think I should do, then?'

'Well, the first thing is to tell the girls to come back down and let them eat with you. But also, you must go and apologise to Anna. She feels it very keenly if she does not have your approval.'

'Well, that's a surprise. Have my approval? She never seeks it! She drives me to distraction at times, with her hair brained schemes that she launches into, with no thought for the consequences. But, I suppose you have persuaded me. I'll go and speak to all the girls. You stay here. In very truth, you and Anna together are a potent influence. I can see that I'm going to have to keep a close eye on you both. Oh and by the way, I've invited the Butlers from Thurcoss over for dinner tomorrow evening. Could you tell Mrs Hardcastle when you see her?' With that he left the room, leaving Sarah wary of what he now thought of her, and what it would lead to.

Eventually, Sarah was joined by all the girls, and a chastened Josiah played the host to perfection. After the meal, Mrs

Hardcastle came in to ask about the Butlers coming for a meal the next day. Sarah hadn't seen her since she was given the duty, but assumed that the jungle telegraph that existed in these large houses had been at work. After she had gone, Josiah explained that the Butler's were their closest neighbours and also friends.

'And Jenny Butler has been in love with Josiah for years, ever since she was a girl of eight. Josiah was fifteen at the time, and mightily embarrassed by it all. You should marry her, she's getting as long in the tooth as you, Josiah,' laughed Anna cheekily.

'That's enough. You've made enough trouble for one day lady. Now who cares for a walk in the garden and we can look at Mama's chapel.' Both Anna and Sarah jumped up at the invitation and accompanied Josiah down the garden. They were both surprised by the progress that had been made. They had both been so involved with Bella's exercises and daily visits to the garden at the front of the house, that they had not even been to see the chapel. The external building was completed now, and they were able to go inside. Josiah outlined his plans for the furnishings. The furniture was going to be simple, so as not to offend the anti-catholic people that were still plenty in number, but it would be beautiful enough to please the family's tastes. A special reredos was being made in Italy and was due to be delivered within the next few days, dependent on the ship arriving at Liverpool as planned. It would then rely on a carter bringing it over the Pennines as soon as possible. Josiah was obviously very proud of his achievement and pleased that the girls approved of all his plans and ideas.

Whilst Josiah had been showing them round, the workmen had stood respectfully to one side. Now Josiah drew the chief stonemason into conversation, and praised the man and his team for getting on with the work so quickly.

'You've worked very hard, all of you. There will be a bonus for you all when you have finished.'

'Why thank'ee mi lord, that's very kind of yer. The good Lord has helped as well by giving us all this fine weather. We couldn't have got on so quick if it had rained some.' Josiah nodded his agreement and walked away, leaving the workmen looking very pleased with themselves. Anna and Sarah walked slowly behind Josiah, and then the impish Anna couldn't resist another jibe at her brother.

'Now I know why there is such a rush. Josiah has decided to marry and wants to get the chapel ready so that he can be the first person to marry in it. Ha-ha, that's right, isn't it?' Josiah only glared at Anna, and carried on his walk back to the house.

The next evening, the Butler family arrived for dinner. The parents were in their mid-forties and their two surviving children, Jenny and Jed, accompanied them. Jed was a tall, slim, dashing gentleman with long blond hair, and a neat moustache. He hovered a little too long over Sarah's hand and gave the gentlest of squeezes to her hand. A little flustered, Sarah turned to say hello to Jenny. She too was tall, blonde and strikingly beautiful. Her dress of a deep russet satin set off her lovely hair, and the dress seemed to hover over her shoulders, as if held up by magic. She wore a lovely amethyst necklace that covered most of her neck and chest, resting on the tips of her breasts. It was the sort of necklace that made you notice her breasts as you admired her necklace. She was definitely out to turn heads tonight, and no mistake. Sarah felt quite dowdy in contrast, even though she had one of her new dresses on, which had been made by the dressmaker in town. As soon as she opened her mouth, Sarah was disappointed in Jenny.

'So this is the new companion that Josiah keeps talking about. Really Josiah, I'm surprised that you have companions to sit at table with you.' She said 'companion' as if she was saying servant, and it rankled with Sarah, but she kept her head down and said nothing.

'Actually, she came as a guest, and her parents are both deceased, so we asked her to stay on and be Anna's companion, especially as Mama is still at her sister's house,' replied Josiah frostily.

Mr Butler cut in and rebuked Jenny for being so rude. He was a smaller man than Jed, and wore the old-fashioned powdered wigs that many older gentleman still wore when dining out. His wife smiled pleasantly at Sarah and asked her where she came from. Fortunately, they had never heard of Read, so didn't ask her any more questions. Mrs Butler was a small plump lady who wore a stiff satin dress of dark grey, with fussy white frills around her neck. Her hair was streaked with grey and she wore it in a severe bun at the nape of her neck.

'How is your Mama, Josiah?' asked Mrs Butler.

'Mama is fine, but her sister is not well, and she is staying a little longer for now.'

'And how is the building of the chapel coming along?' asked Mr Butler.

The servants brought the food in at that point and the next hour was taken up in eating and further small talk. They then moved into the drawing room, and Sarah found Jed beside her.

'Can you play for us, Miss Sarah. It's good when a new person joins us. It makes for greater entertainment.'

'I'm sorry, I don't play.'

'Sing perhaps?'

'Er, no, I don't sing either,' Sarah stammered.

'Quite unaccomplished for a companion,' said Jenny with a drawl, and a pointed look at Josiah. He failed to rise to her comments, merely saying that she had other talents.

'Really?' said Jenny with an arched eyebrow, 'yes, I'm sure she does.' Sarah felt embarrassed. There was obviously an innuendo here, but she wouldn't rise to it either. She would just play it down. She had obviously made an enemy in Jenny. As if to show she had other talents, she picked up her needlework and started stitching. Thank goodness that Tessa Halfpenny had taught her how to do needlework. In the long dark evenings, she had gained considerable skill with her stitching and was glad of it now. But Jenny merely looked to Josiah for conversation and didn't comment on Sarah's stitching. Jed came over to talk to Sarah and was a little over the top to say the least, but she merely answered him in simple statements and tried to get Anna to come over and join her. Anna studiously ignored her.

At long last, the evening was over, and Williams was calling for the Butler's carriage to come to the front door. Jenny made a great play of saying goodbye to everyone, but merely nodded in Sarah's direction, as she swept through the door. As soon as they had gone, Sarah turned to Anna.

'Why didn't you rescue me from Jed?   I was most embarrassed.'

Anna laughed. 'I just thought I'd let him make up to you. You could do a lot worse than Jed. Do you admire him at all?'

'Not really, too soppy for me.'

'Soppy? Do you mean foppish? Because that is what I think he is.'

'Er, yes, foppish, that's what I meant. At least we both agree.'

'I don't think Jenny liked you very much.'

'Well, that's an understatement. She positively ignored me, and tried to humiliate me.'

'She sees you as a threat to her plans with Josiah. She thinks that eventually he'll ask her to marry him.'

'Do you think he will?'

'Never,' said Anna quite vehemently. 'Why, are you interested?'

'No, just curious,' replied Sarah. The two girls giggled as they made their way up to bed.

Chapter 19

Anna was up early next morning and banged on Sarah's door.

'Will you come to the village with me, today? I need to do Mama's visitations. I have been quite neglectful. Do say that you will come.'

'Of course, Anna, but you will let me finish getting dressed and have some breakfast first, won't you?'

'Sorry, Sarah, I do tend to get carried away with an idea once I think of it.'

'Do you? You do surprise me,' replied Sarah sarcastically. 'Right, that's me dressed, have you had your breakfast?'

'Ages ago. I was up so early, I broke my fast with Josiah, and you have to be up early to catch him. He was very quiet, by the way. Probably had too many drinks with Jed Butler. They both forget to stop once they start drinking. I'll go and see that everything is ready for you and get some fresh tea.' Sarah followed Anna down the stairs a little later, and found Anna pacing around the small dining room. On seeing Sarah, she nearly dragged her to her seat, and plied her with breakfast and tea. Anna asked Agnes to bring Mrs Hardcastle in and Agnes left the room. Shortly afterwards, Mrs Hardcastle arrived.

'We'll be going to the village to do some of Mama's visitations today. Could Cook prepare us a basket?'

'Certainly, Miss Anna. It will please your Mama that you are not neglecting your duties. I will see Cook now.' With that, she left the room. As soon as she had gone, Anna dragged Sarah upstairs

'Come on, we need to make an early start; there are many cottages to visit. Now here is your scarf and I'll lend you Mama's old cloak, as yours is far too sumptuous for going visiting.' Anna handed the scarf and cloak to Sarah, who noticed a pungent smell emanating from the scarf.

'What's the smell, I can't think of its name?'

'It's sandalwood, it helps deaden the senses in the cottages. Come, we have no time to waste.' Anna set off downstairs and headed for the kitchen. Martha and Peggy were bustling round filling large baskets of produce, and sending them out to the carriage outside via Myrtle and Agnes. Young William, the gardeners' boy was also helping put the baskets into the carriage.

'That should be enough fer yer, Miss Anna, that's about what yer muther teks.'

'Thanks Martha, it all looks very wholesome. Miss Sarah is coming with me, so we won't be back for luncheon.'

'I thought as not, so I've put yer a few bits i' th' blue basket fer yer own meal, if there is anywhere yer can eat it i' safety.'

'Oh, good, Martha, I'm sure we will find somewhere.'

'An' I'll 'ave th' water ready fer when yer gets 'ome.'

'Excellent, see you later.' Anna left the kitchen followed by a mystified Sarah, who wasn't quite sure of the relevance of all the conversation. She didn't get a chance to ask, because the coachman, Jacob, was waiting to set off.

'We'll go to the mill workers cottages first, Jacob. We'll leave the riverside cottages until last. I've heard that there is fever down there again.'

'Very good, Miss Anna. The mill cottages it is.'

The carriage rolled along the bumpy, poorly formed track that was the main road into the village. The ruts were quite deep in places and Jacob had his work cut out avoiding them. They passed other carriages and ponies and traps along the way, and the people all waved merrily, or doffed their caps on seeing the Grace carriage, dependent on their station in life.

Eventually, they arrived at some mean looking cottages, that seemed to consist of one large room upstairs and one downstairs. Sarah had noticed that Anna had covered her mouth and nose with her scarf, and now she understood why. The stench was overpowering. It was the worst smell that Sarah had ever encountered, even worse than Leeds. Now, she was going into the houses, not just passing them by. Sandalwood was certainly stronger than lavender, but it still did not compensate for the stench. Here again, the raw sewage was running in the street, and children were playing near to it. There seemed to be no discreet place where anyone could perform their toilet, although judging by the contents of pots that were being thrown through the upstairs windows, some did have rudimentary privacy. Sarah would have dearly loved to vomit, but didn't want to offend these poor creatures. If nothing else, this experience she was having had taught her the difference between the rich and the poor in no uncertain terms.

'We'll go in the end cottage first, Sarah.' Sarah nodded, unable to trust herself to speak. She followed Anna in through the door. It took a while for her eyes to adjust to the gloomy and smoky atmosphere. There was a wizened little girl sitting by an open fire, stirring a foul looking broth over the fire. It looked and smelled like overripe vegetables, with one piece of maggoty meat floating on the top.

'Good morning, Jessie. This is Miss Sarah, my companion. My mother is away at present. How are you today?' The little girl just nodded and said nothing. 'How's your mother?' Anna tried again. The little girl just pointed upstairs. Anna set off upstairs, asking Sarah to give the child some home-baked bread and bacon, and a small twist of tea. Sarah doled them out and tried to engage the child in conversation, to no avail. Anna soon returned looking grim.

'The mother has had another baby. We'll leave her some fresh milk, and some baby clothes as well. That should tide her over until she can get back to work.'

'Back to work?' said Sarah astonished.

'Oh yes, she'll have to be back next week, or she'll lose her position.'

'But who will look after her baby?'

'Why, young Jessie, she stays home and looks after the little ones.'

'But she's only about five years old at the most' said Sarah appalled.

'Yes, that is why she stays at home. She is too young to go to the mill yet. She'll stay at home until she is seven, then she will go to the mill with the rest of the family, and the next one in line will care for the babies. That is what happens all the time.'

'But if there are so many working, why are they so poor?'

Anna looked at Sarah as if she was a child.

'Because the miserable mill owners don't give them a decent wage. And they make them buy their food from their own mill shops. The shops are usually run by unscrupulous people, who charge interest and give poor quality goods. They can never get out of the pitiful state they are in. If they try to buy their goods elsewhere, or they can't work, they are thrown out of their cottage, so they are worse off than ever. We try and do our best, but we have to go carefully. Many of the families are proud, and don't like to be treated as charity cases.'

'But can't you get to the mill owners? Surely they have no idea how their workers live.'

'Faith, Sarah, where were you brought up? How can you be so naïve? Of course the mill owners know what state their workers live in. But all they are interested in is their profits. They usually say that they are badly done to, and remind you about the Luddite attacks. The most that we can do is avoid meeting them socially and we never entertain them. Nor do we buy woollen goods from their mills. But it is little enough. Josiah sits on the Poor Relief Committee and tries to bring pressure to bear on them. His main stalwarts are the vicar and the new doctor, Doctor Perry.'

'Talking about me again, Miss Anna? Should I be honoured or dismayed? Especially as it is to a young lady who is not of my acquaintance. I dread to think what infamies you were saying.' Sarah turned to see who was talking, but not before she noticed that Anna was blushing furiously.

'Oh, er, hello Doctor Perry. May I introduce my companion, Miss Sarah Evans. I assure you I was not saying anything irregular about you. Indeed, I was praising your work with my brother on the Poor Relief Committee.' Dr Perry's eyes closed for a few seconds at this point, and he looked very sombre.

'If only I felt that I was doing any good,' he said quietly. The tension in the room was unbearable. The doctor looked as if he was going to break down.

'I'm sure you are doing the best you can under the circumstances, Doctor Perry. And I've heard only good about you, I assure you.'

'Well I'm glad that I have an advocate in Miss Anna, then, as I have many more enemies than friends in this area.' Anna blushed deeper than ever. Hmm, thought Sarah, do I detect an interesting spark here? Or is it just interest of a medical nature on both sides.

'Miss Sarah comes from your side of the Pennines,' said Anna trying to change the conversation.

'Oh, whereabouts?'

'Read.'

'Never heard of it. I come from Rufford, near Southport.'

'Oh yes, I've heard of that. My nearest town is Clitheroe.'

'Oh, yes, where the castle is.'

'That's right. Why did you pick this area if you are from Lancashire?'

'Doctor Griffiths is my uncle. He paid for my medical training and promised me a position on qualification, but we don't exactly see eye to eye. He thinks that I'm far too new fangled for his liking. He sticks by his old methods and won't listen to the new ideas. It's very difficult, but I am so grateful for his support or I wouldn't have been able to undergo the training. My father died young and left us unprovided for. But I'll just bide my time, and eventually the practice will be mine. Well, I must get on. Folks won't get cured if I stay gossiping to you two young ladies, much as it may seem the better option.' He bowed to both of them, and made to leave the cottage.

'Doctor Perry, I wonder if I could consult you on a personal matter?' asked Sarah. Doctor Perry laughed.

'Oh, I'm afraid I would not be allowed within a furlong of Roding Hall. Only my uncle is competent enough to deal with the gentry,' he said ruefully. 'And besides, you are a young lady, and it would not be seemly for me to visit you, even as a doctor.'

'It is not about me that I want to consult you about.'

'Then who is it about, pray tell me?'

'It's about a young girl who lives at Roding Hall. She is six and had weakening of the legs, following a bad labour, and her feet are twisted and she can't walk.' There was a sharp intake of breath from Anna.

'I know a young man with a similar complaint at home and I wonder what your thoughts would be, with regard to her chances of walking. The boy I know has regular exercises and he has been able to walk.'

'Come with me and we will talk of this outside,' said the doctor, and steered Sarah by the elbow and across the grass to the roadside.

'Would this be Miss Anna's young niece, Bella? I'm not supposed to know about her, but my uncle has told me some of her history. He has also told me of the work that you have been doing with her. I'm mightily amazed at what I hear. My uncle is going down to London tomorrow for a conference, so I could visit whilst he was away, quite legitimately, if you sent for me.'

'Yes, we'll do that and see what happens.'

'I look forward to conferring with you on this case. And seeing the inside of the Hall. My uncle has always made me stay outside when he visits!! Goodbye for now.'

Anna seemed to watch him dreamily as he walked away and Sarah teased her about him.

'He is so full of new ideas and understanding. I admire him greatly and would love to work alongside him in his work. And in his life, too,' Anna added quietly, 'but there is no chance of either happening. He is not suitable for me as a suitor in Josiah's eyes, as he is a workman after all. And I'd never be allowed to do any real medical work. Oh, I hate being a girl sometimes.'

'But surely he is a professional man, and as such would be considered worthy?'

'Professional? Why, I don't think that Josiah would consider a doctor a professional man. Anyway, I just know that I won't be allowed to even consider him. Now stop this talk and let's get into the next cottage, before I start crying and really bemoan my lot.' Anna briskly walked into the next cottage, her happy face restored as she helped the family to some food. Sarah could only admire this young girl even more. Instead of bemoaning her lot, she was doing her best to help others less fortunate than herself, but without being patronising. The girls carried on their duties, but spent so much time at the mill cottages, that they did not have time to go to the riverside cottages.

'We'll have to go there tomorrow. It is even worse down there. Don't let the name riverside cottages give you a false impression. The mill owner who owns them is even worse than this one, if you can imagine it. Ah, here is Jacob. Let us get into the carriage and go home.' Sarah noticed that Jacob had spread a blanket over the seats and straw on the floor. As she climbed into the carriage, she realised why. Her hem was coated in mud and sewage, her shoes in a filthy state, and she generally smelt pretty badly. They had a bumpy return journey home and when they arrived, they were rushed round the back of the house to the servant's entrance, and into a back room that Sarah had never seen, behind the kitchen. There, they were unceremoniously stripped off by Agnes and Myrtle and led into a hip bath apiece, that was heavily scented. They were scrubbed from head to toe quite vigorously, and their hair washed. Sarah realised that it was the first bath that she had had since arriving in 1825, and was very grateful for it.

'It's worth going into the cottages just to have a bath like this,' she quipped. 'I could get a liking for this.'

'Why Miss Sarah, we can give you a bath any time you like,' said Myrtle, 'why didn't you say? We can pull the bath into your room and bring the water up for you.'

Sarah then realised why nobody had many baths. It would be a terrible strain on an over burdened household, having to drag jugs and jugs of water up to the bedrooms. And from what she could see, or smell, nobody was too strong on cleanliness. They relied on perfumes to keep the body odours at bay. Not always successfully, she mused. They appeared out of the room looking more like their usual selves, only to find the rest of the household in turmoil. Thorndyke had arrived with a message from Lady Grace. Her sister had died after the doctor had bled her again, and Josiah was to return immediately for the funeral. Sarah assumed that Anna would be going too, but she explained that only the men in her family went to funerals and so she would be staying. Sarah watched as the household bustled around, getting Lord Grace off on his journey.

Chapter 20

The house seemed quieter without Josiah, and Sarah realised how much she and Anna relied on him, for news, information and stimulus. With Josiah's departure came a change in the weather. There were days and days of squally showers alternating with persistent rain. The young girls, especially Bella, objected to being cooped up in the house. Tempers were frayed, as the frustrations became greater. In desperation one day, Sarah told the girls that she was going to teach them to read and write. For once there was silence. Anna was the first to recover.

'But why do we need to read and write? As long as we can run a household, say the catechism and bring babies up, there is no need for us to learn.'

'Anna, I thought I could rely on you to support me in this. Why should just the boys learn to read? Reading is such an escape from the world. There is so much joy to be found in books. You can read about countries across the sea, and the strange people who live in them. Come, let me read a story to you.' Sarah found the Bible on a shelf in the girls' room and opened it to the book of Ruth. She settled the girls on to the window seat in the nursery and sat facing them. As she was about to start, she noticed the servants hovering.

'Come on you four, come and listen too.' The servants looked sheepishly at each other, but when Sarah chivvied them, they sat on the floor, a little away from the window. Sarah read the story of Ruth, paraphrasing some of the words so that it was more understandable for their young minds. All the children, including Anna, were spellbound.

'Now wouldn't you like to be able to read like this?'

'Oh yes, Miss,' blurted out Meg. All the other maids and children laughed at Meg.

'You can't learn to read, you're just a servant,' said Elly. Meg blushed and looked away from Sarah.

'Why not? Meg has got the same brain as you. Why shouldn't she be able to read?' This silenced the children as they thought about what Sarah had said, but nobody could think of an answer.

'I'll set you all a challenge. We will have one hour of tuition in the morning and one hour in the afternoon, for all of you, and we will see who learns the quickest by the end of the week.' Anna did not look too pleased by this, but Sarah thought that this was a little pique that she was not going to be the only one who could read, but that she would also have to work hard to be better than the little ones. Sarah ignored Anna's thunderous look, and proceeded to look for something that she could draw on. Elly remembered that Josiah had had an easel when he was a boy, and she went rooting in the old toy box in the other room. She brought the easel and chalks to Sarah, and for the next hour, all the children were fascinated as Sarah showed them the alphabet.

As they showed signs of getting bored, she got the children to make the letters of the alphabet by putting their bodies into the shapes of the letters, so that they could remember them better. This was a great success. Sarah remembered that this had been a ploy that was used to educate the young in the Little Women series, some of her favourite childhood books by Louisa Alcott, and she silently thanked her for giving her the idea. She then laughed to herself, when she realised that Louisa Alcott had probably not been born in 1825, never mind Little Women having been written.

As the bad weather continued, the children worked tirelessly at their studies. Like all children who have been starved of the opportunity to learn, they soaked up the information like a sponge, their little minds eager for anything they could learn. Because the servants were taking part, it made the Grace children far more studious than they would probably have been otherwise. Sarah was pleased that there was no difference in the capabilities of the two groups of children. Anna was less pleased, not liking the fact that the servants were on a par with them. Sarah just smiled and said nothing. Mrs Hardcastle did not approve of the servants being taught to read and write. She said that it would give them ideas above their station, but Sarah persevered and tried to keep the peace with all parties.

After two weeks, a message was received from Josiah that he, his mother and his sister would all be returning from his aunt's. The household was set into a furore. Carpets were taken out and beaten, paintwork was washed down, woodwork polished, and immaculate cupboards were emptied and scrubbed. It was almost fit for a royal visit. The day dawned when the party arrived home. It had taken them three days, with overnight stays at a coaching inn. They were saddle or carriage sore, and looked strained and weary.

'Next time, Mama, you will travel by train. The journey would have been done in a portion of the time. I shall go to the next meeting of the railway company and offer some of my land for the tracks to be laid. At least you don't get highwaymen on a railway.'

'Oh, you didn't meet a highwayman did you?' asked Anna.

'No,' replied Josiah, 'but we could have done. The roads are so dangerous nowadays. Now all we need is some refreshments and a rest. And a bit of peace.'

'I was sorry to hear about your sister, Lady Grace,' said Sarah quietly. 'Is there anything that I can do to help?'

'Thank you my dear, but no. It has all been taken care of. Have the children been well behaved whilst I have been away, Anna?'

'Yes, Mama,' replied Anna too quickly.

'Well that's worrying,' Lady Grace laughed. 'I shall see them for myself in the morning. For now, I am exhausted and am going to bed. Goodnight to you all.' Lady Grace left the room, leaving Anna and Sarah speculating on what Lady Grace would find in the nursery on the morrow.

'You two are very quiet. Do I detect some more mischief afoot?'

'Oh, no,' Anna and Sarah chorused together.

'Humph, we will see,' said Josiah as he too went to bed. Sarah and Anna soon repaired to bed as well, both pondering in their minds how to explain what had been going on if Lady Grace disapproved.

They were to find out in no uncertain terms the next morning. Sarah woke to the sounds of the maids scuttering up and down the stairs, and Mrs Hardcastle looking flustered. As Sarah passed her on the stairs, she gave her a murderous look, and told her very brusquely that Lady Grace wished to see her at her earliest convenience. Sarah went in to the small dining room to find Josiah and Lady Grace in heated argument. It stopped as soon as they saw Sarah. Sarah sat down quickly on the nearest chair and accepted some tea from Agnes.

'Miss Sarah, from what I hear you have been overstepping the mark whilst I have been away. I was very shocked to find Bella in the same room as the other girls this morning. What have you to say for yourself?' Sarah was at a loss what to say.

'I'm sorry if I have offended you My Lady, it was certainly not intentional. I just found the little girl by accident, and felt sorry for her, and wanted to help her.'

'And that's another thing, Josiah, why did Miss Sarah find out about her? Was that girl Meg not doing her duty? She should be sacked.'

'Oh please do not sack her because of me. I was curious when I heard a cry in the night. Dismiss me rather than Meg. It was not her fault. I went up to the top floor myself.'

'Mama, please calm down. Sarah was only trying to help. And look at the difference that she has made to Bella already. She is a different child. You must acknowledge that.'

'Yes, but for what purpose? She will probably die anyway.'

'But she may not,' Sarah burst in, 'Doctor Perry thinks that she may get better.'

'Doctor Perry? Why on earth has he been here, the young whippersnapper. We only have Griffiths here. What was Griffiths thinking about? I shall have words with him as well.' Josiah now looked at Sarah aghast as well. 'Well, I'm waiting for an answer. Did you know about this Josiah?' Josiah shook his head slowly.

'I sent for him when Doctor Griffiths was away in London at a medical conference. He approved the exercises that we were doing and said that Bella had a full life expectancy.'

'Well, I agree that is good news, but what of the stigma. We won't be able to keep her hidden away anymore and what will people think if they find out that there are imbeciles in our family. Tainted blood, they say.'

'But she isn't an imbecile,' shouted Sarah, 'I've taught her to read and write with the other children, she's the brightest of them all.'

'Read and write?' Lady Grace exploded. 'What has been going on in my absence? I come home and find all my instructions have been ignored, that new staff have been taken on, and my girls have been taught to read and write. This is all too much. I know that you think of yourself as a modern miss, but you are going too far, and too quickly. Oh, oh, dear, my heart is pounding. This could send me into a decline so soon after my sister passing away. Oh, deary, deary me. Agnes, get my smelling salts, girl.' Lady Grace fanned herself with her napkin, until the salts arrived. Agnes fussed round her with the salts and then Lady Grace had one further thing to say to Sarah. 'And you, young lady, can go to your room, until I think what has to be done with you.' Sarah bowed to Lady Grace and rushed out of the room, making a speedy ascent to her bedroom, where she flung herself on the bed and sobbed long and hard.

She must have eventually fallen asleep because, as she woke up, she realised that the sun was coming into the bedroom from the west, so it must be mid to late afternoon. There was a tray on the side table with some soup and bread, but the soup was cold. Sarah supposed that Myrtle would have left it for her. She got up to use the commode and, when she came out of the bedroom, Myrtle was in the bedroom, straightening Sarah's bedcovers.

'Evenin' Miss, can I get yer sum supper? Yer've not eaten all day. Yer must be 'ungry. Eh, but yer've caused a reight rumpus i' this 'ouse, choose 'ow. Lady Grace aint 'alf mad. I've never sin 'er like that before.'

'I know, she sent me to my room, like a naughty schoolchild. I didn't mean to cause any trouble. I just wanted to help. I have no idea what she is going to do about it. I think I'll stay up here until she comes to see me.'

'Mm, sounds like a good idea ter me,' replied Myrtle mournfully. Her mournful tones did nothing to relieve Sarah's anxiety. Nobody came to see her that day, not even Anna or Josiah, and Sarah felt completely miserable, and had a restless night.

Chapter 21

The restless night transferred itself into a blinding headache next morning. Sarah flinched as Myrtle opened the curtains and let in the light.

'A luvly sunny mornin', Miss, meks a change from all that there rain we've 'ad jus' now,' chirruped Myrtle brightly. She stopped as she saw Sarah shielding her face from the sun. 'Ooh, yer luk rough this morning. Are yer not well?'

Sarah groaned. 'Just a headache.'

'I'll get yer some feverfew, a brew o' tha'll set yer up reight an' proper.' Myrtle disappeared again, bringing back a steaming liquid that smelt better than it tasted. Sarah sipped at it slowly, refusing Myrtle's offer of any breakfast. As Myrtle pottered round the bedroom and dressing room, Sarah found that her headache was clearing. She said as much to Myrtle who commented that herbs always did better than the doctor's horrible elixirs. It must be more natural because it was grown in their own garden. Young William was a dab hand at growing herbs. Sarah let Myrtle chatter away about the garden and herbs, as it saved her having to talk for a little longer. After an hour, Sarah felt much better and gingerly asked if she could now have some breakfast. Just some toast and tea, she suggested.

Whilst Myrtle was downstairs, Sarah got out of bed and went to the dressing room to wash and dress herself. She was sitting by the window idly watching the world go by, when she saw Josiah talking to the building foreman. She hoped that it was good news about the chapel. If Lady Grace was happy about the chapel, she may treat Sarah with more sympathy. But Josiah seemed to be getting agitated with him and shouting. Their voices were muted, and Sarah couldn't make out what was being said, but Josiah walked off looking very angry. The foreman stood rooted to the spot, twisting his hat in his hands. He looked very worried before he walked slowly away. Sarah hoped that the lovely reredos that had just arrived wasn't defective in any way. It would spoil all the pleasure that Josiah would have in the chapel building scheme. She heard heavy footsteps pounding up the stairs, and wondered idly what was happening now to upset the household. At least it wasn't her fault this time; she hadn't even left her room yesterday or today. Her door burst open and Josiah appeared without even a knock.

'What will you do next?' he demanded, stalking right into the room and over to her side. Bemused, Sarah looked at him, for once rendered speechless. 'Well, what have you to say for yourself? What part of our life will you interfere in next?' Sarah apologised and said that she didn't know what he was talking about.

'I've just had the building foreman asking to speak to you. I told him that you were indisposed and he said to tell you that the frame was ready. What frame I asked. The frame that she has asked me to make for the little cripple girl he replied. Not content with raising Bella's hopes unnaturally, you go and tell the whole world that we have a cripple in the family. I despair of you. We take you in, give you a home and even give you a position to save your embarrassment. I thought we were treating you with respect and dignity in the circumstances and all you do is undermine my whole family structure and make a laughing stock of all the family. I've a good mind to send you away.' Sarah suddenly found her voice.

'Well, do so then. I have been grateful for the way that you took me in and looked after me. I have tried to show that gratitude by helping your family, but I see that you only perceive my help as hindrance. If that is how you feel, I will take my self away immediately and not offend your family anymore.' Sarah stopped dead in her tracks, shocked at the venom in her own voice, but also petrified that he may take her up on her suggestion and throw her out. Where would she go to? The sheer misery she was feeling overwhelmed her and she burst into tears. Josiah came over to her and held her, as she sobbed against him. He waited until she had calmed down a little and asked what he was going to do with her. He promised that he would never send her away as she had made such a difference to the household, even though his mother was still a little angry with her. He was still holding her when an astonished Myrtle appeared at the door. He sent her off for some more coffee and toast and two cups. Never had Myrtle moved quicker. Josiah laughed in spite of himself.

'Oh dear, did you see Myrtle's face? I bet she can't wait to get downstairs and tell everybody. I've really compromised you now. Alone in a bedroom together, and no chaperone, and in my arms. Dear, dear, your reputation is irredeemable now. Perhaps I had better marry you and keep my mother quiet. Although just at present I don't think she would be too pleased at my choice. At least I would never be bored with you, would I? Annoyed, angry, amazed, shocked, delighted, mystified, bewitched, yes. But never bored. Are you a witch? Is that your secret?'

'No, I'm not a witch, so don't send for the ducking stool,' she managed to joke. At this point there was a loud and obvious knock on the door. They both laughed as they separated, but the door was ajar, and there was no need for Myrtle to knock.

'It's alright Myrtle, it's quite safe to come in. Miss Sarah was upset and I was consoling her. No need to let your imagination run riot. Come in, girl.' Myrtle placed the tray on the low table by the window, and turning to Josiah asked, 'Will tha' be all yer Lordship?' He replied that it would. Myrtle curtsied, and with a sly glance at Sarah, left them to themselves.

'How's the chapel coming along?' asked Sarah after they had eaten the toast, and were companionably sipping the coffee.

'Don't upset me again girl, I may still throw you out yet. Although life here would not be as lively without you. It was the chapel that upset me. I hear that you have been getting the foreman to neglect his duties and make you a wooden frame to help young Bella to walk. It made my blood boil. Here am I offering a bonus for him if he finishes early and you are delaying him, by asking him to make a useless frame.'

'But you are wrong. I asked the foreman if he could make it in his evening spare time, especially so that it wouldn't hold up the building of the chapel. I know how important that work is to you and Lady Grace, especially now with the bereavement. And a frame would help Bella to walk. She can stand for a few seconds on her own now, and with the frame to help her, she should be able to walk, and eventually take her own place in the world, instead of the prison that you have consigned her to.' Sarah dropped her head as she finished her sentence, not daring to look at Josiah. There was a long silence. Eventually Josiah leaned over and held her hand.

'I am sorry, Sarah. I have misjudged you. I should have known better. Where did you get the idea for the frame?'

'It's the little boy that I knew at home. He had one until he could walk unaided. It made a big difference to his confidence in trying to walk. He was about Bella's age when he first walked. And besides, Doctor Perry said he thought that it would work as well.'

'Ah, Doctor Perry, yes, I forgot about him. I've had words with him, and he is quite bowled over by your ideas. I can see that I am going to have to watch you or you will be off and marrying him. I could quite see you as a doctor's wife,' Josiah laughed to himself, 'even though he is a little beneath you.'

'I wouldn't find a doctor beneath me if he was an honourable man. But I won't be thinking of marrying him, not when I've got competition.'

'Why, is he already betrothed?'

'Not that I know of, but Anna appears very attentive when he is around. She seems to think that he is very good at his work. She would be happy to be that particular doctor's wife, I think.'

'There you go upsetting me again. Of course Anna couldn't think of him as a suitor. Anna will probably marry my cousin, John Grace. Or Jed Butler. Or one of the Percy cousins in Durham is quite keen. Most likely John. He will inherit from me if I die intestate. His sister Emily would like to marry me and has made it quite obvious, but I am not interested in her. A silly little girl she is, with no thought beyond fripperies and fashion.'

'And isn't Anna allowed an opinion?'

'No, Anna probably won't be allowed an opinion. She would probably choose someone frightfully unsuitable.'

'But what about all the girls? What do you expect? All the girls are bred to think only about fripperies and fashion. They are denied education and a worthwhile place in society. No wonder they are vain and helpless. That is all that is required of them.'

'You talk as if you are not one of them yourself.'

'Well, I had a father who believed in educating girls. I was educated to the same level as my brother.'

'A shame that you were denied entry to university being a mere woman, or else you may have been our next Member of Parliament, or even Prime Minister.' Josiah fell about laughing at these wild imaginings. Sarah stayed quiet. She had nearly spilled the beans then, and told him that she had been to university. Oh how she would dearly love to tell him that she had got a First Class Honours degree. That would silence him for a while.

'Well, I must go and see what is happening in the rest of the house. And stop scandalising the household. We've been here for two hours now. Whatever would Mama say?' Josiah left without her even thinking of a reply. What 'Mama' would say would probably be to send her back where she came from, but that was easier said than done. Sarah sighed and wondered just how long she could keep the saga going before somebody found out that she didn't live where she had said that she did. Well, not in 1825 anyway.

A message was sent up to Sarah in the late afternoon, that Lady Grace wished to speak with her in her study at 4 o' the clock. Sarah changed into a more demure day dress, to try and make herself look less like the trouble maker that everyone thought that she was. She knocked on the door softly and waited, holding her breath.

'Come in,' Lady Grace's voice sounded out haughtily. Sarah took a deep breath and opened the door into the small study. Normally she liked this very feminine room that Lady Grace had made to her own requirements, but today she had eyes only for the owner of the room, who was sitting in the deep chair by the fireside. Sarah wasn't invited to sit, so stayed standing in front of the fire near to her chair.

'Oh do sit down, girl, you make me feel so small standing there like that.' There was another knock at the door and Agnes came in with a tray of tea and started to place cups on saucers, ready to pour the tea. 'You may go, Agnes. We will see to the tea things, thank you.' Agnes curtsied and left the room. Sarah wondered what Lady Grace was going to say to her. There seemed to be so many things that she was being accused of, according to Josiah. And Josiah, he was another issue. If Lady Grace had got wind of them being caught by the servants embracing in her bedroom, she would probably be branded a harlot as well. Feeling very sorry for herself, Sarah wished that Lady Grace would hurry up with pouring the tea, as the suspense was getting to her. But her wishes weren't granted. Lady Grace leisurely poured their tea, and proceeded to drink hers before she started to say what was on her mind.

'Well, Sarah, I must say that you seem to have turned my household upside down in my absence. I was very angry when I returned, as I left you behind as a calming influence on Anna and find that you have been far from that. Indeed, you seem to have made Anna more wayward than before.' Sarah stared down at the carpet beneath her feet, admiring the patterns, unable to think of any answers at all. 'And you seem to have upset Josiah as well. He won't tell me what, but he accuses you of interfering in some plan of his as well. And as for Bella.

What did you hope to gain by doing these exercises? Why couldn't you wait until I returned? I would gladly have discussed these things with you. Instead, I return from my sister's home, shortly after her passing away and find my household greatly changed. Now I've had a long talk to Josiah this afternoon, and he requests my leniency when I deal with you. And so I have decided to take his advice. Although I must say, it is against my better judgement. But Josiah says that he has plans for you that will alleviate the situation, so I'll wait and see what happens. Perhaps he plans to marry you off to someone. We will have to see. For now, you may go, and you may rejoin the family meals, but please, before you try and do anything else, please ask myself or Josiah first. It leaves us in a very untenable position in the household otherwise. Are there any questions?'

'Er, am I able to carry on with the exercises with Bella and teaching the young girls to read?'

'Humph, you do take things to their extreme don't you? Yes, you can carry on with what you have instigated, but please don't talk about it to anyone outside this family. Understand?'

'Yes,' said Sarah in a very small voice, 'and thank you. I didn't mean to upset you. I was only trying to help.'

'I have heard about your helping from the doctor and the villagers, as well as Anna. It is this that has swayed me. Your help with the poorer villagers was very commendable, I understand.'

'Why thank you,' said Sarah, quite amazed at how the situation had turned out.

'You may go now, and we'll see you at dinner.' Sarah smiled and left the room, relieved that she was being let off the hook very lightly. As she walked slowly upstairs, Sarah decided that she would go up to the nursery and tell the children that they were to be allowed to continue with their lessons and Bella's exercises. There were cheers all round, from both children and servants. Sarah returned to her room later in the day, promising to go up to the nursery early after breakfast on the morrow.

Chapter 22

Next morning, Sarah was up bright and early and breakfasted with Anna and Josiah. She was pleased to see Anna, as they had not seen anything of each other in the last two days. They were full of the plans for the children and gabbled together for some time. Josiah listened to them indulgently, but then asked if he might be allowed to get a word in edgeways. Both girls looked embarrassed.

'Yes dear brother, what do you wish to say?'

'If you two busy young ladies could spare me the time out of your hectic social lives, I would like it if you could spare me some time around about eleven of the clock. Could you manage that?' he asked somewhat sarcastically. Anna replied in the same vein, speaking rather haughtily.

'Well, Josiah, I'm not sure that we can. You'll have to tell us why you need us first, and then we will gravely consider it, and weigh it against our other commitments. Really Josiah, we ladies need more notice if you are to disrupt our lives all the time.' Josiah laughed heartily.

'I want to take Mama down to show her the chapel today, before she takes it into her head to go for a walk herself. Thanks to you Sarah, she has had other things on her mind and has not wanted to go for a walk round her precious gardens.' Sarah blushed, but Anna rushed over to Josiah's side and flung her arms round him, in a rare show of emotion between them.

'Of course we will come with you. We can hardly wait. Come on Sarah, we need to get the children organised so that we can be ready in time.' With that, she dragged Sarah out of the room by the hand, leaving Josiah chuckling to himself.

By eleven, the entire household seemed to be astir with the excitement about the chapel. Anna had asked if the children could come too, but Josiah had said no. He felt that Lady Grace may be upset the first time that she saw the chapel, and didn't want to embarrass her in front of the children. So the children had to wait for now. Sarah agreed with him, and felt strangely pleased that he had been so sensitive to his mother's feelings.

He really did have many sides to his character. Often womanly intuition was evident, other times he appeared strong and macho, and yet at other times, reckless and daredevil. A real mystery man. Josiah made a big mystery of why he wanted his mother to walk round the garden, and she didn't really seem too keen to go. Eventually she was persuaded to go for just a little walk, with Josiah, Anna and Sarah.

They walked round the side of the house down the gently sloping grass towards the river that flowed through the bottom of the garden. Josiah then steered them towards the right and through the small grove of trees, where Lady Grace and her late husband had liked to walk together in the cool of the evenings. They passed through the grove and came out into a large flat area of the garden. As they emerged from the grove of trees, Lady Grace stopped dead in her tracks and gasped. There was the little chapel in all its glory, with the workmen lined up outside the door, hats in their hands. As Josiah gently led his speechless mother forward, the chief stonemason stepped out of the line of men, bowing low before her Ladyship and handed her a velvet cushion with a key on it. With trembling hands, Lady Grace walked towards the door, and opened the door slowly. She walked inside the chapel, looking round at the pews, the leaded windows, the very plain statues, the candles burning, but then she caught sight of the reredos and gasped again.

'Oh, it is so beautiful, just like the one that we saw in Italy on our marriage tour,' she said, her voice husky with emotion, and then finally she cried. Josiah held her tightly and Sarah and Anna walked outside and left them alone together. The workmen were shifting around a little, wondering whether they should stay or not, but the chief stonemason made them stay. After a few minutes, Lady Grace and Josiah emerged into the sunlight and Sarah was impressed at the way Lady Grace had recovered. She thanked the chief stonemason, and had a word with each of the men who were lined against the wall. She asked them what each man's job was, and what part he had had in the building of the chapel. She was very gracious to them all, and was far more friendly with the working classes than Sarah was used to seeing in this century. The gentry were often aloof, condescending and even rude to the work people. Lady Grace reminded Sarah of the Queen Mother at her 100th birthday celebrations in 2000. Always a kind, considerate, courteous lady. Josiah was explaining that the chapel had not yet been blessed by a priest, so it was not able to be used for services yet.

'No matter, I shall come down here and say my own prayers each day. And thank God for the children that I have left to me. This has been such a splendid gift for me, Josiah. I can never thank you enough. Now, send for the priest and we will arrange a blessing as soon as possible.'

'There's something else that he can do whilst he is here, Mama.' Lady Grace looked quizzically at him. 'He will consecrate the lands at the back of the chapel, so that we can make a burial area for the family. They still have to make a fence all round the chapel to enclose the garden.'

'But I want to be buried with my own dear husband, your dear Papa, Josiah.'

'I know Mama, but we will see if we can have Papa brought here, then you can go and visit him every day, instead of having to take a carriage trip each time.' Lady Grace walked towards Josiah and drawing his head down, kissed him gently on the forehead. Josiah looked embarrassed in front of the workmen and started to walk away, back to the house. At dinner, Lady Grace was asparkle with the plans for the chapel blessing. Because of the mourning period, they would only invite close family and friends to the blessing, but it gave Lady Grace a focus to work towards, and seemed to help in restoring her to her normal self. Letters were sent to Cassie and her husband, Isabella and her husband and children, and John Grace and family, Josiah's cousin. After some deliberation, she decided to invite the Butlers as well. Although they were not family, they had been a great help when her husband had died, and they were after all, their closest neighbours.

When Sarah got back to the bedroom, Myrtle told her that the wooden frame was in the dressing room. Sarah ran and got it and bounded up the nursery stairs. She showed it to Bella and all the children, and the servants crowded in to see as well.

'Tomorrow, young lady, tomorrow your hard work will start. We will see what you can do with it.'

'Eh, Miss, I'll never get 'er to sleep now, she were wound up enough as it were. Now cum on Miss Bella, or yer won't be fit fer nowt in th' mornin'. Sarah made a quick exit, laughing to herself as she went down the stairs. Most of the next day, Sarah worked with Bella and the servants, until Bella got quite cross and threw the frame on the floor.

'Bella, I will not stand for this nonsense,' Sarah reprimanded. 'How can I get you to walk if you won't try? Anyway, I think that you have had enough for today. We'll try again tomorrow.'

The whole focus of the family and house was now on the coming chapel blessing. The date was fixed for October 1st. The servants were kept busy opening up the wing of the house, to accommodate the visiting family. It was hardly used, but kept fully furnished and under covers. Now, all the covers had to be taken off, and the furniture highly polished. The carpets were beaten, panelling waxed, and the curtains washed and rehung. It was like a major spring clean, and extra staff were hired from the village to help in the major undertaking. Mrs Hardcastle went round with a permanent frown on her forehead, but in fact, she ran the whole set up like a military battle. Everybody knew their role and their individual part in the operation. And it was not just the house. Extra gardeners were brought in to tidy the gardens up after the long hot summer. The workmen finished creating a graveyard round the sides of the chapel, ready for the consecration. Sarah kept out of everybody's way by spending a lot of time up in the nursery with the children. Bella was improving by leaps and bounds. The wooden frame seemed to have given her a whole new lease of life. Sarah started to teach the children some little hymns and songs to while away the time. The nursery servants were called in more and more to help with the housework, so a lot of the nursery work was left to Sarah and Anna, but they soon involved Elly, Mary and Charlotte.

162

The family started to arrive during the last week of September. Isabella and her brood were the first. Josiah and Lady Grace took Isabella and her husband, Jake Heywood, straight into the library when she arrived, barely giving them time to take their coats off. Sarah could guess the content of the conversation. Voices started to be raised, and there was the sound of tears. Sarah sloped off out into the garden to keep out of the way. She was dreading meeting Isabella, as she could tell that Isabella was unhappy about the news that she was hearing. She walked down towards the chapel. She too, was finding this a place of solace, as well as Lady Grace. They sometimes met there, and had gentle chats, as well as having little walks together round the rest of the gardens.

Josiah's cousin John had arrived during the afternoon, with his sister Emily and younger brother Frederick. Their parents had not come with them, as they were both getting over an illness, and were frightened of getting a chill as well. They were lively cousins, and Josiah was obviously fond of them. Sarah noticed that Emily seemed very keen on Josiah. What was it with this man? He had all the women after him, he was ever so courteous with them, but never seemed attracted to them, however hard they were trying. And try they did, Sarah laughed to herself. She was quite embarrassed at times for them.

Sarah went down to dinner that evening in some fear and trepidation, but Isabella was not present. She had retired early with a headache. Sarah felt even guiltier, knowing that the headache was of her making. She sat next to Isabella's husband. He was a short, fairly plump man, with receding hair and Sarah was surprised that the lovely tall Isabella was married to him. Still, she now understood that there was a lot more to marriages than love and romance in 1825. He perhaps had a healthy bank balance, or the promise of great wealth, or a title. But after sitting next to him, Sarah realised his attraction. He was a witty and erudite man, who teased Anna mercilessly. He had a natural gift of involving people in conversation and that rare gift of making people think that they were the most important person in the whole world.

The day before, Sarah had not met their two children Carrie and Polly, as they were too young to come to the evening dinner. They ate in the nursery with the other children. Next morning, Sarah met them when she went up to the nursery. Polly was tall and slim like her mother, but Carrie was short for her age and looked quite plump already. She was obviously going to take after her father. The two girls welcomed Sarah. It was obvious that they were mystified by Bella. Nobody must have told them who she really was. They just assumed that the child was staying there, and just expressed sympathy for her when they watched her doing her exercises and trying to walk. Nobody enlightened the children.

At luncheon next morning, Sarah met Isabella. Isabella gave Sarah a cool nod, said that she would like to talk to her afterwards in the library, and then ignored her for the rest of the luncheon, keeping Anna in conversation. Anna was not too interested in her talk, as she only wanted to talk about the forthcoming Season, and what a pity it was that they would not be able to go because of their bereavement. Anna commented that it was a relief to her and Isabella looked disgusted at her.

'How on earth will you be able to keep up with the haut monde stuck down here all the time? You need to be in London for the Season so that you can be seen and, perhaps get an offer. Or several offers, even.'

'I couldn't think of anything worse,' replied Anna.

'Oh, you are incorrigible. I despair of you. I think that I will ask Mama if you can come home and stay with me for a while. You are obviously not getting the correct training here for your future role in life. I wonder if she would let me take you up to London. I will ask her at dinner.'

'Don't bother yourself. I would rather stay here in the country helping Mama.'

'Well, you are a little ingrate. I do not know why I bother.' Isabella flounced out of the small dining room, obviously in a bad mood.

'Thanks Anna. She will probably tear a strip off me when I go to see her.'

'Tear off a strip? What do you mean?'

'Oh, you know, be cross with me.'

'She would be anyway, she's good at being cross. She was a very strict older sister. Almost as bad as Cassie,' Anna laughed to herself.

'I heard that Anna,' came a squeaky voice from outside the door. 'How dare you, you young scallywag. You should show respect for your older sister.'

'I would if you earned it, but anyway, you are only four years older than me. Not exactly elderly.'

'But I am a married woman and so you should show me respect, and anyway, I'm. . . . . .' Cassie stopped in mid sentence.

'Well, go on, you are what?' asked Anna.

'Nothing for little sisters,' replied Cassie, emphasising the word little.

'Huh, I suppose you are enceinte. It's about time.' Cassie gasped.

'Who is enceinte?' asked Lady Grace as she came through the door.

'Mama, how lovely to see you,' gushed Cassie. 'You are looking very well considering all the sadness you have had. How do you feel? I am looking forward to seeing the chapel. That must have been a lovely surprise for you. Shall we go and look now?'

'No Cassie, we will not. You will have to wait. And stop trying to divert me. I asked who was enceinte?'

'Oh trust Anna to ruin everything as usual. She always was spiteful. I am enceinte Mama, but I wished to announce it at dinner as a big surprise. I was beginning to get worried. After all, I have been married for three years now. And James' mother had been so pointed. Asking me if I am breeding yet, every time I meet her. She is so common. It has been a trifle embarrassing for me to say the least. I couldn't wait to tell you all, because I know that you would be pleased. And now Anna has gone and ruined my surprise.' Cassie stamped her dainty little foot petulantly. Anna sniggered to herself, and said in an aside to Sarah, that she had probably wanted to make a grand show of the whole thing, and she was glad that she had spoiled it. Sarah was surprised at the tone of Anna's voice in talking about her sister, but she suspected that there had been a lot of disagreeable discourse between them in the past.

Lady Grace said that she was very pleased with Cassie, and that she must take plenty of rest. Mother and daughter went off together arm in arm, Cassie telling Lady Grace that her husband James would be arriving on September 30th, as he had appointments in London. Lady Grace explained to Cassie that the Percy family from Durham would not be joining them for the chapel blessing, as it was too soon after the bereavement. Sarah decided to go in search of Isabella. The family seemed to be far more volatile now the sisters had come home. Life could prove to be very interesting. But first she had to see what Isabella was going to say about Bella.

. . .

Chapter 23

'I was very shocked at what had happened to my daughter, especially as I was not consulted about it,' Isabella began. Sarah started to answer and also apologise but Isabella stopped her. 'Hear me first, and then you can explain yourself afterwards.' Sarah sank back down into the dark green leather chair in the library. This was one of her favourite refuges usually, but today it was beginning to feel a little menacing. Isabella looked very fierce, for all she was younger than Sarah. But being a married lady took precedence over an unmarried spinster in this society. 'My first reaction was a great deal of anger against you, I must be honest. That is why Mama and Josiah would not let me speak to you yesterday. But I have been up to see my Bella now, and I have been amazed at the changes in her. You have worked hard with her, but I am sorry that you may have wasted all your time. What kind of life do you think

Bella could have if she leaves here? She would not be welcomed in society circles.'

'Then society does not deserve her,' interjected Sarah crossly.

'I don't make the rules for society. If she had been a boy, it may have been better. Men can still make their way in the world as a cripple.' Sarah shuddered again at the use of that word. 'I cannot take her home; everyone was told at the time that the child had died. I can never acknowledge her as my own daughter. She will have to stay here. Perhaps they can pretend that she is an orphan girl from the workhouse that they have taken pity on. So you see, Miss, whilst I am pleased you cared enough to help my child, you have put me in an untenable position. She was so happy to see me, and thrilled with the progress that she had made. I think perhaps that she thought that I was going to say that she could come home with me now. But I couldn't. She has grown to look so like Polly, that people will recognise her. Or worse, they may think that I have taken pity on a bastard of my husband's. I do not think that I could live with that. I would be the butt of all our friends' jokes, and laughed about amongst our circle. No, I cannot take her home.'

With growing horror, Sarah listened to Isabella, and the full impact of what she had done was revealed to her. Far from being a help to this child, she had made a terrible situation even worse. She just had to get involved. Jumped in with both feet as usual. She remembered that Josiah and Lady Grace had mentioned unreasonably raising her hopes too much, but it was only through talking to Isabella that she fully realised what she had done.

'I am so sorry for putting you in this position, Isabella. I never meant to hurt you, or Bella, or anyone else. I really wanted to help Bella. You see, I knew a boy that . . .'

'Yes,' cut in Isabella, 'I have heard about your boy, but as I said earlier, it would be different if she was a boy. You should have realised this. I am surprised that a woman of your obvious knowledge and maturity did not. However, I have thought about the situation and talked for a long time to Josiah and Mama. Anna also has leapt to your defence in no uncertain terms. We have decided that Bella will stay here, but will have a more active role in the house than she has done previously. We have decided to say that she is a distant cousin who is an orphan, and that we have taken her in. I would be obliged if you would hold to this story yourself, should you be talking to anyone outside the house. Do you agree?'

'Oh yes, of course Isabella. Thank you for being so understanding.'

'You may go now.'

'Thank you.' said Sarah as she fled from the room. She ran straight into Anna who was about to come into the library.

'Issy, come up to the nursery and see the children. They want to put on a show for you,' burst out Anna.

Isabella, Anna and Sarah went up to the nursery, and found that Josiah, Jake and Lady Grace were already there. The chairs had all been arranged in rows in the middle of the floor. The children ushered the adults into their seats and after a lot of giggling, started their performance. Bella was sitting on a small chair, and the other children grouped around her. Each child read a poem or a short passage of scripture. The family showed their approval for each child's performance. The crowning glory of the show was a hymn that Sarah had taught them. It was one of John Newton's hymns. It was an adult hymn really, but she had struggled to find a children's one in the hymnal that was in the house. In her own time, the hymn was a golden oldie, but in 1825 it was more like an up to date modern Graham Kendrick song. Their childish voices blended together, as they sang their hearts out, singing words that were timeless.

'How sweet the name of Jesus sounds
In a believer's ear,
It soothes his sorrows, heals his wounds,
And wipes away his fear'.

Tears, rather than fears were the order of the day as Sarah noticed Isabella and Lady Grace fumbling for handkerchiefs.

Loud applause was given to the children, with all the adults expressing their pleasure at the little impromptu concert.

'That is not all,' said Anna quietly. Bella stood up, and using the frame to support her, started to walk slowly round the room. Now, even Anna and Sarah were fumbling for their handkerchiefs. Bella sank after a few steps, but not before everybody was amazed at what she had achieved. The children were as happy as the adults at having given them a surprise, but little Mary couldn't understand why everyone was saying that they were happy, but were crying. At that, they all laughed out loud, leaving Mary even more bemused at the actions of the adults.

'Perhaps we could give the show again tomorrow for the rest of the family?' shouted Mary, pleased that everyone was laughing again, but the tone of the room changed again.

'I think not, my dear,' said Lady Grace quietly. 'This is just nursery fun.' Sarah reflected on this, realising that they didn't want the outsiders to know about Bella. Some of the joy seemed to have left the nursery and everyone moved about the room, straightening the furniture, and looking busy.

That evening, James, Cassie's husband arrived. He was the complete opposite to Jake. He was tall and slim and very fanciful. He took to posing about the room, turning this way and that in front of the mirror over the fireplace, when he thought no one was looking. He was quite interested in Sarah and totally ignored Cassie. Indeed, he sometimes belittled her during the dinner conversation. Sarah was very uncomfortable with him, and was glad when all the men went to the billiard room for a game, leaving the ladies to gossip. Sarah found society gossip so boring, especially as she didn't know anyone that they were talking about, and the topics were so trivial. She drifted to the side of the room where the candles were and picked up her sewing. After two stabs with the sharp needle, Sarah abandoned her sewing and decided to go outside for a stroll before bedtime. It was not long before she realised that someone was following her. It was James.

'Well, my dear, how are you enjoying your stay here?' James asked mincingly. Sarah cringed.

'Quite well, thank you Sir.'

'Oh come, call me James. I am sure that we are going to get on famously.' Over my dead body thought Sarah to herself. What a creep. She wouldn't trust him as far as she could throw him. Suddenly she was reminded of Darren. She didn't know why. Or was it that smarmy way of talking. Yes, that was probably it. Creeps united, she thought to herself.

'Perhaps you would like to walk down to the chapel with me. I am really looking forward to seeing Josiah's pet hobby.' He said Josiah with just the hint of a sneer and Sarah shuddered at the thought of going anywhere with him.

'I'm sorry James, I've just gone very cold. I must go back inside. I do not want to risk catching a chill.' Goodness, she thought, I sound like one of Jane Austen's soppy heroines. James took his jacket off and moved towards Sarah. Sarah did a neat sidestep, and walked quickly towards the house.

'No thanks, I really am tired. I want to retire early.' As she ran through the doorway, she ran into Josiah. He caught her and asked her what was the matter. She started to say something, but James appeared behind her. Josiah's eyes narrowed as he took in the situation.

'Well, Boothroyd, out for a stroll?'

'Yes, I was just going to have a look at the chapel but I changed my mind,' he replied smoothly.

'You would be better seeing it tomorrow, when we have the ceremony. It's your turn on the billiard table now.'

'Thanks, I'll go inside then.' Josiah waited until he had gone and then turned to Sarah.

'Was he giving you offence, Sarah?'

'No, but I think that he would have done if I hadn't run back inside,' she laughed. 'Thanks for saving me.'

'My pleasure. Be careful with him. I do not like the tales that I am hearing about him when I go up to town. He appears to be moving in very fast circles. I can only hope that paternity will settle him down. He needs it.'

'I can look after myself, Josiah.'

'I know, but he is a dangerous man, and not one that I would like you to get to know better.'

'I am honoured at your concern for me.'

'I am getting a little fond of you, Sarah, and I wouldn't like to see you get hurt.' He may have said more, but Jake came out at that point to have a cigar in the garden. Lady Grace would not let the men smoke anywhere in the house. She wouldn't even build a smoking house in the grounds for them. She said it was far too dirty a habit for gentlemen. Sarah was inclined to agree with her. Jake's appearance gave her the excuse to go inside. She took a candle off the side table in the hall, and lighting it from the candelabra on the wall, she hurried upstairs. She had had enough excitement for one day!

Chapter 24

The next morning dawned fine. It was one of those warm Indian Summer days of October. The household were up and about early and breakfast was finished quickly. James had not come down for breakfast and Sarah was glad not to have to face him. The service was set for eleven, after which there would be a large meal. This was an unusual arrangement for the family who often just had a light luncheon. But as the days were drawing in, they wanted to make the most of the daylight.

The family gathered in the chapel, along with the Butlers who had arrived for the ceremony. Sarah found herself seated next to Jed Butler and found him to be an amusing, if trivial, companion whilst they were waiting. His sister gave Sarah a frosty nod of acknowledgement and purposely moved to another seat rather than sit next to her. Just after eleven o' clock, the musicians started to play pieces from Purcell's church music for strings. One of the violinists seemed to be much more proficient than the others. He seemed to be fairly bouncing about in the musicians' gallery at the left hand side of the chapel. At one point, he played a solo and the air was electric. She had never heard a violinist like it. His mastery was breathtaking. She leaned over to Jed and asked who the violinist was, but all he knew was that he was a friend of Jake Heywood's. Sarah watched him carefully during the service and was impressed by his professionalism, far above what she would have expected to hear in such a rural area. Perhaps he had come from London or somewhere. She would have to have a word with Jake afterwards. The musicians suddenly stopped for a few seconds and then started a different tune. Lady Grace walked down the aisle of the chapel on Josiah's arm, following the procession of the priest and the other religious people. The little congregation rose to their feet, and the chattering ceased.

Josiah led his mother to the front pew, and helped her to sit down. The priests moved to the front of the reredos, and stood behind the simple carved oak table that was to take the form of an altar. Josiah had kept the furnishing very simple, so as not to antagonise the more puritanical priests that abounded in those times. The only stained glass consisted of three windows. One depicted Christ dying on the cross and was at the centre of the chapel, high up on the wall above the reredos. The other two were coats of arms, one of the Grace family, and the other of the Percy family which Lady Grace had been born into. No extra pictures or icons had been added apart from two simple statues. One represented the Madonna and child, and the other was of Moses with the tablets of stone containing the Ten Commandments.

The service of dedication was simple and beautiful. The smell of incense and burning candles was quite overpowering to Sarah. After the dedication, they had the full Mass from the Missal. It was conducted in Latin and Sarah struggled to follow the words, as her remnant of schoolgirl Latin left a lot to be desired. But the beauty of the Mass enthralled, as she listened to the priests.

Following the service, the priests led the way out of the chapel. Josiah led Lady Grace out, followed by her daughters and their husbands. Anna and Sarah took up the rear of the family procession, and then the Butlers joined in behind. In the garden, a simple ceremony of consecration was held, so that the garden could now become a burial ground for the family.

The family was followed back to the house by most of the servants and the workmen, who had been told that they had to report to the house after the service. It was a solemn group that followed in procession back to the house. The workmen all looked ill at ease, being inside the great house, but Mrs Hardcastle took them into the small dining room, and told them to wait there. They did not have long to wait. Lady Grace and Josiah came into the dining room and spoke to the men. Lady Grace explained to the men how much it meant to her to get her own chapel in the grounds, and especially to have her husband buried there, too. They commended the men on the speed that they had finished the chapel, and said that they were pleased with the minimal disruption that they had made to the rest of the gardens. Lady Grace then took a blue velvet bag from Josiah and went to each workman in turn. She gave each man a golden sovereign. The first man gasped as he saw what the gift was. He had never held a coin of such great value in all his life, and couldn't believe it. All the other workmen looked equally pleased by their gift. Finally, she gave the chief stonemason and the foreman five sovereigns each. They all heartily thanked Lady Grace, and then the oldest man amongst them shouted 'Three cheers for Her Ladyship' and all his colleagues bellowed out a mighty roar that brought Williams into the room, wondering what was happening. His appearance stopped the men mid-cheer, until they realised who he was, then they all laughed at themselves.

Josiah and Lady Grace then left, but not before telling them that a special meal was to be served to them. The maids brought in tray after tray of food for the men, and encouraged them to eat heartily. They all ate to the full, and Martha the cook brought small baskets for them to take some food home for their families. Some of the older men were almost in tears at this point, but the young men decided that this would be a nice snack on the walk home if they got hungry. They all decided that they had never been treated like this before by the gentry, and they would like to work for Lord Grace himself again.

'Perhaps he will want a house building when he gets married,' suggested one wag. Another answered and said that this was Lord Grace's house, but perhaps he would need a dower house for his mother when he did get married. And what about the rest of the family, wouldn't they all need new houses building? The suggestions got wilder as more porter was consumed, but eventually, partly prompted by Mrs Hardcastle, the foreman told the men that it was time to go home. They all shambled off a little sheepishly, mumbling their thanks to Mrs Hardcastle as they left.

As the men were leaving, the family had already gathered in the large dining room. Sarah noticed that the strange violinist was present, but he was at the far end of the table, and appeared to be talking vivaciously to young Anna. 'Ah,' thought Sarah, 'is this going to be a rival for Doctor Perry?' She would have to pump Anna for the gossip afterwards. She felt shocked at herself. She had never been a gossip, yet here she was, joining in like an inane fool with the other young women. This century was definitely having a deleterious effect on her brain.

The family was treated to a more sedate luncheon. Martha had excelled herself. They had started with white mushroom fricassee, followed by broiled salmon. Next there had been a choice of roast rib of beef, fricandos of veal or dressed breast of lamb. The sweet course had been a choice of either raspberry or lemon syllabub, followed by the usual sweets and fresh fruits. Martha had even made a cake in the shape of the chapel and decorated it. Lady Grace made Martha come up to the dining room when it was served. She was a long time coming. Mrs Hardcastle had had to practically drag her up the stairs. Martha was flustered and ill at ease when she arrived in the room, and stood just inside the doorframe. Lady Grace asked her to come forward and stand next to Lord Grace. She did so, whilst trying to curtsey at the same time. Lord Grace then cut into the cake, despite the fact that the girls had pleaded with him not to cut it, or spoil it in any way. Josiah carefully cut a single piece, gingerly placed it on a delicate china side plate, and gave it to Martha.

'Thank yer Sir, who is it fer?' she asked. Josiah laughed.

'Why Martha, it is for you. I hear that it was your idea to make this cake, without telling us. That was so kind, so you must have the first slice. Come now, eat it up.' Martha looked like she could no more eat the cake in front of the family than she could drink poison. She hesitated, and Sarah felt sorry for her. She was saved by Charlotte.

'Mama, I know that Peggy helped Martha an awful lot. She told me that she helped mix the icing and decorate the cake. Shouldn't Peggy be here as well?'

'What a good idea, Charlotte. Trust you to know who did what in the kitchen. You are always in there. I'm sure that when you are married you will run a very good household, because you spend so much time in the kitchen.'

'But I find it so interesting watching how all the ingredients go in together and come out as something else. And anyway, now that I can read and write I can . . .' she stopped mid sentence, remembering that she was not supposed to tell anyone outside the family that she was learning to read and write. Lady Grace, as usual covered the gaffe, and made it into a natural comment.

'Yes, aren't we fortunate in having Sarah? She has done so much for our family by teaching all the girls their letters. Apparently her dearest Papa used to believe in educating girls, and so this is a great remembrance for him. Sarah is able to continue upholding his beliefs with our girls. It has certainly made family life much more entertaining.' By this time Charlotte had recovered from her blushes.

'Why is it more interesting now that you can read and write, Charlotte?' asked Cassie. 'What need have you to read and write?' There was a trace of peevishness in her voice, and Sarah suspected that Cassie was more than a little jealous at this revelation. She hated to think that any of her sisters were getting more of something than her.

'Why, I am writing all Martha's receipts down, as at present they are all in her head. That way we will always have the receipts, even when Martha has long gone. Oh, I do apologise Martha. I did not mean to be rude, but you are such an excellent cook, we would like your cooking to be remembered forever, even when I am an old grandmother.' Martha blushed furiously at this and was speechless. Josiah ordered Peggy to be brought up from the kitchen.

Peggy was even more flustered than Martha. Never in her whole life at Roding Hall had she been asked to go upstairs. Her mind was racing about what fate could befall her. She knew Martha had been sent for and had not returned. Perhaps one of the guests had found a bone in the fish course, and choked on it. Perhaps Martha had told them that Peggy had made the fish dish. But she had been very careful with it, and was sure that there were no bones in it. She knocked on the dining room door, with great fear and trembling. Peggy was thinking that she would probably be discharged now. Well, whatever it was, she would just have to bear it, and hope for the best. A deep voice bade her to enter. She peeped round the side of the door, and stood just inside the door. 'Come here, girl,' boomed Lord Grace from the far end of the room. Peggy had to walk the full length of the room, and kept her head bowed. She stood next to Lord Grace, still with her head bowed. She jumped when he spoke to her.

'Here you are girl. Have a piece of cake. I have it on the highest authority that you had a hand in making this confection. Is that true?' Peggy nodded her answer, took the cake from Lord Grace with trembling hands, and fled to the back of his chair, where she had spotted Martha. She was so relieved that she was not in trouble that she could hardly stop her hands trembling. Lord Grace then cut another much larger piece of cake and told Martha and Peggy to take it back downstairs for the other servants. They fairly fled out of the room, after curtseying their thanks.

Sarah sat back in her chair, looking at Josiah. He really was a kind man, although the poor servants had looked petrified when they had entered the room, so perhaps on second thoughts, he was not so kind after all. He could have told them what he wanted them for. But overall, Sarah was impressed by the family today. Both with their dealings with the workmen and then the servants. Perhaps they were becoming more human and less aristocratic after all. Or was she just getting used to it all? Following the meal, Lady Grace invited everyone into the ballroom for a musical soiree. They were really bucking custom today, as musical events usually took place after evening dinner, but apparently the guest violinist had to leave that evening, as he had an engagement in London the day after next.

The chairs were arranged in short rows round the front of the ballroom. The Minstrels' Gallery was not being used as there was only a single musician, and it was a performance rather than incidental music for listening or dancing. Sarah asked Anna who the violinist was. Anna laughed.

'Surely you are teasing me. You don't know who the great Paganini is?' Sarah gaped at Anna.

'You mean he's the real Paganini, from Italy?' Sarah knew that she was sounding like a simpleton, but she couldn't believe that she was meeting one of her own favourite composers in the flesh. Anna laughed again.

'Well it would not be an imitation one, would it my dear friend. You are funny. Sometimes you know so much, and yet at other times you know so little. Of course it is the real Paganini. Had you not heard that he had left Italy? He has been travelling Europe for years, playing at different houses, and moving on quickly. He has quite a reputation with the ladies you know,' Anna laughed. Sarah remembered how he had been talking far too intimately to Anna during luncheon. But now she could see him closer, she realised that he must be about twice or even three times older than her. Anna leaned down to whisper in Sarah's ear.

'It is rumoured that he has got the phthisis. He certainly looks like he may have, does he not? He is so pale and thin. But it just adds to his air of magic when he performs. Although it is rumoured that he is in league with the devil too, because of the way that he plays. You will see what I mean, look he is about to commence.' Anna settled back into her chair ready to listen.

The familiar strains of Paganini's 'Variations on a Theme' came flooding into the room. It was her favourite piece. It always reminded Sarah of the South Bank Show, which used the piece as their theme tune. Her father had been a great fan of the show. She knew that it was technically a very difficult piece of music to play, but Paganini made light work of it. His fingers seemed to float all over the strings. He jumped about all over the front of the ballroom, and Sarah realised why they hadn't put him up in the Minstrels' Gallery to perform. He wouldn't have had room! The very air seemed to be charged by his presence, and all the family held their breath whilst he played. After that piece, he played many more, playing for over two hours. Nobody became bored or shifted about in their seats. They were all spell bound. Tumultuous applause broke out after each piece, and they didn't want to let him go.

Eventually Jake insisted that he had to go, as he was accompanying him to London. Their carriage was booked and they had to go. Not tired or seemingly wearied by this stupendous performance, Paganini thanked Lady Grace for inviting him to such an important occasion as the blessing of the chapel. He said that it was a privilege to have been asked. Lady Grace replied that the privilege was all theirs. He kissed her hand, made a deep bow, then walked briskly out of the room. There was silence in the room for a while, whilst everybody remembered the maestro's playing. Then slowly one by one, people drifted out of the ballroom, making their own amusement for the rest of the afternoon.

Chapter 25

The next day became a flurry of leave takings, as Cassie and James left first thing in the morning. They were going to stay with friends outside Leeds, and then on to some more friends near Harrogate. Cassie was trying to make the most of visiting all their friends before her condition started to show. Whilst the ladies were together in the drawing room last evening, Cassie had been bemoaning her lot.

'Once I get bigger, I will have to go into hibernation. Lord, it will be so boring. I cannot wait for the child to be born, so that I can be rid of it to the maids, and can get on with my life again. It is a pity that the maids cannot have the babies for us and save us the bother of either begetting them or parting with them. I do not know how I will keep an eye on James as it is, whilst I am enceinte.' Sarah was shocked by the attitude that Cassie was displaying. Especially as she had been so proud of her condition when she had arrived. It was sad to realise that she only saw the baby as yet another possession, or a necessary evil to produce the inevitable heir. Sarah worried about the baby's prospects, but then many of these people didn't look after their own children. It was the way of the world amongst the gentry, she reflected sadly.

'Really Cassandra, you should not be talking in this vein, especially in front of others. You should be on your knees thanking God that you are enceinte. Think how you would feel if you did not have children? What would happen to the estate then?'

'I do not care about the estate. It is a paltry one compared with this, even though they have more money than us. The house down in Sussex is better but, of course, his uncle has taken that. It should not have happened. Just because he lost a leg in the war. Why does that mean he needs a bigger house? It is not fair,' said Cassie peevishly.

'Cassandra, I am tiring of your petty words. If you cannot join pleasantly in our conversations on a general level, then pray remain silent.' Cassie flushed, and took to walking restlessly about the room, picking up ornaments and putting them back down again, and generally irritating her mother even more. Eventually she left the room, saying that she was going to leave early as she was bored. Lady Grace pulled her lips together in a thin line, but refrained from saying anything further. The other ladies said goodbye politely to her, but nobody was sorry to see her go.

After Cassie and James had left, Isabella decided that she would go, too. She had had a run in with her mother about Anna. Isabella had suggested taking Anna back home with her, so that she could groom her for the Season, and secretly thought she could get rid of some of Anna's more outlandish ideas. She would then take her to London for the Season. To Anna's relief, Lady Grace left the decision to Anna, who vehemently refused to go. Overhearing the conversation, Charlotte begged to go instead, and eventually Lady Grace agreed to the idea.

'This is only because I have need of you over the next few weeks, Anna. Next year you must go to London for the Season, or you will become an old maid and all the best suitors will have been betrothed. Charlotte, you must behave for your sister, and help her with the little children. If you cause any difficulties, you will be sent back.'

'If she becomes difficult, I do declare that I shall put her in the kitchen with Fanny. She is not as amenable as your Martha. She would probably make her stand in the scullery all day and do all the greasy washing up. She would not take it kindly if a young lady of the house tried to help or give advice in her kitchen.' Isabella laughed at the images that this invoked.

'I will be good, mama, I promise. I was ever so good at Aunt Marguerite's was I not?'

'You were very well behaved, my dear. A credit to the family. Now run along and find Agnes and get her to pack your clothes. What time were you thinking of going, Isabella?'

'As soon as possible after lunch, Mama, if that is convenient for you.'

'I'll let Mrs Hardcastle know, then she can tell Martha that we will be reduced numbers at dinner tonight.'

'I shall go up to my room now, and write some letters, so that they can be posted from here.' With that, Isabella left the room. Sarah picked up the book that she was reading. It was Jane Austen's 'Pride and Prejudice'. To the family this was the latest bestseller, but to Sarah it was a timeless favourite. It was strange to read it in the time that it was written. She came to realise that some of the images that appeared strange to her twenty first century mind, were no longer strange, but becoming the norm where she was now. It certainly helped her to understand some of the mores and customs that she was encountering. She only wished that she had read it prior to coming on the holiday. Then she would have known what to expect.

After luncheon, Isabella and her entourage were loaded into the carriage, and set off back to her home. It was a subdued party at dinner that evening. Lady Grace seemed quiet, and Sarah suspected that she had been drained by the effort of entertaining her children with their spouses and grandchildren. But of course, she wouldn't admit to that. Also, she was still feeling quite raw after the bereavement, and some of the emotions that she had gone through during the last few days had touched a nerve. So soon after losing her sister through the effects of childbirth, Lady Grace was now worrying about Cassie, and how she would fare when her time came. That was one confinement that she was not looking forward to. Cassie would not cope with the pains like Isabella had. Especially when Bella had been born, Isabella had been amazingly stoical. Cassie would be more likely to scream and shout and generally blame everybody for her pain. Lady Grace sighed in anticipation of what was to come, and then decided that she would go up to bed early. Anna and Josiah followed her, all deciding that they would benefit from an early night.

The next morning, Sarah decided to take a walk in the garden, and as it was quite mild, she took her book with her and sat on the new bench that had been made. It was placed near the path going down to the chapel. She had been there some time before Josiah came round the corner.

'So there you are, I thought that you had disappeared. I have been looking for you.'

'I have been enjoying this lovely autumn day. It is so warm for the time of year, and the leaves are starting to turn such lovely colours. Look at that lovely maple tree. What lovely shades there are to be seen.'

'Do you like the autumn best?'

'Yes, but only in autumn.' Josiah looked at her quizzically.

'What do you mean?'

'Well, I like autumn best when it is autumn, then when the trees are bare, and the snow falls, I like the winter best. But then when the buds start appearing on the trees and in the gardens, then I like spring best, until summer arrives, with all its glory, and then, . . well, I suppose you have guessed the rest,' Sarah said laughingly.

'I know what you mean. All the seasons are so different. And each season has its own beauty, with different fruit and flowers in their turn. I was in a house in Kent where they had built a small extra house made of glass on the side of the lounge. They kept the room very warm and were growing fruit and flowers all year round, and also fruits that are not native to these shores. It was incredible. I would like to have one here. Just think, to have fresh fruits out of season without having to send to London. It would make Martha's day, as well as Mama's. She does so love to surprise her guests with something out of the ordinary.'

'You mean a conservatory or glass house,' said Sarah feverishly trying to think what they were called in 1825.

'Yes, that's what I mean.'

'I have a small one at my house.'

'Really? What do you grow in there?' Sarah thought about her little conservatory, with its cane furniture and cacti.

'Not much yet. It has not been finished very long. There are only some succulent plants. My brother may be sending some plants over from Amer. . , er, er the New World later,' said Sarah remembering to use the correct terminology.

'Perhaps you could advise me on having one built, then Sarah. I would welcome your advice.'

'Of course, Josiah, I would be delighted.' She would have to change the topic pretty soon, or she may say the wrong thing. 'It seems to be getting chilly now, I think that I will walk back inside,' added Sarah.

'I agree. But I wanted to have a talk to you Sarah. Will you come to the library with me? It may take a long time.'

'Of course.' The two strolled back to the house and after ordering chocolate, they settled down in the comfortable old leather chairs, by the fire. Once the chocolate had arrived, Josiah started to talk.

'What I have got to say may shock you, Sarah, but I want you to hear me out.' Sarah looked at him, wondering if this was going to be a proposal scene in this real life drama that she appeared to be living in. But why would he expect her to be shocked? Perhaps he was going to confess that he had sown his wild oats. Well, she could easily match him on that one, she reflected ruefully.

'As you know, it is imperative that I marry, and marry soon. My mother has brought a selection of girls to my attention, but I have not found one who is to my liking, or who I feel that I could spend the rest of my life with. Until I met you. I am wondering if you would do me the honour of becoming my wife?'

'I, er, er, I' stammered Sarah. Josiah interrupted.

'Please, let me finish. I do not want an answer yet, because that is only half of what I have to say,' Sarah nodded.

'Now it is I who will be stammering,' said Josiah looking a trifle disconcerted. 'I do not know how worldly wise you are Sarah. You seem to be a very modern woman and have a lot of ideas that are before your time. That is what gives me the courage to tell you the whole story, and I hope that I do not offend you, and lose your friendship. But I could not let you marry me without telling you everything. It would not be fair.'

'Goodness,' thought Sarah, 'perhaps he is a serial killer or something.'

'I am very fond of you and I admire you greatly. I also enjoy your company, you are so lively and provocative, challenging everything that I hold dear. But, and this is a serious but, I do not desire you, as a man should desire the woman he marries. Do you understand me? I tend to desire men rather than women. There, I have said it.'

'Oh, you are gay,' burst out Sarah without thinking.

'Gay?' asked Josiah with a look of puzzlement on his face, 'Yes, I do try and be gay at all times. Most people describe me as a gay man.'

'No, no,' laughed Sarah, 'that is the word we use where I come from to describe men who prefer men to women.'

'It is hard to conceive how words can change their meaning in just a matter of miles. But at least you seem to understand what I am saying to you, regardless of the actual word. Gay just means happy, frivolous, or merry in this part of the country.'

'It does in mine too, but there is also this hidden meaning. But if you are gay, or prefer men as you say, why are you asking me to marry you?'

'I have no option. I have my duty to the family. I must beget an heir. My proposal is that if you would consent to marry me, we would act as a normal married couple until we had an heir and a spare, and then afterwards we would be married in name only. After that, we would still live together to keep up appearances, but you would be free to go elsewhere with your favours. As long as you were discreet and did not bring the family name into ill repute. Please do not give me an answer today. You need to think about all that I have said. I know that it will have been a great shock for you.'

'No, I can see now why you were very polite, courteous, and charming to every lady you saw, but there never seemed to be an attraction with any of them. But why me then?'

'You seemed different right from the start, and as I have said, you always seem to have ideas that are years ahead of us in this rural backwater. I thought that you might be able to understand me. But I have offended you now.'

'Not at all. Just surprised me, that is all. Well, you have certainly given me something to think about.'

'So you will think about it. You won't just dismiss me out of hand?'

'Of course not. As Anna pointed out to me, I am getting a bit long in the tooth, and I ought to be glad of any proposal that I get, so I shall consider it.'

'She didn't?' Josiah replied, quite scandalised at this revelation about his younger sister.

'She did,' replied Sarah seriously. Suddenly they both burst out laughing.

'What a pair we are to be sure,' said Josiah. 'Perhaps we deserve each other.'

'Perhaps so,' replied Sarah, 'and I will think about it carefully and let you know.'

'Thank you Sarah. You are the first woman that I have ever thought of marrying, and have even been slightly attracted to.'

'I might get you to change your feelings then,' teased Sarah.

'Who knows?' he teased back in return. Sarah got up to go and as she left the library, she turned and spoke to Josiah.

'Thank you for being honest.' Sarah smiled and left the room slowly, then rushed up to the comfort of her room to try and think about what she should do.

Chapter 26

Sarah spent a long time thinking that day. She was quiet throughout dinner and pleaded a headache, so went early to her bed. She dismissed Myrtle early, and getting a good supply of candles, she sat by her window, and thought long and hard. She was not shocked by what she had heard, as she knew that homosexuality had been around as long as there had been people. But obviously it was an unspeakable topic in this era. Probably illegal as well, she reflected. She couldn't really remember when it was legalised, but was sure that it was only in the late twentieth century. But she wasn't sure when it officially became illegal in the first place. But that didn't matter anyway. What on earth was she to do? Could she marry under those circumstances? Actually, it was the best of both worlds, as she would only have to produce two heirs, then she was free to do what she wanted. But that was not what she wanted from her marriage. Could she stand to live in a loveless marriage? Would she survive childbirth? What if she had six girls first?

She did like Josiah, but she certainly didn't fancy him. He was more like a brother to her. But life would not be dull living here with him. And she could certainly enjoy living in this beautiful place. And she would never have to get up early to go to work again. Now that had its attractions, much as she loved her work and her life back in Read and Whalley. But did she want to stay here in this era, and the answer was a definite 'no'. As much as she was enjoying life, it was not what she wanted. But she had tried several times to get back to her own time, to no avail. Was she stuck in this time warp forever? Would she never get back to her former life, and her new love, Joe? Thoughts of Joe threatened to overwhelm her. She still felt exactly the same about him, even though she had not seen him for four months. Tears brimmed over and spilt down on to her nightie.

The questions went round and round in her head all night. She eventually went to bed when it was nearly dawn. She woke later than usual, and would have slept longer if Myrtle had not come into the room.

'Mornin' Miss. Lovely day. What are yer wearing terday, then?' Sarah stirred in her bed and started to stretch.

'Morning Myrtle. You choose. I can't be bothered to think today. I've got a headache.'

'Lord Grace wer askin' after yer this mornin' at breakfast. Wanted ter knew if yer were up yet.'

'Oh, he probably had some job that he wants me to do,' Sarah said far more lightly than she felt. Sarah completed her toilet and went downstairs for breakfast. Fortunately, the family had all long gone, and she breakfasted in peace. As she was settling down to her second cup of coffee, Josiah came into the room.

'I do not want to apply any pressure to you, but have you thought about what I said last night?'

'Good morning Josiah. I have thought about little else. All night. And now I have a raging headache for my efforts,' she laughed. Josiah commiserated. 'But I do want to talk to you.'

'Let us go into the library again. It's my favourite room. I never feel as comfortable in my study. I think it is because it was my father's, and I still think of it as his room.' They walked slowly towards the study and Sarah noticed that Josiah was as nervous as she was.

'Thank you for the honour that you have bestowed on me by asking for my hand in marriage . . .'

'But' interrupted Josiah.

'Yes, but' laughed Sarah, 'and there is a but. A big one. I listened carefully to what you said to me last night, but I think that it is only fair that you listen to my story as well.'

'I am sure that it cannot be as terrible as my story,' pleaded Josiah hopefully. Sarah leaned over and stroked his hand.

'Josiah, I am very fond of you. The feelings that I have for you are like that of a sister to a brother. I could marry you on your terms and be quite happy, but I do not know if you will still want to marry me if you know the full story of my circumstances.'

'Let me guess, were your parents not married? Or something equally awful? It does not matter. I will marry who I wish.'

'I wish that it was so easy. I know that you will find it hard to believe what I am going to tell you, but I could not promise to marry you if you were not fully aware of my predicament. Do you remember when I arrived on that first night in June?' Josiah nodded. 'Did you not think that it was odd that I just appeared with no baggage, and no invitation? And no-one knew who I was? Oh dear, I do not know where to start.' Sarah got up from the chair and started to pace the floor. 'The night I arrived, I came here on a visit with some friends, but the year that I arrived in was 2001, not 1825.'

'I am sorry. I already do not understand what you are trying to say. What does 2001 mean?'

'I mean that I really live in the year 2001, in the twenty first century. Nearly 200 years after you.' There was silence for quite some moments.

'How can that be, Sarah? How can you have arrived in 2001 but are now in 1825? I just do not understand it.'

'Neither do I,' replied Sarah quietly. 'I came here for a dinner and dance. We were made to dress up in costumes that were fashionable in another age, and pretend to be the characters from another era who actually lived in this house during that time. During the evening, I came down to the kitchen to get a drink of water. I fell down the stairs and knocked myself out. When I came round, I found that I was in your kitchen, surrounded by Martha and Peggy, and then eventually the rest of the family arrived. I was as bemused as you. I thought that all the people were actors who were taking the part of the staff who would have lived here in 1825.' There was another long silence. Sarah felt that she should stay silent for a while, until Josiah could start to take in what she was saying, before she told him anything else.

'That is why you asked for a newspaper,' he said dully.

'Yes,' replied Sarah quietly. There was another silence.

'To check the date.'

'Yes.'

'So have you tried to get back to your own time?'

'Of course I have. I thought that if I had another head injury, it might send me back to my own time.'

'But it did not work'.

'No. I just got headaches and bruises.'

'And do you think that you will ever go back to your own time?'

'I have no idea. I do not know how to do it, or I would. I am sure you can understand that as much as I have been welcomed and made happy here, it would be infinitely preferable to return to my own time. I do hope that you understand that.'

'Yes, of course. I do not know what to say. I am sure that you laughed at my simple attempts to explain my predicament. How you must have been amused at my proposal. And what a loaded proposal!' Josiah laughed ruefully.

'No, I did not laugh at your proposal. What I said still stands. I would happily marry you on your terms, but I am frightened that I may just go back to my own time without being able to stop myself. Then what would you do?'

'Well, leave me an heir, and it wouldn't matter, would it?' said Josiah harshly.

'Please do not say that. I would hardly like to bear a child and then disappear again. Much as it would be convenient for you.'

'Sarah, I am so sorry, I did not mean that. Please forgive me. It is just that it is all so hard to comprehend.'

'Perhaps you should come back with me. Homosexuality is legal in the twenty first century. Has been for quite some time. About 40 years I think.'

'Legal? You mean that I would not risk imprisonment if I were to be caught?'

'Certainly not. It is quite common for men to be seen together as a couple in the streets. And it is acknowledged that men live together as partners. Or women for that matter.'

'Women? They too live together?' Josiah asked incredulously.

'Yes. They even adopt children nowadays.'

'You live in enlightened times. It is hard to comprehend. I think you are right. Perhaps you should take me with you if you return to your own time. I think that I would like it.'

'I wish that it were so easy to return. I would gladly take you if I only knew how to get back myself.'

'My mind is finding this all too hard to take in. I think that I will have a walk around the gardens and think about what you have said.' With that, Josiah left the room, and Sarah picked up a book and tried to read, to distract her mind. But her own mind was racing. Had she gone too far in what she had told Josiah? Did he really understand what she was saying? How much more should she tell him? Could he take in what sort of world she really came from? She doubted it. Not knowing where he had gone, she felt that she could not go into the garden, or he would think that she was following him. Instead, Sarah paced round the library. At one point, Sarah noticed Josiah heading for the chapel. Perhaps he was going there to pray, and try to sort out his feelings about what he had heard. Sarah felt guilty that she had really unsettled him. She suddenly remembered that she was no longer a virgin, and that was an important issue in 1825. She wondered if that would be a problem on her wedding night. Well, she would have to blame the tampons, and leave the rest to luck.

Agnes came into the library and asked Sarah if she knew if Lord Grace would like his chocolate now. Sarah replied that Lord Grace had gone into the garden for a walk, but that she would dearly love a drink of chocolate. Agnes bustled off, almost colliding with Anna as she came into the library.

'Oops, sorry Miss,' said Agnes.

'No, I am sorry, Agnes, I was rushing without looking. I was looking for Josiah.'

'He's outside in the garden. I am just going to have a drink of chocolate. Why don't you join me, Anna.'

'Excellent. Make that two drinks of chocolate Agnes, please.' Agnes left the room, soon returning with a daintily prepared tray. As well as the chocolate, there were some newly baked oat biscuits, and a silver vase containing a single red rose. The two girls tucked into the small repast and didn't notice the door opening.

'Ha ha, what is going on in my absence? Drinking my chocolate, I see. Well, where is mine?' It was Josiah. Sarah looked carefully at him, but he seemed to be more at ease, more like his normal self. Anna jumped up and ran over to Josiah.

'Josiah, I was looking for you. I need some advice on one of the villagers. Please advise me,' she pleaded.

'It will have to wait young lady. I need to talk to Sarah first, and then I will speak to you later.' Anna looked quizzically at Sarah, who remained silent and just smiled at Anna. Anna looked at Josiah, but he did the same. Mystified, Anna shrugged her shoulders and left the room, leaving the door ajar.

'And shut the door, Anna. You always were a listener at open doors.' The door slammed. Josiah pulled a rueful face, and suggested to Sarah that they go for a walk, so that they could talk in peace. As they got down to the far reaches of the garden, they sat companionably by the river, on a little wooden bench. Josiah started the conversation after a short period of silence.

'Would you still be prepared to marry me, then?'

'Yes, if you are prepared to marry me.'

'Why yes, I think we are a well-matched couple. We both appear to have problems.' Josiah laughed. 'I will do my utmost to make you happy. And thank you. You have solved my problem. How could I tell any young woman what I have told you? Young women of this age would be scandalised. But I knew you were a woman of modern ideas. I just did not realise how modern. I am sorry to make haste, but could we announce our betrothal soon? I know it will cheer Mama up, and make her quite relieved.'

'Why not? We really do not have to make much of a fuss, do we? Especially with the house being in mourning.'

'Oh lor, that is true. I had quite forgotten. Perhaps Mama will be so grateful that I am to be married that she will forego the usual period of mourning. But even if she does, we cannot have a large society wedding in town.'

'Good. I would hate that. Couldn't we just get married here?'

'What, in the chapel?'

'Yes, I would really like that.'

'We will go and ask Mama and see what she has to say.'

'See what Mama has to say about what, Josiah?' asked a grinning Anna as she appeared from behind a tree.

'You minx. How long have you been listening?'

'I just heard the last sentence, so tell me I pray, what else I missed?'

'All right, but you must not say anything yet. I have just asked Sarah to be my wife and she has agreed.'

'Well I am pleased for you, Josiah, it is about time. But Sarah, I did not realise that you were so desperate to marry. I could have found you a much better husband than Josiah if you had told me.'

'That is enough Anna,' said Josiah trying to put on a stern voice. 'You won't be asked to attend Sarah if you make such disparaging remarks about the future Lady Grace.' It was Sarah's turn to stare. Lady Grace. She had forgotten about the title. How could she become a Lady when she hadn't been born to it? She would have to learn from Lady Grace before her marriage to Josiah.

'We had better go and tell Mama now, before this young lady tells everyone,' laughed Josiah.

Chapter 27

Josiah caught hold of Sarah's hand and led her into the house. Josiah knocked on the door of the small parlour where his mother was, and entered the room after her quiet 'come in', with Sarah following nervously behind him.

'Josiah and Sarah. What can I do for you? You look so serious, both of you.'

'Well, actually Mama, I have just asked Sarah to marry me, and she has agreed.' For a split second, Lady Grace looked stunned, and then her breeding took over.

'How marvellous. That is good news. You have both kept very quiet about your courtship.'

'There has been so much going on in the house that we never got round to it before. It has just happened this morning. And as she has no parents or available elder brother, I am unable to formally ask for her hand.'

'Of course, you will have to wait until the period of mourning is over before you could marry.'

'Actually, Sarah has said that she would prefer a very quiet wedding in the chapel, if you approved.' Lady Grace's face lit up with a smile.

'If I approved? Of course I do. That would be so wonderful. For you to marry in the chapel that is dedicated to my own dear husband, that would make me very happy indeed.'

'Have you thought of when you wish to marry?' Josiah said yes and Sarah said no simultaneously. Then they both laughed.

'Disagreeing already? Does this bode well for your marriage?' laughed Lady Grace.

'I would like to marry on Christmas Day, but I have not discussed this with Sarah. What do you think, my love?'

'Sounds fine to me, Josiah.'

'That is settled then.'

'Do you mean this Christmas Day?'

'Yes.'

'But that is less than three months away. How on earth can we get Sarah ready for then, and plan the whole wedding?'

'But it will only be a very small wedding Mama, because of the mourning period. We can only ask the closest of family and friends. Besides, most people will be in London for the Season and will not attend. It will not need much arranging.'

'What would you know about these things Josiah? You are only a mere man.'

'But I would not need much, Lady Grace. You have already bought me so many fine things. Surely I would need little beyond my bridal gown.'

'But what about your Grand Tour? You would need lots of clothes for that.'

'We would not go on a Grand Tour. Not immediately. We would need to stay here during the period of mourning. We could think about that in a year or two. Unless the babies have come along by that time.' Josiah almost leered at Sarah, who daintily blushed like a vestal virgin.

'Do not be so coarse in front of your betrothed, Josiah. I do apologise, my dear, but men will be men.' Sarah smiled graciously at Lady Grace, thinking if only she knew the truth.

'I will send for a dressmaker today. We have no time to lose. Do you wish to go into Leeds to choose the material for the bridal gown?' Sarah remembered the smells and bumpy ride into Leeds.

'No, I would rather the dressmaker brought some swatches of material for me to choose. Unless that would be inconvenient.'

'Not at all, it would be very convenient. Good,' said Lady Grace. 'I knew that you would be sensible. I must say that I admire your choice, Josiah. It will stop all the speculation about you not marrying. And stop all those tiresome girls making up to you,' Lady Grace laughed as she went over to the bell pull. Agnes answered the call, and was sent off to get Mrs Hardcastle.

'You had better choose a ring Josiah. Are you having my large diamond that was your Great Grandmama's? I will give it to you now.' Lady Grace started to pull the ring off her finger.

'No, Mama, I will not take that whilst you are alive. Besides, I want Sarah to have the large emerald ring, which belonged to Great Aunt Charis. It will exactly match her eyes. I thought that the first time that I saw her.' Sarah was surprised that, given his disinterest in women, he had noticed the colour of her eyes on their first meeting. But then, she was continually being surprised by him. There was a knock on the door, and Mrs Hardcastle entered.

'Ah, Hardcastle. I need you to contact the dressmaker urgently.'

'Yes, your Ladyship. And what is she to bring with her?'

'Bridal attire.' Mrs Hardcastle's eyes widened in surprise.

'Bridal?'

'That is correct. You may inform Williams and the rest of the staff that Lord Grace and Miss Sarah are to be married.' Mrs Hardcastle recovered herself quickly.

'May I be the first of the staff to give you my sincere felicitations, Lord Grace. And you as well, Miss Sarah,' she added as an afterthought. Sarah nodded graciously. 'And when is the happy day to be, may I ask?'

'Christmas Day'

'Christmas Day?' repeated Mrs Hardcastle. 'This Christmas Day?'

'Yes, and it will be a very quiet nuptials, given the circumstances. Thank you Hardcastle, that will be all for now.' Mrs Hardcastle left the room, after bowing respectfully. Sarah could just imagine her running down to the kitchens and telling everyone. There would be some shocks down there today, Sarah reckoned. And around the rest of the county too, when some of the girls who fancied Josiah found out. Ah well, it couldn't be helped. She would just have to ride the storm.

The next few weeks seemed to fly by. The days were concerned with dressmakers, floral arrangements, guest lists, and the receiving of presents. All the presents had to be carefully logged in a book, and thank you letters written. Presents appeared from all over the country, mainly from people that Sarah had never heard of. Because the wedding was to be so quiet, the presents arrived in advance of the wedding day, rather than guests bringing them nearer to the wedding day.

Lady Grace had decided that Sarah would not need the usual linen and bedding that a bride needed, as she would be living in Roding Hall, which had its full complement of linen. A new set of linen for the bridal bed would be all that was required. Lady Grace had already asked Sarah if she would like her to leave Roding Hall, now that she was to become the new Lady Grace. Sarah was shocked.

'Indeed not. There will always be a home for you here. I do not want you to leave; I need you to teach me how to run a house as efficiently as you do. I will need lots of help from you.' Lady Grace smiled.

'That is so kind of you to say so, my dear. I will help you all that I can. Some day, I think that I will get Josiah to build me a dower house so that I can live on my own and please myself as I get older. But I will not stay all the time. I will take the girls away to my dear brother-in-law's house. It will help him during his bereavement, but also be a change for the girls. It will give you and Josiah a chance to have some time on your own whilst you are newly married.'

'There is no need, really. I feel that I am pushing you out of your home.'

'As soon as I bore Josiah, I knew that one day his wife would usurp me. And it will also happen to you. Be prepared for that, dear Sarah. Make the most of being mistress of all you survey whilst you have the chance. When you have children, enjoy them, for they are not babies for long, and then they leave you, one way or another.' Sarah felt quite sad when Lady Grace said this, as she knew that most women in this era had lost babies. It suddenly dawned on her that she too would be having babies in this era, with no National Childbirth Trust, pethidine or gas and air. And water births would definitely not be on the cards here. She remembered the dirty frockcoat that Doctor Griffiths had on, and she shuddered. She would try and stick with a midwife. They were probably safer than the doctors, certainly cleaner. It was quite a frightening thought. Sarah suddenly realised that Lady Grace was talking to her.

'And I can only wish that you have such a delightful daughter–in-law as I am going to have.'

'Why thank you, Lady Grace, that is so kind of you. I do hope that I match up to your exacting standards.'

'I am sure that you will. And please, do you not think that you could call me Mama from now on?'

'All right Lady Grace, er, Mama. I will try.' Lady Grace beamed and then left the room.

By the middle of November, plans for the wedding were well in hand. The dress had been presented for Sarah to try on and be adjusted. It was made of shimmery white satin, and was gathered under the bust. The sleeves were puffed up at the shoulder, and then were tighter on the rest of the arms. There were satin ruches trimming the sleeves, with filigree lace around the wrists. Flowers were appliquéd onto the bodice of the dress, with little seed pearls at the centre of the flowers. The skirt of the dress was wider than some of her other dresses, as befitted the new fashion. The satin ruches were repeated all around the hem of the skirt, which tapered into a long train behind her.

Sarah was to wear a fine gossamer veil that had been Lady Grace's on her marriage. It was to be worn under the headdress of orange blossom flowers. Sarah was to carry orange blossoms as her bridal bouquet, as it was thought that they were lucky for a bride. The flowers had had to be grown specially and brought from London because it was a winter wedding, where they had been raised in one of the new glass conservatories. Special satin shoes had been ordered and fitted. Fine white silky stockings had also been purchased. As it was a winter wedding, a long cape of fine swans' down was made for her, so that when she walked to the chapel, she would not be cold. A muff made of swans' down was to complete her attire. Sarah loved the whole outfit, and felt every inch a bride when she tried it all on.

Anna, Charlotte, Elly and Mary had all been measured for their dresses too. They were to wear replicas of Sarah's dress, without the headdress and veil, but in different colours. Anna's dress was the palest lilac satin, her favourite colour. Charlotte's was mint green, Elly's was the palest blue, and Mary's was pink. After a lot of discussion, and a lot of insistence from Sarah, it was decided that Bella could attend the wedding. Although she was unable to be an attendant as walking was still difficult, she was to be carried onto the front row of the chapel, where the other attendants would sit. Sarah felt that she had won a battle that they were even letting Bella be seen at the wedding, and she was glad that she could monitor this little girl's progress in later years. Bella also had the same dress as her aunties in a delicate lemon shade. When the girls were all dressed up in their finery, Lady Grace cried.

'They look like little flowers in their different coloured dresses. I am so pleased Sarah. You have an eye for colour.' As they walked away from the nursery, Mrs Hardcastle was coming up the stairs.

'Mr Martin is here, your Ladyship.'

'Ah thank you, Hardcastle. Come Sarah, you need to meet Martin.' With no further explanation, Lady Grace swept down the stairs into the small dining room where Mrs Hardcastle had put the man.

'Martin, good of you to come so promptly. This is Josiah's betrothed. The wedding day will be on Christmas Day. Will you be able to execute the commission by then?'

'Certainly your Ladyship. When would you wish me to start?'

'Immediately if you can.'

'Indeed. I brought all my palettes just in case that was the request. Is there any special pose or clothing required?' Sarah wondered again at these people who just expected everyone to drop everything and serve the family, regardless of any other commitments that they may have.

'I will leave that for you to discuss with Josiah. It was his idea. Young William, the gardener, has just gone to get Josiah from the stable.' Sarah was mystified by this conversation and was unable to comprehend why she needed to be there. However, shortly afterwards, Josiah came in and shook hands with Mr Martin.

'Congratulations Lord Grace. And may I commend you on your lovely choice of bride. It will be a pleasure to paint her.'

'Paint her' thought Sarah to herself. 'I am going to be painted.' She couldn't believe it. And then her mind drifted back to when she first arrived at Roding Hall, and the young maid had gasped at the similarity of her appearance to the picture on the wall. No wonder the picture had looked like her, it was her! She must be the only person in the world who could have seen the portrait before it was even painted. That was a turn up for the books. When she and Josiah were alone that evening, she told him that she had seen the original painting when she arrived in 2001.

'Well if it is still around in 2001, we are getting our money's worth,' quipped Josiah. 'But who was I? Was my descendant a good chap?'

'Actually, there were no descendants, or at least not living here. The house had been sold to a state Trust called the National Trust. A committee looks after it and they have a chap looking after it as a curator. Visitors pay to go and look round the house. Many of the big stately homes have had to be sold off. The family wealth just got used up, and many of the families could no longer afford to live in them.'

'I have so much to learn about the future. Tell me more. Why did they lose their money?'

'I don't actually know how it happened for your family. The Great War changed a lot of things for people with wealth. After the war, men and women were no longer prepared to work for small wages in the big houses, and live in at the house. They preferred to go into the factories and get more money, and have their own household. They were also prepared to move to other towns to find better jobs.'

'What was the Great War? When did that happen?'

'There have been a lot of wars. There was the Crimean War in the 1850's, then the Boer War with South Africa at the turn of the century. The Great War or First World War was from 1914 to 1918, when England fought Germany. They said that that was the war to end all wars, as thousands were killed unnecessarily. But there was a Spanish Civil War in the 1930's and then the Second World War from 1939 to 1945. This again was started by Germany. Since then there have been smaller wars, in the Falkland Islands, the Gulf States and Israel. There always seem to be wars, rumours of wars or civil wars going on somewhere in the world. Although I suppose that we hear about them more easily nowadays.' Sarah stopped talking as she realised that Josiah had gone very quiet. After a long time, Sarah touched Josiah's hand.

'Are you all right, Josiah?'

'Yes, I am just a little grieved that my estate is no more, and there is no longer a Lord Grace living here. It makes my building plans a little futile.'

'Oh no. It is good that ordinary working people can come and see how you used to live and admire and enjoy the house and chapel.'

'Was the chapel still there?'

'I don't know. The curator didn't mention it. And we didn't go for a walk in the gardens.'

'I've heard too much. I think that I do not wish to know anymore today. My head is hurting with all these new fangled ideas. I wish you goodnight.' Josiah bowed, avoiding her eye, and slowly left the room. Sarah decided to go to bed as well. She hoped that she had not upset Josiah too much. Perhaps she should have been more circumspect

Chapter 28

Next morning, Mr Martin the painter was up bright and early and asking for his model. Josiah had requested that she be painted in her green dress, which she had first worn when she arrived. He also gave her the enormous emerald ring and insisted that she wore it. He asked Martin to include the ring in the painting, as it was to be her betrothal picture. Sarah asked if she could have a picture painted with Josiah as well, and Martin said that he would see if time would permit. Sarah found sitting for the picture quite irksome. She had to stay perfectly still and she found it difficult. To while away the time, she gazed at her beautiful emerald ring. She loved this ring and couldn't have chosen better if she had chosen herself. The emerald was very large, and had been set in a circlet of twisted gold round about it. There were no other stones in the ring, and so it enhanced the emerald. Sarah wondered about the previous owner of the ring, one of his great aunts, Josiah had said. She must ask him about it some time. When Mr Martin had gone, Josiah came in to look at his sketches. He commented on how much progress had been made. Sarah laughed, and told Josiah all about cameras. When he finally understood about cameras, she then made it worse by telling him about digital cameras.

There followed a long conversation about printing, typewriters, and telephones. These were difficult enough concepts for him to grasp, but email and computers were beyond him. Josiah found it incredible that Sarah could email her brother James in the New World thousands of miles away, or even hear him talking on the phone. He later asked about transport, wondering if railways were still around. Sarah replied that they were, but Josiah couldn't believe the speeds that they travelled at. When she told him about cars, he laughed, until she explained that that was how her parents had been killed. He was full of remorse after that. Planes, helicopters, Channel Tunnels were like a fairy story for Josiah. Especially the Channel Tunnel.

'Well, how will you keep the French out if you have a tunnel under the sea?'

'We are allies with the French now. We have not fought wars with France since the nineteenth century. Except about imports and exports, or football,' she laughed. Josiah shook his head disbelievingly. At practically every occasion when they were alone, Josiah asked Sarah more questions about her life. She seemed to be functioning in only two areas. What was happening in 2001 for Josiah, and arrangements for the wedding.

Every day there seemed to be more decisions to be made about some aspect of the wedding, whether it was food, arrangements, guests, wedding apparel and a myriad other details. Sarah couldn't imagine what would have happened if it had been a big society wedding, as befitting a peer of the realm. She was only glad that this was a so-called quiet wedding. It seemed to take up all of her time and most of the household staff as well. The dressmaker's young seamstress was spending the whole of her time at the house now. Although she had finished all the attendants' dresses and the bridal gown she still had to make outfits for all the other members of the household. Even the staff were to have new garments, in honour of the wedding.

The house was scrubbed from top to bottom in December, even though it had all been done in October for the opening of the chapel. Clean bedding was put on all the beds in the wing, and fresh curtains hung. Fires were lit in the bedrooms, to thoroughly air the beds, and furniture was rearranged in different bedrooms to suit the coming occupants.

The gardens came in for their own bit of spring cleaning again as young William and Calvert, the head gardener, were given orders about their contribution to the nuptials. The chapel grounds had to be completely finished as well, so that Josiah's father could be re-interred before the wedding.

Poor Martha and Peggy were busy preparing food for the wedding and fretted over the wedding cake. Sarah had to go down to the kitchen to stir the ingredients into the cake. This was a superstition in Martha's own home village, and she would not make a cake without the bride being involved.

'Keeps the devil away,' she explained to Sarah, when she asked the reason. Sarah became quite fascinated by the cake. It was very large, and built in the shape of Roding Hall. Sarah was surprised that it did not have tiers like cakes in her own time, but Martha had decided to honour the house. The little chapel had also been built in cake, and was set to one side of the house cake on the enormous board that was supporting the cakes.

Sarah was feeling very mixed as the days of December sped by. It was exciting that she was going to be married, but she would have preferred to be marrying Joe. 'Some chance now,' she said sadly to herself. Josiah caught her sitting in silence in the library one day. She was so engrossed in her thoughts that she didn't hear him come in.

'Having second thoughts, Sarah?'

'No, not really, I'm just mourning for the way of life that I had. Life was so different in my century.'

'Tell me more. What did you do all day?'

'I worked in a library.'

'Worked? You mean that you went to work and were employed by somebody who paid you money?' Josiah said aghast.

'Yes, most people have to work in the twenty first century. There are very few people who can afford not to work. Even people like you, peers of the realm, cannot always stay at home nowadays. They have to earn a living.'

'Perhaps I will stay here then,' he laughed, 'I do not think that I would like to go out and have to work. I enjoy my life as it is. And where do you work in a library? If the peers of the realm are having to work, how can they afford to employ someone to work in their library?'

'I work in the town library. All villages and towns have a lending library now. People can go and borrow books for nothing, so that they don't have to buy them.'

'But what is the point? How many people can read them?'

'All people can read now. Education for all children was set up in the late nineteenth century. Often by people like yourself.'

'But how could the people afford to pay for their children's education?'

'They don't. It's free.' Josiah pondered on this and stayed silent for a while.

From education, they talked about health and politics. Josiah was aghast when Sarah said that all people had the vote from the age of eighteen, even women, and that ordinary people without land, wealth or position could be a Member of Parliament. State benefits and free health care were beyond him, and Sarah realised just how lucky she had been to live in the twenty first century.

'Now I realise why you sometimes look sad, Sarah. I hope that you can bear to marry me and stay here.'

'I don't have much option, do I? But I will be happy. I just hope that I don't have six girls before I have the heir and the spare!' Sarah laughed. 'At least my brother's wife has had twin boys, if I managed that it would save us both a lot of trouble.'

'I do appreciate how much you are doing by marrying me. What ever I can give to you, I will. I will try to make you happy. Money is no object.'

'I do not crave money. But I would like to do some things. To give me an interest. I would love to set up a school in the village for the poor children. Would you do that? I could teach some of the older girls and then let them be the schoolteachers.'

'Hold fast, that is a big plan that you have got. I cannot promise you that, but I will look into it. The village parson is always saying that the common people have got brains and they should be educated. But many of my friends feel that that would give them ideas above their station, and they are not fit to be educated.'

'Well, convince your friends that they are wrong. I am the daughter of working people, but I have a first class honours degree from the university. And I am sure Anna could go to university. She's so bright. In my age, Anna would be a doctor. More women are in training to be doctors than men, nowadays.' Josiah laughed.

'Perhaps you should take Anna back with you if ever you go back.'

'I'd love to. She would love life in the twenty first century. She is definitely a woman born too early.'

Christmas seemed to be taking a backward place that year. Although the yule log was brought in, and presents were prepared for each other, the main focus of the whole house was the wedding. Sarah reflected sadly that she should be visiting her little nephews in America this Christmas. She had been so looking forward to it. If only she could let them know what had happened. They would be wondering why she hadn't turned up. They would be two years old tomorrow, and growing every day. How she would have liked to see them, but then there was a lot of things that she would have liked to do this Christmas. And getting married to a gay man had not been one of the things that she had thought of. Oh well, it could be worse. She could have landed in the workhouse, instead of this lovely household and family.

It was decided to have a dinner on Christmas Eve, prior to the midnight service in the village church. During the dinner, the picture of Sarah was to be unveiled. Mr Martin had not had time to paint a picture of the two of them together, but promised to return after Christmas. All the guests would be assembled for the wedding by then. All the Percys from Durham arrived, and Cassie and James, and Isabella and Jake and their brood. The Grace family from Sheffield only arrived late in the afternoon of Christmas Eve, so there was a little flurry of activity before the dinner. Extra staff had been taken on to help in the kitchens, and in the house generally for the wedding. It was quite daunting for Sarah. She kept meeting people, and was not sure who they were.

In a fit of sentimentality, Sarah decided to wear her green velvet dress for the Christmas Eve dinner. She knew that Josiah would be pleased, as he always said that that dress was his favourite one. He would probably have wanted her to get married in it if his mother had allowed it, but she insisted on the traditional white. As she was fastening her emerald choker, Myrtle came into the room, chastening Sarah for dressing without her. Myrtle had effectively been promoted now that Sarah was going to be Lady Grace, and was very pleased about the situation. Prior to Sarah arriving, Myrtle had had only general duties in the house. For her, her rise in the household had been meteoric, and she looked forward to being the personal maid for the new Lady of the house.

'Eh, Miss, what 'ave I told yer 'bout dressin' yersel'. Yer mun wait fer me now.'

'It will take me a long time to get used to that Myrtle. And anyway, you weren't here. So I started getting myself dressed. You can dress my hair, though. I hope my hair behaves tomorrow. I love the style that you practised on me last week. It will look so pretty underneath the veil.'

'Are yer excited, Miss?'

'Yes, I am. And worried too. I just hope that everything works out all right. I'm just a little nervous about mishaps. Also, it feels strange that I won't have any of my family there to watch me marry. It's times like this that I miss my mother.'

The two girls remained silent whilst Myrtle titivated Sarah's hair, both thinking of their long-dead mothers. Myrtle was worried that Sarah was having morbid thoughts the night before her wedding, so she tried to change the subject.

'I've sin yer cake. Martha 'as done yer proud. Yer should 'ave a look at it on yer way down ter dinner.'

'Thanks, I will. Now do I look all right?'

'Yer look luvly, Miss. Proper pretty. Yer'll mek a luvly bride termorrer. I bet I cry mi eyes out. I'll 'ave ter get used ter callin' yer 'yer ladyship.' Oh, it will feel funny at first.'

'I wish you could still call me Sarah. Her Ladyship sounds a real mouthful. Besides, I'll keep thinking that they mean Josiah's mother.'

'Oh Miss, it wouldn't be reight. I'll 'ave ter practice.' Sarah stood up and did a twirl.

'Will I do?' Myrtle nodded, and watched Sarah as she left the room to go downstairs. As she got downstairs, Sarah realised that she was the first to arrive in the formal dining room. She looked at the clock on the large marble mantelpiece. She would just have time to go and look at the cake. She hurried along the dimly lit corridors with her candle, and went down the stairs into the kitchen. Suddenly she caught her foot in the hem of her dress, and fell down the last three stairs. She banged her head and was knocked out.

Chapter 29

Sarah first became aware of noises buzzing in her head, before she fully came round. It was a noise that she couldn't christen straightaway. Her head was sore, and she supposed that she would have a whopping bruise on her head. She could just imagine it. 'The bride wore white satin but had a black eye.' It wouldn't look too good; they would think that Josiah was knocking her about. Thoughts of Josiah made her startled. It was her wedding day in the morning. If he knew that she had fallen again, he would be angry with her. Even for going down the kitchen stairs in the dark. Ah well, it was too late now. She suddenly decided to get up and check where she had banged her head in the mirror. She lifted her head and instantly put it back again on to the pillow. That's strange, she thought, where had the pillow come from? She gingerly opened one eye and didn't recognise the room that she was in. She could hear someone talking outside the room, but couldn't hear what they were saying, or who it was. She closed her eye again. It was less painful that way.

Hearing footsteps coming towards her, she opened her eyes carefully. Then her eyes flew open in surprise. 'Joe' she cried. She couldn't believe her eyes. 'Joe, I've missed you so much.' Joe laughed.

'Well I'm glad that you are awake. You have really had me worried. I've just rung the doctor. I've missed you too. I thought you were dead; you were lying there so still. What were you doing in the kitchen?'

'I was looking at the wedding cake for tomorrow.'

'Wedding cake? Tomorrow? What are you talking about?'

'Oh, I think I've been dreaming. What time is it?'

'Midnight.'

'And what date?'

'Same date as it was when you arrived. What is the matter with you? It's a good job that I've sent for the doctor, I think that you have got concussion.'

'2001?'

'Yes, I said that, didn't I?'

'I think that I've been dreaming. I thought it was 1825.'

'I think you have. You were playing the part of your character too much perhaps.' Sarah looked round the room. Yes, she was back in her own time. There was a big silver grey television in the corner of the room, where the noise had been coming from. The volume had been turned down low, so that there was only a quiet sound. There was also a stereo unit. And bliss upon bliss, there were electric lights. Whilst being overjoyed at being back with Joe, Sarah suddenly remembered that she should be getting married. What a rumpus there would be when they found that she had disappeared. How would they explain it? What would Josiah do now? What would happen to poor Anna? Sarah realised that Joe was speaking to her.

'The rest of your party have gone home, but they have left your clothes here. They were a little upset when you fell in the kitchen. What were you doing there, now you have woken up from your dream?'

'I remember now. I was very thirsty, and the servants had cleared away all the food, ready for the next round of snacks. So I nipped to the kitchen for a drink of water, and slipped in these dratted shoes.'

'Sarah, I am so glad you are all right. I felt terrible when they found you. All sorts of thoughts went through my head, and they were all selfish. I thought that I had just found the woman I wanted to spend the rest of my life with, and now there you were lying at the bottom of the steps. It was awful. I love you Sarah. Do you really feel the same way about me? It is so strange how we both fell in love at the same time. I'm sure that is pretty rare. They always say that one partner loves more than the other, but with us, I feel that we are equal.'

'I agree Joe. I really thought that I was in 1825. It must have been a very vivid dream.'

'Oh, there's the doorbell. That'll be the doctor.' Joe returned with a youngish woman carrying a bag.

'Here's the patient, Doctor McClure. I think that she was knocked out for about half an hour. One of the guests was a retired doctor and he said that there were no broken bones, and that it was safe to move her into the cottage. But he did say that I should send for you.'

'Yes, that's right,' smiled the doctor pleasantly. 'Now young lady, what can you remember?' Sarah recounted the story of her fall and blackout. Dr McClure carried out a full neurological examination. Bit more thorough than the last one, reflected Sarah. Her hands and clothes are a bit cleaner too.

'Can she stay here for a few days? Will that inconvenience you? Can you find her a bed?'

'You can share my bed anytime,' whispered Joe with a meaningful look at Sarah. 'No, that will be fine, Doctor McClure. She can stay here; my housekeeper has offered to be resident whilst she is here. I rang her earlier. Got to have a chaperone, I suppose.' Joe laughed. Dr McClure gave a trite smile.

'Very good then, if you think you can cope. She seems to have made a full recovery. But I think she ought to take it easy for a few days. I'll give you a leaflet with head injury instructions on, just in case. Take her to Casualty if you are worried, or call me out again.'

'She will be better staying here. She lives alone, and over in Lancashire.'

'I'll pop in tomorrow and check her over again.'

'Thanks a lot Doctor.'

'Goodbye to both of you.' The doctor left the house and Sarah settled down on the settee, closing her eyes. She felt quite exhausted, just with having an examination. Perhaps she should stay here after all whilst she recouped her strength. Besides, it would be delicious staying here with Joe. Her toes curled up in the happy anticipation of what might happen in the next few days. As she was drifting off to sleep, the outside door opened.

'Hello, Lord Grace, are you there?'

'Josiah,' Sarah cried out wildly. When she looked round, all that she saw was Joe and a plump middle aged lady with suspiciously jet black hair. Joe was rooted to the spot staring at her.

'How do you know my name?'

'Joe, I'm sorry, I was dreaming again.'

'But how did you know that I was called Josiah? I keep that a very closely hidden secret.'

'I don't know. I just heard the lady say 'Lord Grace', and I remembered that that was the name of the character you were playing at the dinner.'

'Well, I was playing the character, but I am Lord Grace as well. I was playing the fifth Lord Grace. I am the eleventh Lord Grace. And my real name is Josiah, but I let people think that it is Joseph.'

'But you are the curator.'

'Sadly yes. We had to sell the house to the National Trust in the eighties. We were crippled with death duties when my father died. The money had been dwindling over the last century anyway. I still own this house and am allowed to live in this house forever, and my family after me. It wasn't sold with the big house. This is just the lodge house. Fortunately, when I left university, the curator's job was vacant and I got it. It's so good, that I can still live in my house and show people round it, but get paid for it. Far better than struggling along, wondering whether you can pay the next tax bill. I've got the best of both worlds.' Sarah was becoming befuddled with all that she was hearing. At that point, the lady housekeeper who was called Joan, came in with a tray of hot chocolate.

'Here you are, your Lordship, two hot chocolates. I know how much you love the drink. I hope your companion does too.'

'My companion is called Sarah Evans. She fell into my life tonight, and is going to be the next Lady Grace. How about that Joan?'

'I always said that one day you would meet someone and fall head over heels. It's a good job that the young lady feels the same way.'

'Oh I do,' Sarah replied. 'But it is a bit of a shock. Actually, I fell down the stairs, as well as in love. And he forgot to tell me about the Lord Grace bit.' Joe and Joan both chuckled.

'He always does that, Miss Sarah. Says it sorts the wheat from the chaff.'

Sarah sipped the chocolate, remembering the last time that she had sipped chocolate with Josiah and Anna in the library. Must be a family failing, this liking for chocolate, she decided.

'So who was your father then?'

'I've told you. The tenth Lord Grace.'

'So are you directly related from the fifth Lord Grace that you were playing the part of?'

'Oh no, not directly. He died without issue. His fiancée disappeared the night before the wedding, and they never found her. He went a bit strange after that and never married. He developed an interest in new inventions, and poured a lot of money into harebrained schemes. His cousin John became the sixth Lord.' Sarah didn't know what to make of the story. She desperately wanted to hear about the rest of the family but didn't dare ask too much. It might raise his suspicions. One day she would have to tell him what had happened, but she was frightened of telling him too soon, in case he ridiculed her. 'And besides, what if she went back in time again.' Her heart started pounding at the thought of that, until she realised that she must not have gone back in time, as Joe said that they never found her. That was a relief, and she hoped that she would stay in her own time forever, especially now that she was reunited with Joe.

Later in the night, Sarah was escorted up to the guest bedroom. Joan had been very thoughtful and had brought a nightie for Sarah to wear. It was high necked and made of flannelette, with lots of frills round the yoke of the garment.

'I thought that I had better bring you something to wear, my dear. I knew that his Lordship would be unlikely to have anything suitable in the house. It is not his habit to bring ladies home after a date. Well, not unless he sends them home before 8am, before I arrive,' she chuckled to herself. Sarah was pleased to hear that. It was obvious that he wasn't a womaniser, or Joan may have told her another story. After Joan had retired herself, Joe sneaked quietly into the bedroom.

'Well, that's a passion killer nightie if ever I saw one,' he laughed. 'Not that anything would stop the passion that I feel for you at the moment. But I will control myself, because you have been ill. But be warned, I'm not a patient man. Watch out tomorrow night!' Sarah smiled her response, and stretching out, pulled Joe towards her, and gave him a long lingering kiss. Joe responded with equal passion and pulled away suddenly.

'Kiss me like that and I may have to take back what I said about waiting until tomorrow,' he said hoarsely. Sarah laughed and suggested that she would prefer to wait until tomorrow. Although she hoped that she would never use this excuse in future, she had a terrible headache, and would welcome a peaceful night's sleep. Joe pulled a face and said that he would forgive her just this once, but that excuse was banned starting from tomorrow. Sarah watched him go out of the bedroom, and snuggled down under the duvet. Her head had hardly hit the pillow before she was fast asleep. Joe peeped in later on as he was going to bed and stood by her bedside for quite some time, just taking in the wonder of the feelings that he had for her, and watching her as she slept peacefully.

Chapter 30

The next morning Sarah woke early, the sound of the early morning traffic waking her. Her headache was gone and she felt full of life. She lay and listened to the sound of the traffic for a while and realised how much the noise was part of modern day living. Almost a soothing part of life. To say that she had missed the travel noises in 1825 was going a bit too far, but it was pleasant to hear the traffic. Eventually she got out of bed and opened the curtains. The front of the lodge house was very close to the main road. It was amazing to reflect that the house had been in such a rural area in 1825, and yet it was in the middle of a town now. Sarah looked round at the bedroom.

Although it was only the lodge house, the proportions of the house were spacious. The room had large windows with window seats, covered with padded cushions. There were some elegant pieces of furniture in the room. The bed was a four-poster, and the drapes were in a material matching the curtains and window cushions, in a heavy brocade. Sarah was surprised that she had not noticed the room last night, but then she had been desperate to get to sleep, and anyway, she only had eyes for Joe.

A gentle tap on the door roused Sarah from her thoughts.

'Come in,' she called. Joe opened the door and came in.

'Joan wants to know what you would like for breakfast. And are you fit enough to get up?'

'Just toast and coffee would be fine. And yes, I do feel fit enough to get up.'

'Hum,' said Joe appreciatively, 'that augurs well for tonight. I think that I had better tell Joan that we don't need her to stay tonight. What do you think?' As he was saying this, Joe took Sarah in his arms and held her tight. A kiss ensued and Sarah felt her body responding fiercely to Joe. A voice from downstairs disturbed the moment.

'Coo-ee, coffee is ready,' shouted Joan. Joe and Sarah both laughed and went downstairs together, hand in hand.

The breakfast was served in a small dining room, which was elegantly furnished.

'You have some lovely furniture, Joe.'

'Yes, I took some from the house before it was sold. I really love this house. Originally there were two matching lodge houses, one on either side of the drive. The other one was where the gatekeeper lived. It was knocked down when cars were invented to make more room for parking and access. This one was a little larger and was built for Lady Eleanor Grace in 1849. The fifth Lord Grace died that year, and his cousin John became the heir. Lady Eleanor insisted on having the dower house built, so that she didn't interfere with John's wife.'

'What did Josiah die of?'

'He fell from a horse during a hunt.'

'Oh, just like his dad,' replied Sarah without thinking.

'How do you know that?'

'Oh, you must have told me last night.'

'I don't think that I did.'

'Well perhaps one of the other people there told me.'

'Hmm, I suppose so,' muttered Joe looking at Sarah suspiciously.

'Could I go for a walk in the gardens today? I feel like I want some fresh air.'

'Certainly, I have some paper work to do, before I open the Hall to the public, but I can take you later.'

'No, I'd really rather go alone. You can take me later, and tell me all about the family and the house.'

All right, why don't you go for a walk and then come across to the café for lunch. That way Joan can go home and do her own chores. She usually has the weekends off and only came in specially.'

'That sounds lovely. Where's the café?' Joe gave her the instructions and Sarah asked Joan if she could borrow a pair of walking shoes. Joan rooted in the cellar and found an old anorak and a pair of stout shoes.

'Will these do for now?'

'They will be fine, thank you. But first, I would love a bath. It seems ages since I had one.' 'Several months to be precise,' she thought to herself. She made her way to the bathroom, and had a long luxurious soak, revelling in the feel of the water cleansing her. After she got dressed, Sarah donned the anorak and shoes and set off into the garden. The house wasn't open to the public yet, so Sarah was able to wander about unhindered. She made a beeline for the chapel. She went through the little gate that was now made of wrought iron. The railings too, were made of wrought iron and the tops of the black railings were tipped with gold colouring. They had obviously replaced the original wood, and would be far more substantial. She found the spot where the fourth Lord Grace, Josiah's father, had been re-interred. She was pleased to see that Lady Eleanor was in the same grave with him. So they were reunited in death, Sarah breathed to herself. Lady Grace had lived to a ripe old age of ninety-two. That was an incredible achievement in those days.

She moved to the next grave. It was Bella's. She had died in 1827. Sarah felt very sad for the little girl, and wondered what had happened. Still in those days, with no antibiotics, life was very precarious, as hers would have been if she had stayed in that time. As she moved over to the farther side of the garden, Sarah found a smaller stone. It was Anna's grave. It felt very strange to be reading about her friends. Sarah read down the gravestone.

Anna, daughter of Josiah and Eleanor
born 1810, died 1835.
Sadly missed by her beloved husband
Doctor Thomas Perry.

'Yes,' shouted Sarah in exultation. 'She did marry him.' She wondered how on earth it had come about and decided she would carefully ask Joe at lunchtime. She looked further down Anna's gravestone and noticed that there were the names of several small children who had obviously died in childhood. There was no mention of whether Doctor Perry had been buried there, and Sarah wondered what had happened to him. As she looked at the names of the children, she noticed that the firstborn child had been a girl, and that she was called Sarah. So Anna had remembered her friend. And remembered her with affection, even though the rest of the family probably thought badly about her. It was a strange feeling, thought Sarah.

All these people that she was involved with, and she would never know what had happened to them, apart from the stark history of the gravestones. Sarah was overwhelmed by sadness, remembering the times that she had spent with Anna and the children. A little tear trickled slowly down her cheek, as she sat by Anna's grave. She would try and find some flowers whilst she was there, and put them on Anna's grave. And Josiah's and Bella's. She owed them that much. She took comfort in the fact that the graves were nicely tended. Someone obviously took great care of them, unlike many of the gravestones in the public cemeteries.

She was so obsessed by her thoughts that she didn't hear someone coming up behind her. Sarah jumped when she felt a hand on her shoulder. She turned round quickly to find Joe standing next to her. She wiped her eyes on her anorak sleeve, having no hanky with her.

'Joe, you gave me such a start.'

'Hey, what's this, tears? What on earth is the matter, my love?'

'Oh, take no notice of me. I was looking at this gravestone of a lady called Anna. She must have been Josiah's sister. But I noticed that her first child was called Sarah, like me.'

'You are such a tender soul. Crying about someone you never met.'

'Do you know any of the history about this Anna? I am curious, with her having called her first child Sarah.'

'I know some of the history, but it is not a good story. A family skeleton I suppose. But all families have them. I actually came to see if you were ready for lunch.'

'Yes, I am. It must be the walk in the fresh air.' To be honest she wasn't hungry, but didn't want Joe to think that she was very upset. They walked slowly, hand in hand towards the National Trust café. It had been built in the stable block, at the side of the house. Sarah found a table whilst Joe went to the food area, selecting them both a dish of homemade broth and dumplings and coffee. Sarah was a little hesitant about hearing the story, so she talked to Joe about the chapel generally.

'Is the chapel still used?'

'Yes, it is still licensed for the Grace family to hold services in and marry in. Hey, would you like to get married here?'

'I'd like that very much, Joe,' Sarah said softly. 'Is that a proposal?'

'It's about the best you'll get!' he laughed. 'I sort of just took it for granted really. Well, will you marry me?' Sarah blushed when she saw the waitress hovering to deliver the broth. Joe followed her gaze.

'Hello Rebecca. I'm just proposing to Sarah here. Why don't you stay and listen to her answer, then I've got a witness.' The waitress laughed. She was obviously used to this eccentric Lord of the Manor.

'Well, come on, the broth is going to be cold, and Rebecca hasn't got all day, they're busy.'

'Yes, I'd love to marry you Joe. I've thought of nothing else since I met you,' she said looking straight into his eyes, completely forgetting her audience.

'Hurrah,' shrieked Rebecca. 'His Lordship's getting married at long last. Are you having the wedding here?'

'Where else? I couldn't afford anywhere else, could I?'

'Let us know the date as soon as you can, then we can all make sure we are free to work. That is one wedding we will not miss. Isn't that right girls?' The other kitchen staff nodded their agreement and added their congratulations. They obviously all liked working here. It seemed a happy place to work. Rebecca went back to the kitchen with the dirty pots from the next table, leaving Sarah and Joe alone. As they sipped their lunch, Joe started telling Sarah the story.

'It all started with the girl whose part you took at the dinner. I'm sorry that you were picked to play her part, because she wasn't as nice as you and she caused havoc here in 1825.' Sarah felt uneasy; this was no interesting story about someone that she had never met. This was her story, but seen from the family's perspective, and she knew that it wouldn't show her in a good light. She kept silent, wondering what Joe would say.

'She turned up at the house one evening and quickly inveigled herself into all aspects of the family. The current Lord, number five, was dallying about getting married, to the exasperation of his mother. Suddenly he announced his betrothal to this mystery girl, whose family background was a little suspect to say the least. But she upset most of the people in the house even before the betrothal. She started teaching all the daughters to read and write, and as if that wasn't enough, she taught the servants too. Scandalous in those days. They were frightened that they would get ideas above their station.' Gosh, thought Sarah, he even sounds like Josiah now.

'Then she interfered with the care of a young girl with cerebral palsy that lived here. In those days, they were called cripples, and were kept hidden away. This woman . .' he stopped mid-sentence. 'Now that's strange, she was called Sarah too. Oh, what an insult to you. Anyway, that is beside the point. This Sarah taught this child some exercises to help her. She actually did wonders with her.'

'So she wasn't all bad then, was she?' Sarah asked feverishly, trying to put herself in a good light with Joe.

'Wait, you haven't heard the worst yet.' Sarah's heart sunk

'For her engagement, she chose a family heirloom. A big emerald ring that had been handed down the family for generations. Fortunately she didn't choose the real diamond engagement ring that passed down to each consecutive Lord's wife. She said that because the Lord's mother was still alive, she wouldn't use the ring. It's a good job, Sarah, isn't it? Or else I would have no family heirloom to pass on to you.' Sarah swallowed. Hard. For once she couldn't think of anything to say, so just smiled at Joe.

'But the worst is still to come. They were to marry on Christmas Day. They held a pre-nuptial dinner the night before the wedding and she disappeared before the dinner. Just disappeared, like a puff of smoke. But, of course, she took the ring with her. Neither her nor the ring was ever seen again. Some of the extended family and friends thought that she must have been a sneak thief who had an accomplice working with her. But both Josiah the fifth and Anna would hear nothing bad about her.'

'So what was bad about Anna? You mentioned a skeleton.'

'Oh yes, well a few months after her disappearance, Anna disgraced herself with the local doctor. She made it very obvious that she wanted to marry him, but the family would have none of it. A doctor wasn't good enough for a sister of a Lord in those days. They were just seen as workmen. Even when she told them that she was pregnant, they still wouldn't give in, and they were going to send her away to a convent in the South of England. A much bigger scandal in those days you know. So one night, she and this doctor eloped. It caused ructions at the time. The doctor was the nephew of the family doctor, and he came in for a lot of blame with the family. Nothing was heard of them for quite a long time, then he turned up here with two little girls. Anna had died in childbirth. He was gutted, and blamed himself because he was a doctor and couldn't save her. He left the girls here, and went off to Africa to be a missionary doctor, and nothing was heard of him again. He probably died in Africa, for all I know.'

'And what about the girls?'

'They were brought up here by the next Lord and his wife.'

'And the sixth Lord was his cousin?'

'Yes.' Sarah was relieved. At least Joe wasn't the direct descendant of Josiah. That would have felt a little too incestuous for her.

'So that's the family skeleton. There are probably many more that I don't know about. Would you like another coffee and some cake?'

'No. I'd prefer some chocolate, but yes, I would like some cake.'

'What sort?'

'Any, I'll let you choose.' Joe went back to the café counter. He came back smiling.

'This is a special cake. It's called Martha's currant slice. Apparently there was a cook here called Martha in the time of Josiah the fifth, and when the girls were taught to read, one of the daughters of the house wrote down all of Martha's recipes. She was very interested in cooking herself. I think that she was called Elly.'

'Charlotte,' Sarah corrected without thinking.

'How would you know? Anyone would think that you had been there.' Sarah paused, wondering whether she should tell him anything. She took a deep breath.

'Joe, about some of your stories, I felt like I knew what was going to happen. Do you think that I was that Sarah, that I did go back in time?' Joe fell back in his chair laughing.

'Of course not, you goose. You were talking to that man sitting next to you at the dinner. He had researched all my family history before he came on the holiday. Why, he knew more than me. He filled your mind with facts. And then when you hit your head and were unconscious, you had a long and powerful dream. That was all, you had a long dream. Going back in time. Ha ha. I've never heard such an idea. No Sarah. You couldn't have been that person. You are far too sane to believe that. You are far too sweet, anyway. The only way I would believe that it was you, was if the ring turned up again. What a likely story!' Sarah forced a smile at Joe, her mind in a turmoil.

'Perhaps you are right, it was a long dream after all.' Sarah was even beginning to convince herself. 'At least I promise you that I will not leave you the night before our wedding. There is no chance of that. Now I have found you I will not let you go.'

'Then marry me quickly. Next week if we can, but don't ever come up with those daft ideas again, or I'll doubt your sanity. Well, I'll have to go back to work now. Got to earn a crust, especially as I now have a wedding to pay for and a wife to support. Tonight I will get you the diamond engagement ring out of the safe.' Sarah smiled her assent and leaned over and kissed him. As he turned to walk away, she slid her right hand down to meet the left hand and stared at the ring on her finger. A dream it must remain, if he insists, she mused to herself. She slowly slipped the large green emerald ring off her finger, and into her pocket. She would have to find a good hiding place for this, until she could get back to Read. And for the next few years, for that matter. Perhaps in the chapel. Yes, that was a good idea.

'I think that I will just go over to the chapel again. I found it so peaceful there,' she shouted.

'Good idea, and start thinking about a date for the wedding,' Joe replied.

'Anytime except Christmas Day,' Sarah quipped back. She smiled as he walked away. Some day she would tell him. Well, maybe, maybe not.